SHADOWS

CONRAD JONES

Copyright © 2016 CONRAD JONES
All rights reserved.

ISBN: 9798389971479

The Inspector Braddick Books
Brick
Shadows
Guilty Until Proven Innocent
Deliver Us from Evil

Detective Alec Ramsay Series
The Child Taker
Criminally Insane
Slow Burn
Frozen Betrayal
Desolate Sands
Concrete Evidence
Thr3e

Soft Target Series
Soft Target
Soft Target II 'Tank'
Soft Target III 'Jerusalem'
The Rage Within
Blister
The Child Taker
Unleashed

The Anglesey Murders

Unholy Island

A Visit from the Devil

Nearly Dead

Dark Angel

What Happened to Rachel?

Pure Evil

Unravelling

Circus

A Disturbing thing happened

CHAPTER 1

She clung to the girder as tightly as she could, the metal cold as ice against her cheek. The wind howled and whistled between the stanchions of the bridge, threatening to rip her from her perch and toss her into the abyss. Her heart was beating so fast that she thought it would explode at any second. Fear pumped through her veins. She hated heights. It was a real phobia. Climbing the bridge was the hardest thing that she had ever done. If the stakes weren't so high, she couldn't have done it. Not for all the money in the world, not for anything. Tears blurred her vision and the contents of her stomach churned, threatening to come back up. Her body shook from head to toe. She looked down and wretched, bitter tasting bile spewed into the wind, splattering the windscreens of the traffic far below. The vehicles had come to a halt, their owners staring upwards in disbelief. They seemed so small and far away. Just a glance down was enough to bring up another mouthful of bile. She squeezed her eyes closed and tried to control her breathing. The air was bitterly cold, and it bit into her lungs each time she inhaled. She spat the bitter fluid out and the wind took it away into the darkness. Her heart was pounding in her chest; cold sweat ran down the small of her back. The wind blew harder and harder, lifting her from the structure. Her hands gripped the rough metal edges, desperately clinging on as the wind pulled violently at her. The gusts were like ice cutting through her clothes, her exposed flesh was numb. If she waited too long, her limbs would be too numb to move. She sobbed as her feet found purchase against the rusty bolts and pushed upwards, higher and higher, every inch agony. Her goal was above. She had to reach it, or the consequences were dire. The wind dragged at her body, freezing her scalp, whistling painfully into her ears. Her tears poured and were taken by the wind. Saliva drooled from the corners of her mouth. She crept upwards, inch by inch, yard by yard. Her palms were cut and scratched; blood trickled from her nails, making her fingers slippery. Clinging on became more difficult with every minute that passed. It was twenty minutes of bitterly cold and painful progress before she was high enough.

Finally, she was there. She had reached the designated point. They had been specific about where she must be. If she didn't climb that high, then they would kill them. It was that simple. A black and white choice. Do it, or they die. All of them, except her sister and her children. Their fate would be worse than death. They said they would force them into the sex trade, and she believed them. Her fingers cramped as she clung to the metal.

When she stopped climbing, she looked over the edge and her stomach lurched again, and she almost let go as panic set in. She felt dizzy with fear. Her head was spinning. The wind blew stronger, each gust lifting her body away from the metal, edging her closer to the drop. Her thoughts were a quagmire of regrets, her emotions in turmoil. The cold was sapping her strength. Life had taken her down a one-way street and she couldn't go back. There was no way out. This was her only option. She had pushed too hard against an irresistible force and when it pushed back, she realised that she was nothing in comparison. They searched for her weak points and utilised them, quickly and brutally, leaving her no choice but to do as they said. She had begged and pleaded, promised to back off and destroy the evidence that she had gathered but there was no mercy forthcoming. They had warned her several times, but she thought that the force would protect her. Her position was her armour, her strength and shield but she underestimated the power of her foe. Its reach and ruthlessness had no boundary. No laws restricted their response. They had their own laws, their own code. Anyone threatening their existence was made to suffer and then eliminated. She was part of an awesome organisation but despite the strength of the law enforcement agencies, the reality was that she was an individual and easily crushed. Her family were her weak point. They were vulnerable and she couldn't protect them. No one could.

Her vision was blurred with tears as she looked over the edge, the vehicles below like insects crawling across the bridge. She heard sirens approaching and blue lights flashed on the approach roads. They couldn't help her now. They couldn't stop what was about to happen. No one could. It was too late. The lights of the power station down river twinkled through her tears, rainbows surrounded each glowing gem. A tugboat floated silently on the Mersey, heading for the estuary and the sea beyond, the water as black as oil. The lights of the bridge penetrated the darkness for only a few metres before being swallowed up by the night. Below the bridge was nothing but inky darkness. She wondered how long it would take to fall and hit the water. Her stomach flipped, anguish, fear and deep regret gripped her like a giant fist. She thought of her mother, how scared she had been. The image of her father, stricken with dementia, unaware of what was happening to him as they bundled him into a van. His eyes were childlike, terror and helplessness behind them. She thought about her pregnant sister and her other children. She thought about what they had said they would do to her and her unborn baby.

The images floated by in her mind as she took a deep breath, closed her eyes and rolled off the girder into the abyss. Her journey to the river took much longer than she thought and her impact with the water was catastrophic. She was dead before the Mersey engulfed her body and claimed her for its own.

CHAPTER 2

The old fish factory was dark, damp and the stench of its past pervaded the air, finding its way into their nostrils. They could almost taste the decay on their lips. Another odour filled the air. The smell of fear. Sweat ran from every pore, running down their foreheads, trickling down their backs. It was cold, painfully cold. Fear made them perspire, soaking their clothes, increasing their discomfort. The sound of rainwater dripping through holes in the roof echoed through the cavernous factory. Their trawler swayed gently with the swell, protected from the powerful waves in the harbour, by the dock wall. They were cold, tired and frightened, very frightened. The thick cable ties that bound their wrists and ankles, bit deep into their flesh. Their muscles cramped and burned, their fingers and toes were numb. Six men, with hopes and dreams, stared death in the face. Their skipper eyed each of them, regret and guilt weighed him down.

'A simple drop-off,' he had said. 'The easiest money you will ever make,' he said. It had seemed easy enough when he recruited them but with hindsight, he had stepped into a world that he didn't belong in, unwittingly placing his crew in danger.

They sat shivering on the dock, the sound of seagulls drifted on the biting wind. The headlights of a car swept over the scene, dazzling them, making them blink. It came to a stop and the doors opened, engine still running, heavy footsteps splashed in the rainwater. The murmur of foreign voices reached them. Orders were barked in an alien tongue. Men ran here and there, shadows in the darkness. The frightened six looked at each other, their eyes wide with trepidation. They wanted to talk but dare not. Powerful torches swept the darkness, illuminating the trawler and the dockside and the harbour beyond. The white tips of the waves appeared and then vanished. Footsteps echoed into the night, coming closer, increasing their angst. Men dressed in dark combat clothing materialised from the dark and one figure stepped forward from the group.

'Which one of you is the captain?' a deep voice asked. The accent was thick and guttural, its owner tall, dressed in an Italian suit and black overcoat. His eyes were piercing blue, his hair cropped to the scalp. The six remained silent, scared and unwilling to betray their skipper. 'I will not ask again.' They remained tight lipped. 'Okay, have it your way. Shoot the young one in the legs.'

'Wait, wait! Don't shoot anyone for Christ's sake. I am the skipper,' an elderly man answered. His watery eyes scanned the men on the dock. He was frightened but there was steel in his eyes. His tongue flicked over dry lips, touching his whiskers. 'There's no need to hurt anyone. I'm the captain.'

'Your name, old man?' the foreigner asked curtly.

'Linus Murphy.'

'Where did you sail from?'

'Dublin,' the old man answered. His white beard hid his lips.

'Who are you working for?'

'I don't work for anyone,' the skipper said, shaking his head. 'I was paid to deliver those crates here. It was a one-off job. We're fishermen by trade.'

'Who paid you to carry the crates?'

'I don't know his name,' Linus answered hoarsely. His throat felt like sandpaper.

'You don't know who paid you?' the foreign man chuckled sourly. He exchanged glances with the other men on the dock. Some of them smiled and shook their heads, others grinned and glared at the fishermen, amusement touched their lips. 'I don't have all day. I asked you a simple question, answer me or you will be sorry.'

The old man stared back, defiance in his eyes. 'I don't know his name. I'm telling you the truth.'

'No, you are not but you will tell me the truth in the end. Take the young one,' he said, pointing to the youngest fisherman. Two of the men grabbed him by the ankles and dragged him from the group, cracking his head hard on the moss covered concrete. One of them kicked him in the midriff, knocking the breath from his lungs. A second kick doubled him over. He groaned, gasping for air. Another kick landed to the side of his jaw. Two teeth clattered across the dock. He wretched and the contents of his stomach splattered on the dock.

'Stop, stop. Don't hurt him anymore please!' Linus shouted. The foreigner raised his hand and the men stopped the beating. 'I genuinely don't know who is behind this,' Linus snapped. 'I only know the man who set this up. I don't know who is behind him.' The men on the dock remained silent, waiting for more information. The silence was menacing, their eyes filled with loathing. Linus swallowed hard and carried on. 'All I know is that I was approached two weeks ago and offered a lot of money to bring those crates across the Irish Sea. It seemed like easy money and I couldn't see the harm in it.' He nodded to four huge crates on the dock. Fresh fish packed in ice glistened in the torchlight. The foreign men stared, looking unimpressed with what he had said. 'Look, we don't want to step on anyone's toes here. We've never done anything like this before. Times have been hard,' Linus said apologetically. 'We're fishermen trying to make a living, nothing more. We don't want any trouble. These lads don't know anything, honestly. There's no need to hurt them.'

'You haven't answered my question.' The foreigner nodded and his men kicked the young fisherman in the head repeatedly, taking it in turns until his face was a bloody mess. His lips split against his remaining teeth. A long gash opened above his left eyebrow and blood splattered the other fishermen.

'Stop, stop!' Linus shouted. His crew closed their eyes or looked away. Long seconds went by as the onslaught continued. 'For God's sake!' Linus cried helplessly.

Another nod from the foreigner and they stopped. 'Don't waste my time any longer. I will only ask one more time. What is the name of the man who paid you?'

'Patrick,' Linus mumbled. 'Patrick Finnen. I only met him the once. I was told to sail the crates over here. He said that we would be met here, unload the cargo and sail home, nothing else. It was supposed to be a simple pick up and drop off.'

'Who does Patrick Finnen work for?'

'I didn't ask. I don't want to know who he works for. I didn't ask what was in the crates and I don't want to know that either. Take them and let us go home. We don't want any trouble.'

'You don't know what is in the crates?' The man smiled thinly. His expression was one of mild amusement. 'Come now, Linus. You are a man of many years. Your country has seen more troubles than most, yes?' Linus nodded reluctantly. 'Drugs have become part of life for the young, even in Dublin, no?'

'Unfortunately,' Linus mumbled.

'Then you had a good idea what you were carrying,' the foreigner said, wagging his finger. He paused and rubbed his chin. 'Had you heard of this Finnen man before he approached you?'

'No.' Linus shook his head. He had heard that the local mobs were vying for the routes that Ireland offered into the UK but had no interest in the names of dangerous men, no matter what nationality. 'I swear to you that I had never met him before.'

'You're lying, Linus,' the foreigner said with a twisted smirk. 'You had heard his name. I can see it in your eyes.' He nodded to his men and they kicked the injured fisherman in the head, breaking his nose and splitting his cheek against his teeth. Blood splattered Linus's face. Another kick broke the young man's jaw with an audible crack.

'Stop for Christ's sake!' Linus shouted, his voice breaking. 'He's just a boy. You'll kill him!'

'Tell me the truth, old man or this young lad dies in front of your eyes. Then the others, one by one.'

'Please don't hurt him anymore,' Linus pleaded. 'I honestly don't recall hearing the name before he approached me. That is the truth.' The foreigner nodded slowly. He seemed to believe him. 'Can I ask you a question?'

'You can ask.'

'Who are you and why are you doing this to us?'

'All you need to know is that we are very pissed off with your boss, this Finnen character. He is trying to encroach on our territory. We can't allow that to happen.'

'I am awful sorry about that, truly I am. Like I said, we didn't mean to step on anyone's toes. It was just a delivery. We have no part in Finnen's business. Had I known, I never would have agreed to carry those crates and whatever is in them.'

'You pretended not to know what was in them.'

'I didn't ask what was in them. I should have done but I didn't want to know.'

'You must have suspected what you were carrying.'

'I have to admit that I didn't think it was just fish, but I didn't think it would lead to this, believe me.' Linus nodded again and looked down at his feet, feeling embarrassed. Greed had landed him and his crew in dire trouble. 'I would never have put my men in danger. Like I said, I didn't ask enough questions. These lads didn't know anything. They just do as I tell them. They had no idea what we were carrying.'

'Show them what they were carrying.'

'We don't want to know!' Linus snapped but it was too late. One of the Russians kicked over a crate, ice and fish clattered across the dock. Thick packages wrapped in tape spilled out. Linus shook his head and bit his lip. 'Like I said, take it and let us go home. We won't say a word to anyone about this. You have my word on that.'

'And if we do let you sail away, will Patrick Finnen stop sending his drugs across the sea onto our turf?' The foreigner shrugged.

'I don't...'

'He is attempting to branch out into our territory. We cannot allow that to happen.'

'We'll never have anything to do with this business again. You have my word.'

'Unfortunately, there will always be gullible people who think that they can make fast money. People like you, Linus. People who close their eyes and don't see,' he paused. 'How did you say it?' A wry smile crossed his lips, 'Yes that was it, 'they don't see the harm in it'. Wasn't that what you said?'

'We meant no disrespect to you or anyone else. I had no idea that it would affect anyone else. Honestly, I didn't. These lads are innocent in all this. Let us go and we'll sail home and say no more about it.'

The man nodded and folded his arms. He shook his head as if talking to a child. 'And what will you tell Patrick Finnen about his shipment?' Linus suddenly looked up; realisation hit him like a hammer. 'What do you think your friend Patrick will do to you and your families when you tell him that you lost his drugs?'

'I wasn't planning on losing them. I didn't think about that…'

'No, you didn't think about it, Linus.' The man wagged his finger again. 'You didn't think about it at all. You didn't see the harm, as you said.'

'I'll talk to Finnen. This is on me, not my crew,' Linus said shaking. He could see their predicament clearly. He looked at his crew one by one. They looked terrified. Not one of them had thought that they were doing something wrong. They sat shivering from the cold and the fear, tears were running freely down their cheeks. 'This is not your fault, lads. Don't worry. I'll fix this. This is not your fault at all.'

'Whose fault is it, Linus?' the man said, looking bemused.

Linus shook his head and shrugged. 'This is down to whoever was supposed to meet us here,' he said confidently. 'This is on them. We did our part crossing the sea.' Linus shook his head. 'This is on them. They fucked up. They should have been here as planned. I'll tell Finnen that they didn't show but you did. I'll explain it to him.'

The man frowned. His men sneered. One of them spat on the dock. 'Oh, Linus, how stupid are you?' he sighed. 'They did show up.' He gestured to one of his men. The man aimed his torch towards the rusty metal girders that held up the roof, illuminating the purple bloated faces of four men. They were hanging upside down from the rafters. Their feet and hands were trussed behind them, their features swollen and grotesque, tongues lolling from their bloody lips. Two of the men were clearly dead, their eyes lifeless, only the whites showing. The other two were twitching, close to death, suffering, every second a living torment.

One of the fishermen gasped, another began to cry loudly and muttered the Hail Mary. Linus heard his prayer and felt tears of frustration running down his own cheeks now, all hope leaving him fast.

'Jesus, Mary and Joseph!' Linus cried out. 'Don't worry, lads,' he said, his voice breaking. 'We'll come to an arrangement to pay Finnen back. I'll fix this. I will.'

'Do you have a million euros, Linus?' the man scoffed. 'I think not, or you wouldn't be sitting there pissing your pants. You would be in a nice warm pub counting your money.'

'I'll take whatever I have coming from Finnen. Let us go,' he pleaded. 'These young lads didn't mean any harm to anyone. They didn't know anything about the drugs. I'll square things with Finnen.'

'How?' the man sighed. 'The only way that you could pay him back for his loss would be to sail for him again and again, every day for the rest of your days until the debt was paid. I can't allow that to happen. You understand that, I'm sure?'

'I'll sort something out with him. If not, Finnen can go and fuck himself. I won't smuggle anything for him again. I don't care what he does to me. You have my word.'

'Brave words but when he starts hurting your family?' he shrugged. 'You will do anything that he asks. Your only hope now is to tell me who he works for.'

'I honestly don't know.'

'Then your next voyage will be your most interesting yet,' the man said, waving a hand. 'String them up next to those lowlifes. I want to know what they know. One of them knows something. Let's make sure Patrick Finnen doesn't send anymore of his shit across the sea.'

As the foreigners moved towards the six, Linus and his men began to scream for mercy. Their cries echoed into the darkness, lost on the inky black sea.

CHAPTER 3

Detective Inspector Braddick checked the mirror. His hair and whiskers were speckled with grey, shaved tight to his skin. He climbed out of his Range Rover Evoque and struggled into his heavy leather jacket. His grey suit was no match for the island's winds. The drive from Liverpool to the Anglesey port of Holyhead had taken him two hours. Two hours of overtaking lorries and caravans, motor homes and dawdling tourists. The scenery was spectacular, but it was lost on him under the circumstances. He was stiff and bad tempered. The wind howled across the harbour, chasing moody clouds before it. As he walked from the vehicle the rain poured sideways. His boots splashed in muddy puddles; their thick soles covered by the water.

The order to drive there had come from an Assistant Chief Constable, new to the position. He had been abrupt and knew little about the circumstances of the crime scene that he was sending Braddick to. All he knew was it was a multiple murder scene and that the North Wales Police wanted the presence of Merseyside detectives. The details were sparse at best. At the time, Braddick had to bite his lip, tempted to ask the ACC if he knew his arse from his elbow. He hated walking into joint operations without a proper briefing. It was embarrassing at best. He couldn't imagine why their presence had been requested or why the ACC had singled him out for the job but asking the reasons why wasn't always appreciated by the top brass. 'Shut up and do as you're told'. Thinking for himself wasn't always seen as a strength. He had to bite the bullet and do as he was asked, not for the first time and not for the last.

The rain was almost horizontal as he ran towards the police cordon, wind cut through his clothes and chilled his flesh. Yellow crime scene tape flapped wildly, threatening to snap. A gaggle of journalists were huddled behind a Nissan, trying to keep their cameras dry. They showed only a passing interest as Braddick went by them, snapping a few shots and then returning to their chitchat. A miserable looking uniformed officer lifted the tape and mumbled a greeting. Things could be worse, he thought. He could be him, ordered to man the line in the pissing down rain and a howling gale. A fine example of job dissatisfaction in the force. Braddick half smiled at his plight as he ducked beneath the tape and scurried towards the entrance of the abandoned fish factory. The doors had been opened, making it look like the mouth of a cave. He was pleased to see the miserable expression on a familiar face as his DS saw him. Detective Sergeant Adrian Burns waved as he approached. Braddick's face creased as the stench from inside hit him. The dark lines in his skin deepened.

'What the hell is that smell?' Braddick asked, covering his nose with his hand. His black skin glistened with the rain.

'It is a heady mixture of fish and dead people,' Ade said flatly, his expression never changed. He looked like he had been to bed in his clothes, not slept and then got out the other side to go to work. There were dark circles beneath his eyes. His tussled hair was as unkempt as his black suit. 'In fact, there are lots of fish and lots of dead people to be precise.'

'Fish and dead people? Okay, that explains that then,' Braddick shrugged and nodded, familiar with his sergeant's sarcasm. 'You had better fill me in. What have we got and why have we been called all the way here?'

'What did the ACC tell you?' Ade asked. His face was etched with wrinkles, his mouth a permanent scowl.

'Bugger all to be honest.' Braddick sighed. 'The details were sketchy. I'm not sure if he knows what day of the week it is yet.'

'He's new at the job. It is early days yet.' Ade shrugged. 'Follow me, Guv and I'll show you what all the fuss is about,' Ade said, gesturing for him to follow him. His trench coat was creased where he had been sitting on it during the drive. 'How was your journey down here?'

'Crap. Fucking caravans everywhere,' Braddick said smiling thinly. 'The Evoque was like a balloon in the wind coming across the island. Tell me that we're not wasting our time here.'

'Oh no, we're definitely not wasting our time,' Ade said, shaking his head. 'I didn't expect this when I woke up this morning. You're going to love this.'

'I doubt that very much.' They walked through the cavernous building, avoiding the deeper puddles as they went. The ground was littered with rotting refuse, dumped over decades. An old mattress had turned into a fungus garden, shopping trolleys lay rusting next to washing machines and a burnt-out Ford Escort had been turned into a makeshift den by local kids. A headless doll had been placed into a broken pram and thoughtfully covered in an old pink blanket. The sound of waves breaking on the harbour wall provided a constant backing track to what was going on. He looked beyond the harbour and saw a lighthouse at the end of a long breakwater. Waves crashed over it, engulfing it before landing in the harbour. A huge ferry was navigating the breakwater before heading off to Dublin, leaving thick white foam in its wake. Braddick spotted vehicles from the Coast Guard, Border Patrol, Crime Scene Investigation and the local plod. Uniformed men stood huddled in groups, talking in hushed tones while white clad technicians scoured the scene for clues. 'What's going on here? This is a fucking circus.'

'Every man and his dog are here. I'm not sure who is in charge. No one seems to know yet. It is going to be a logistical nightmare,' Ade muttered to himself. 'Two men have been strung up from the girders. They're over here.'

As they approached the hanging gallery, the magnitude of the crime became clear. 'The local plod has identified them. Their ID's were left on the dock. I've checked their ID's, Guv…' he was cut short by Braddick's reaction.

'Jesus,' Braddick hissed as he studied the battered faces of two men, their bodies hanging upside down, more reminiscent of Iraq or Columbia than a Welsh port. One of the men had a message carved into his chest, his grey hair caked in congealing blood. 'Whoever did this wanted to get someone's attention.'

For the attention of Patrick Finnen, Dublin, Ireland......stay in Dublin...

'Has to be drugs,' Braddick muttered. 'There's only a couple of outfits I know who would leave the bodies on show and make a statement like this.'

'My thoughts exactly, Guv. I was trying to say…'

'What the fuck are they doing this far out of the cities?' Braddick interrupted, stopped and eyed the scene. He imagined it without the white clad figures and uniforms. It was a bleak place where decay saturated the atmosphere. 'A miserable place to die,' he said, shivering.

'Aren't they all, Guv?'

'Some more so than others.'

'I suppose so. Look, Guv…'

'The locals must have a three- or four-hour head start on us,' Braddick said, interrupting him again, gesturing to two detectives who appeared to be coordinating the scene. He walked off before his DS could finish his brief. 'Let's introduce ourselves.' The locals spotted them approaching and turned to greet them. 'I'm DI Braddick, and this is my DS, Ade Burns.'

'Thanks for coming over here, much appreciated.'

'No problem.'

'We met your sergeant earlier.'

'You did?' Braddick said, studying the bodies, not really listening.

'Yes. He's been very helpful so far. I'm DI Grady and this is DS Thompson.' The locals greeted him with a brief handshake and a nod of the head. From the way they looked at him, Braddick didn't think they had many black detectives in their stable. 'I'm glad you're here. We need to put our heads together on this one. Let me explain. Follow me,' Grady said, walking away. Braddick noted that they were dressed for the office obviously not expecting to be called to the coast. They stood directly beneath the bodies and Grady pointed to the rusty girder that they were tied to. Orange patches striped the metal at regular intervals. 'Can you see the other rope burns?'

'Yes. I count eight friction marks,' Braddick said, frowning. It was obvious that other ropes had been wrapped around the beam recently and then removed.

'There were more than just these two hung up there.'

'It certainly looks that way,' Braddick agreed. 'So, where are they?'

'We're still looking.'

'Have you called divers in to check the water for more bodies?'

'Yes. We have divers on the way,' Grady said coldly.

'How long will they be?'

'They are on the way.'

'It's important that they get in there quickly,' Braddick said, pointing to the breakwater. 'The wind and tide will take the bodies out in no time.'

'Yes, we know about winds and tides. That's why we called the divers in.'

'You should get the coastguard to patrol the mouth of the harbour too, in case any of them float up.'

'Funnily enough, we thought of that too.'

'Have you checked the tides today?'

'Yes, we have checked the tides and the coast guard are on the case already. We have dealt with bodies in the sea once or twice before,' Grady said calmly. His face flushed red.

'Of course, you have,' Braddick said, realising that he had offended the Welsh detective. 'No offence meant; I'm just thinking aloud.'

'No offence taken.'

'Ten possible victims?' Braddick looked at the friction burns on the girders above them and grimaced. 'What the hell happened here?'

'Drug deal gone wrong,' Grady shrugged. He looked up at the beam again and gestured for them to follow him. 'Badly, badly wrong,' he added. 'We haven't seen anything like this on our patch before. Come this way.' They approached the trawler and stopped to look over the deserted deck. CSI officers were at work inside. The nets were rolled up at the stern, the deck wet but clean. 'It isn't a local trawler…'

'Can I take a look?' Braddick asked before he could finish, stepping on board before he had the answer.

'Help yourself,' Grady said irritated by Braddick. He rolled his eyes skywards and shook his head. 'Is he always so impetuous?' he asked Ade.

'He's usually worse. I think he's making a real effort today,' Ade replied with a straight face. He shrugged and followed his DI aboard. 'He sort of grows on you,' Ade added as he stepped aboard.

'I doubt that very much,' Grady mumbled to himself.

Braddick crossed the deck and climbed into the wheelhouse, analysing the surroundings before walking down steep wooden steps into the bowels of the boat. A narrow galley was tidy but had been used recently; there were coffee mugs upside down on a tiny draining board. The smell of bacon and eggs lingered in the air. Six berths, three port and three starboard, were made up with sleeping bags and pillows. The bunks were narrow, and the odour of unwashed men drifted to him. He looked beneath the pillows and the mattresses but found nothing but mobile phones and a couple of iPads. There was no sign of a struggle and the men who had made up their bunks that morning had every intention of climbing into them that night. Braddick glanced into the hold and then climbed back to the deck. He stepped over the bulwark onto the dock.

'Where are the crew of this boat?' Braddick asked himself as he scanned the scene and spotted a white van about fifty yards further on up the wharf. Dead fish littered the wharf, their scales still shiny and wet but their eyes sunken. 'These fish are not recent catch. They look like they have been on ice for days. They probably used them to mask a shipment.'

'Agreed. One of the bodies has Irish identification on him. We're assuming he sailed in on the trawler with five crewmembers. It is registered from Dublin Port to one of the dead men, Linus Murphy.

He's the poor bastard with the message carved into his chest. As for his crew, we haven't got a clue where they are.'

'The rope marks on that girder tell me we're looking for more bodies,' Braddick said, looking around. 'An Irish trawler in Holyhead. I assume you have checked if their paperwork is legit?' Braddick asked. 'Any log or manifesto on board?'

'No,' Grady said with a half-smile. 'You know a bit about boats?'

'Liverpool is a port,' Braddick said grinning. 'We have boats there too and I don't need to be Captain Birdseye to see that their nets are completely dry, and the deck is spotless. They weren't fishing. When a dragger that size pulls in its nets, there's crap everywhere. Tons of crap.'

Grady shrugged in agreement. 'There's no ice on board, no fresh catch, no paperwork and they never made contact with the coastguard. They knew the port well enough to know about this place. The covered dock hasn't been used for landing fish for twenty years. Linus Murphy was old enough to have been here when it was operational though. It is accessible from the sea and hidden from view of the town and the port. The Coast Guard told us that it has been used before by smugglers.'

'It seems like the ideal spot for a delivery. This is a nasty one but why call us?' Braddick couldn't see the connection to Liverpool yet. Grady gestured to follow him towards the white van. As they approached, Braddick could see that it was a refrigerated vehicle.

'The logo on the side identified it as belonging to a fishmonger from Everton. Your neck of the woods. Over there is a Ford Focus, a sports model.' Grady pointed. 'Your DS checked the phone number and the plates on the van,' Grady said, gesturing to Ade. 'The business doesn't exist. False name, false number. There's a clipboard inside with a bill of sale for four crates of fish of various description. I think they were making a pickup and then they were going to drive back to Liverpool. If they were unlucky enough to be pulled over by traffic, they had an invoice for their load and appeared legit.'

'Let me guess.' Braddick shook his head. 'The crates of fish listed on the invoice have gone.'

'Bingo. No sign of them apart from what is spilled on the dock.'

'And the Ford Focus belongs to who?' Braddick asked.

'We're still working on that. It is registered to a limited company in a place called, Litherland?' he said, looking at Braddick for conformation. Braddick nodded that he knew the area. 'I think two of the men were planning on driving the fish van and the Ford was their escort. There is a sawn-off shotgun under the passenger seat. The second victim hanging from the rafters is also from your neck of the woods.'

'He had ID on him?' Braddick asked with a frown. He glanced at Ade, who was staring at his feet.

'Yes,' Grady glanced at Ade too. 'Sorry. I thought your DS would have told you. That is why we called you.'

'Sorry, Guv,' Ade said, blushing. 'I did try to tell you, but you interrupted me. I didn't have the chance to finish what I was saying.'

'Sorry, Ade,' Braddick said. He knew he had a habit of not listening when he was thinking. 'Who is it?'

'The second body is, Gary Mason,' Grady explained.

'The Gary Mason?' Braddick said, turning to Ade, eyebrows raised.

Ade nodded and shrugged. 'The Gary Mason, Guv.'

'You know him?' Grady asked.

'We know of him,' Ade answered. 'He was an enforcer for years, mostly low-level stuff. He ran a team of bent doormen who had a habit of beating up dealers and robbing their drugs and money. The family are trouble with a capital 'T'.'

'You never nicked him?'

'No. The usual story. He was a slippery bastard. We had a few complaints of assault, but no one ever carried the charges through. Witnesses had a habit of forgetting what they had seen. We could never touch them.'

'I see. Nothing new there,' Grady said with nod. 'We also found ID for three other men from your area tossed on the wharf, so we're assuming there were two men in the van and two escorting them in the car. Four in total.'

'Another three?' Braddick asked with a frown. 'That makes ten possible victims. Fucking hell,' he said in a whisper. 'They left their ID's so we would know who was here. They want their families and colleagues to know what happened to them.'

'Right,' Grady said, gesturing to the dead men. 'That matches with the number of marks on the beam.' He pointed to a CSI who was processing a pile of evidence. There were wallets, keys and random pieces of paper on the dock. 'The other three ID's are all from the same family. What was it again?' he asked Ade, frowning and checking his notes.

'Farrell, Guv,' Ade said with a cold smile.

'Farrell?' Braddick said, surprised.

'I said you would love this.'

'You're fucking kidding me?' Braddick said, shaking his head. He rubbed his chin with his right hand. 'The Farrells are trying to get back in business?'

'Well, it looks like they had a go, Guv,' Ade said, gesturing towards the hanging corpses. 'Doesn't seem to be going that well so far, does it?'

'Your DS said you're familiar with them?' Grady looked hopeful. 'The Farrells, that is.'

'They're a big family that were fronted by father and two sons. More slippery bastards, I'm afraid.'

'It sounds like you're talking past tense.'

'I am. One of the sons was killed in a fight and then the father and his other son disappeared last year.'

'Disappeared to the Costa Del Crime or were they made to disappear?'

'We're not a hundred percent sure. They either ran or they're dead.' Braddick shrugged. 'They were working with a Russian outfit and that only ever ends in tears. It would appear that the rest of the family has tried to pick up the reins.'

'Like DS Burns said—' Grady gestured to the dead men '—it isn't working out very well for them so far.'

'And long may that continue. Okay, I can see the link to Merseyside,' Braddick said, smiling to himself. 'Anything else that links to us?'

'Yep. We have the nine, nine, nine call,' Grady added.

'What call?' Braddick frowned.

'A call was put through to the main switchboard at Chester, male voice, strong Liverpool accent, obviously very distressed.' Grady gestured to their vehicle. 'I have a copy on my laptop. The caller was hysterical, but he claimed that he saw what happened.'

'Liverpool accent?' Braddick raise his eyebrows. 'That isn't a coincidence. Can I hear the call?'

'Of course.'

The four detectives walked over to a dark blue BMW. Braddick and Grady climbed into the front, the others into the rear. He closed the door, shutting out the biting cold and the relentless whistling sound of the wind. Grady pulled up the file on his laptop and clicked play.

'Hello, emergency service operator, which service do you require, fire, police, or ambulance?'

'Fucking all of them! They've got me mates, they need help. The bastards are hurting them!'

'Calm down, sir. Where are you calling from?'

'I don't fucking know! We're by the sea in some fucking Welsh place, Holywell or Holyhead…fucking Holy something…get the fucking police here,

please…they've got our Gary! They said everything would be sound and nothing bad would happen!'

'Okay calm down, can you see any street names or distinctive features around you?'

'For fuck's sake!'

'I can't help if I don't know where you are, sir.'

'There's a big monument on top of the hill…like a spike…and there are ferries in the harbour. Me mates are in an old warehouse by the sea. I saw the fuckers coming and I tried to warn them, but they wouldn't answer the phone. There must have been no fucking signal or something…then they had guns, the dirty bastards shot our Gary in the legs…they're fucking hurting me mates…'

'Did you say that they had guns?'

'Yes! Are you fucking deaf or stupid? I am trying to tell you that they're hurting me mates. The fucking bastards!'

'Okay, I'm going to connect you to the police. What's your name, sir?'

'I can't tell you my name. Another car is coming…fucking hell they've seen me!'

The line went dead.

'That is all we have,' Grady said, looking out of the window. He pointed to a stone obelisk on top of the cliffs that overlook the harbour, ferry terminal and railway station. 'I think he was up there next to Skinner's monument. By the time the information had been passed on and the possible positions narrowed down, they were long gone. The accent, the van and the dead men, well that is why we called you.'

'He was their lookout,' Braddick said, turning to his DS. 'He saw them coming but couldn't warn them.'

'The phone signals here are crap. It's like being on the fucking moon some days.'

'We've got a witness out there somewhere,' Ade said, looking up at the obelisk. 'He'll be piss wet through, freezing cold, tired, hungry and frightened. But we know he is related to Gary Mason.'

'How so?' Grady said turning.

'He called him 'our Gary'. It's a Liverpool thing. He is related, no doubt about it. I'll get onto HQ and get someone around to Mason's family. If we know who he is, we'll know where he is going. If we bring him in, we might be able to nail these bastards.' Braddick nodded in agreement and Ade opened the door, allowing the wind to scythe through the vehicle until he closed it behind him.

'Was Gary Mason shot in the legs?' Braddick asked.

'No but maybe one of the others was.'

Braddick opened the window to call after Ade. 'Make sure a full risk assessment is done before anyone approaches the Mason family. They'll be trigger happy. Just put eyes on them for now.' Ade nodded that he understood. 'And we need to put DI Cain in the loop,' he shouted over the wind. 'Put a call into her too. She can coordinate things until we get back.' Ade walked away and took out his mobile.

'How do you want to proceed?' Braddick asked the Welsh detective.

'We will handle the Dublin side of things, informing the Garda and coordinating with them. The rest of it is more likely yours than ours, wouldn't you say?'

Braddick nodded, his hands deep in his pockets. The wind made the corpses swing, the ropes creaking against the rusty girders. 'I think whatever happened here will be resolved on our patch, one way or another. We'll need everything from forensics sent direct to MIT and the Drug Squad at Canning Place. DI Steff Cain heads up the DS.'

'No problem. We'll get on it.' Grady saw the divers arriving in a white van. 'First priority is finding the missing men. I'll brief the divers.'

'Guv,' Ade said, tapping on the window with one hand covering the phone. His face was ashen, eyes wide with shock. Braddick lowered the window. 'It's DI Cain.'

'What?'

'They pulled her out of the Mersey this morning.'

'What?' Braddick felt sick. 'What the fuck happened?'

'She jumped off Runcorn Bridge last night.'

CHAPTER 4

Irene Cain looked into her husband's eyes. Norman was drifting in and out of the real world. There were moments of clarity, his eyes clear, frightened and accusing. He looked at her as if she was the one who had tied his hands behind his back, trussed his legs together and gagged him. He was confused as to why she hadn't fed him, hunger and thirst were burning inside him, driving him to the point of panic. The rest of the time, he was lost inside his decaying mind, unaware of their plight, eyes seeing, brain receiving but not communicating properly. Irene wished that he would stay locked inside his own mind. He was safer there away from the danger, the thirst, the hunger and the agonising cramps that being bound caused.

She thought back to the night they were taken. Norman was settled in his armchair, Roy Orbison playing quietly in the background. The music seemed to soothe his troubled mind and he would doze the entire time it played. Sometimes he would wake up humming the tune, but he could rarely remember the words. It was the only time she could relax and catch up with her soaps. Nursing Norman was a fulltime occupation. Sometimes it pushed her to her limits. There were days when her patience snapped. The days when he didn't know her, didn't know where he was, didn't even know his own name. Those were the days when he could be awkward, aggressive and verbally abusive. Changing a grown man's nappy and wiping his arse was difficult enough but when it was her husband, the man she had loved, married, had children with, admired, respected and adored, then it was heartbreaking. Sometimes he would call her a stupid bitch, get his hands covered in faeces and smear it everywhere. They were the days when she felt like giving up, putting him into care but the brief moments of lucidity swayed her to persevere. Now she wished she hadn't. He could have been safe in a nursing home, tucked up in bed oblivious to what was going on outside. The night they were taken, there was a knock at the door and Irene had opened it. They forced the door so hard that she was stunned by the blow and they were overwhelmed in seconds.

The men who had taken them had told her that they would be released unharmed if their daughter did as she was told. She had no idea what that meant. Steff was the smartest woman she had met, attractive, driven and successful. She couldn't have been prouder of her although the dangers of her job were a constant concern. She didn't talk about her job in detail, but Irene knew she dealt with the most violent section of society; drug dealers. She had never met a drug dealer, but she was positive that the men who had abducted them were just that. They were foreign and they were nasty, and they were huge, frightening men who picked them up and carried them like they were dolls. Even at their strongest point in life, the Cains could not have resisted. They were peaceful people. Violence was only for the television or the news. It didn't enter their world. Their world revolved around each other and their family. They doted on their daughters and their grandchildren. Steff had idolised her nieces. She spoiled them silly on birthdays and at Christmas. The family ribbed her constantly about meeting a man and having her own family, but her job dominated her life. Still, they often talked about it. They hoped that she would have a family one day. Until Norman became ill, that is. After that, Irene was devoted to making his life as comfortable as possible while he died from the inside out. She loved him more now than she had when they married. He was her best friend, lover and soul mate. She missed him terribly even though he was still breathing.

Irene looked at Norman. His eyes were closed, and his breathing was laboured but steady. He seemed to be sleeping. She could smell him, the nappy full of two days of waste. Her pleas to be allowed to go to the toilet had been ignored along with her requests for water and the restraints loosened. At the end of the first day, they gagged her to shut her up. Having to urinate in her pants was one of the most embarrassing things that she had ever endured. The warm, wet feeling soon become cold and incredibly uncomfortable. She certainly wasn't looking forward to cleaning Norman. That would be horrific. She had decided that she would sit him in the wet room clothed and peel them off one layer at a time, allowing the hot water to wash off the waste. His clothes would have to be thrown away but that was the least of her concerns. The first things that she wanted were the toilet, a drink, to talk to her daughters and then to smoke a cigarette, not necessarily in that order. Her mind stopped drifting as she heard the driver's door open. She felt the vehicle rock as someone climbed into the van. She couldn't see anything, but she was certain that she could hear the engine turn over, splutter and then start. It juddered and then moved. Her heart raced as the van picked up speed and the radio was turned on. She could hear a deep voice muttering along to the music, not quite singing, not quite humming, somewhere in between. The smell of cigarette smoke drifted to her. It made her craving ten times worse.

She didn't know how long they had been travelling but it didn't seem to be that long before it came to an abrupt halt. The radio was turned down and she heard voices, two or maybe three, one in the front and the others outside. Their language was alien to her, thick and throaty. The type of language that sounds as if they are arguing even if they are not. There were five minutes or so of discussion, some laughing and what sounded like whispering. The radio was turned up again and the van set off at speed. She heard sirens approaching and her heart jumped at the thought of the police surrounding the van and releasing them but as it faded into the distance, she cried again. The sound of children playing drifted to her, and then faded away. After what felt like an age, the van stopped, and she heard the engine turned off. Footsteps and voices seemed to circle the vehicle and then everything went quiet for a moment. Her throat was dry, and she felt sweat trickling down her spine. Fear made her skin tingle as if ghostly fingers were stroking her neck. The silence was deafening, threatening and oppressive. What were they doing? Would they leave them in some remote spot to starve to death? Would they set fire to the van to destroy the evidence? Irene had seen a drama on the BBC where the criminals seemed to know as much about forensic evidence as the police did. She didn't want to burn to death. That would be a terrible way to die. She half hoped that they would shoot them and put them out of their misery. Whatever happened, she would be with Norman somewhere. She wasn't a religious woman, but she believed that their souls would find each other in eternity, wherever that may be. A love that strong couldn't be extinguished by death, it would continue somehow. She just knew that it would.

She jumped when the side door slid open and strong hands reached in and grabbed her. They pulled a hood over her head and she could hear Norman grunting through his gag. She felt herself being lifted upwards and out into the cold night air. She didn't struggle, she didn't have the energy and she didn't want whatever was going to happen to hurt. As long as there wasn't too much pain, death would be a blessed relief. She thought about Norman and how frightened he would be. Of course, he wouldn't understand what was happening to them. All he would know was that he was being hurt. She felt a sob in her chest at the thought, poor Norman. Hot tears stung her eyes and ran down her cheeks. Her breath was caught in her chest.

A door opened and she knew that they had been carried indoors. It was suddenly warmer and the sound pollution from the town was dulled. She was lowered onto something soft, and comfortable, and familiar. The smell of their surroundings was well known to her, her senses ultra-aware, trying to analyse where they had been taken. Then she felt her bindings being cut, first her legs and then her hands. She instinctively moved her hands to her face.

'Do not move the hood for ten minutes,' a voice growled at her. 'We will be watching you. If you are not sure how long that is, then count slowly to six hundred. Understand?' Irene nodded, not really understanding anything. She heard footsteps padding away, two sets, maybe three. She heard Norman breathing, mumbling under his hood. The smell of pine air fresheners, her favourite, drifted to her. Cooking smells from weeks before lingered in the fibres of the house, baked apple pies, roast lamb and bacon. The smells that made her house her home. The smells that never truly left because they were a part of them, a part of their very existence. She was home. She knew that she was. They had brought them home.

Irene counted slowly in her mind, desperate to rip off the hood and the gag, desperate to check if Norman was unharmed, desperate to drink and relieve herself and desperate to call Steff. The temptation to rush or stop at three hundred or four hundred was overwhelming but she daren't. She could not risk it. They had said that they would take them home if Steff did what was asked of her and they had. She could barely believe it. There had been times when she thought they would be left to starve to death. Maybe they weren't so bad after all. They had lived up to their word. Steff had said that drug dealers were evil, completely devoid of empathy. Maybe they weren't so bad after all.

She reached six hundred and pulled off the hood. The house was in darkness, yellow light seeped through the kitchen window from the street. Everything seemed normal. The shadows of her furniture were in the right places. She unfastened the gag and breathed deeply, her jaw aching and stiff. Moving carefully in the darkness, she decided to leave the light off to avoid blinking painfully against the glare. Norman was curled up on the settee. She took off his hood and removed his gag, his eyes wide open, almost catatonic. She walked into the kitchen and took a tall glass from the drainer. Filling it with cold water, she let it overflow for a few seconds before drinking from it. The liquid soothed her throat and quenched her thirst. She refilled it again and took a knife from the drawer before making her way back to Norman. His eyes didn't flicker as she cut through his bonds. She removed the ties and sat him upright, placing the water to his lips. Norman sipped from the glass, water dribbled from his mouth down his chin and onto his cardigan. Irene waited for him to swallow before giving him some more. This time he gulped thirstily from the glass. His eyes flickered against the light, his pupils shrinking to pinpoints. He looked at her and smiled thinly, recognition sparked in his eyes for a moment.

'Irene, where have we been?' he croaked. His voice hoarse. 'I'm hungry. What time is tea?'

'We're home now, Norman,' she whispered and kissed his forehead. 'I'll make you your favourite in a while.'

'I didn't like that place, Irene,' he said, shaking his head. 'My arms are sore.'

'I know, darling,' she said, holding him tight. She missed him holding her. It was one of the things that she yearned for, his embrace. 'Don't you worry now. We'll put you in the shower and then I'll make some tea. You'll feel better after that.'

'I'm hungry.'

'I know you are,' she said, stroking the back of his head. He laid his head on her shoulder. She kissed his forehead. 'I love you, you beautiful, beautiful man. I always will.'

As she kissed him, a plug-in timer switched on, igniting the leaking gas from a severed pipe behind the cooker in the kitchen. A cloud of gas ignited instantly. The burning sensation was brief and excruciating as her skin blistered and peeled. She felt Norman hold her tightly as the delicate tissue in her lungs sizzled and popped before death took them. The blast ripped the front elevation from their home.

CHAPTER 5

Ronny Mason stepped off the bus and looked around. He had spent the night trying to sleep in a garden shed to keep out of the biting wind and torrential rain. His stomach was tied in knots; fear, embarrassment, and absolute shame twisted his insides. Every time he dozed off he was snapped awake by guilt. He felt completely helpless. His phone was dead, and he couldn't call anyone to tell them what had happened. What could he say? 'I left them there and ran away. I saw them being hurt and did nothing.' He was confused, tired, hungry, and frightened. More frightened than anything else. His father would kill him. He would get the blame. He knew it. They had said that nothing bad would happen. They were wrong. They lied.

Sleep eluded him all night. Every gust of wind had brought the sound of demons approaching, every raindrop on the roof was a footstep. He had cowered, shivering and shaking from the cold, for hours. It was all he deserved for leaving his family there. He had done nothing. He had run away.

When daylight had finally arrived, he made his way to a bus stop and got on the first bus that arrived, a double-decker headed across the island and over the bridge to the university town of Bangor. After an hour, the bus stopped outside the railway station and he climbed off, stiff and exhausted. He pulled up his collar and jogged across the road, dodging the busy morning traffic. His dark tracksuit was damp and cold, his Adidas trainers sopping wet. A lorry drove by and splashed his pants with dirty surface water. Ronny swore and flicked a finger to the driver and ran for the shelter of the railway station. The huge slate roof shielded him from the rain, but the wind still cut through him. He checked the timetable, searching for trains that were heading for Chester; there he could switch trains to Liverpool. Ronny struggled to read the station names, his dyslexia a constant handicap. School had been a nightmare for him. He wasn't stupid but he wasn't bright either. Intellectually challenged and born with no drive or ambition, he had left school with nothing but a twenty-five-metre swimming badge. It took him fifteen minutes to work out that there were no trains for forty minutes. He couldn't wait on an exposed platform for forty minutes. If they were looking for him then they would have the station watched. Paranoia gripped him. Ronny decided that he would be safer walking through town, finding a bar that was open, one that had a Samsung charger in their lost property, then he could turn up last minute for the train. He needed to get his mobile charged and find a signal. Letting the family know what had happened was imperative. They needed to pick him up and hide him until things settled down. It was the least that they could do. They always looked down on him and gave him the shitty jobs, especially his father. He gave him one shitty job after the other. He had heard them calling him thick. Once, his cousin had called him a retard. Well, he might not be the brightest bulb on the tree, but he knew a fuck up when he saw one. This one was a monumental fuck up. They had assured him that nothing could go wrong, nothing bad would happen. They lied. It couldn't have gone worse. The fact that they lied cut him deep.

Ronny walked as fast as he could without looking suspicious. Every car that splashed by was a threat, every glance in his direction terrified him. He asked a couple of student types if there were any bars with early opening hours and they directed him to the local Weatherspoon's. Five minutes later, he was walking into the warmth of The Black Bull Inn. It was surprisingly busy, the tables occupied by a menagerie of drinkers, some there to socialise, others to drink alone. Whatever had gone wrong in their lives, alcohol for breakfast seemed to be the solution. The chatter of voices and the smell of ale made him feel normal for the first time in days. He ordered a pint of strong cider and a double whisky and downed them in minutes, ordering the same again before asking for a charger. The barmaid handed him one and pointed to a socket across the room. He carried his drinks to the table and plugged his phone in. The light began flashing and he stared at the screen while the battery light scrolled up and down.

He thought back to the night before, hiding next to the monument, watching through binoculars. When the men with guns arrived, he had called Gary constantly until he heard the gunshots and the screams. Then he called the police and another car arrived. When he looked through the binoculars again, someone was looking right back at him through theirs. That was when he turned and ran. He didn't stop running for over an hour. Gary had always said he was a shitbag, no balls, no backbone, no stomach for the job. Ronny tried to convince him otherwise but when it came down to it, Gary was right. He had turned and ran. Ronny swallowed his drinks and tried to work out who to call and what he was going to say. Ron senior, known to everyone as Big Ron, had gone bananas when Uncle Gary had told him that he had set the deal up. Big Ron had seen it as a threat to his authority. Once Gary had explained that it was a massive payday, Ron had relented and given his consent. He had insisted that his son, young Ronny should be included but Gary was adamant that Ronny wasn't up to it. Big Ron insisted and if Big Ron said something should happen then it happened. He felt like he had let him down. He couldn't phone him. His father would kick him from Monday to Sunday. He had beaten him from as far back as his memory went. Ronny was terrified of his father. Most people were. He racked his brains for the words to explain to him what had happened. His hands were shaking as he watched the battery icon growing. There was no choice. If his father heard the news from someone else, he would be double pissed off. One more round of drinks and he would make the call. His hands were shaking visibly as he emptied the whisky glass.

CHAPTER 6

Patrick Finnen was standing on the O'Connell Bridge watching the River Liffey flow beneath it. He hadn't heard from the trawler crew or the buyers for twenty-four hours and his contacts across the sea in Holyhead had told him that there was an incident near the harbour. A big one. They told him that the police were all over the place and a refrigerated van had been seen arriving on scene and had left a few hours later. Refrigerated vans spelt dead bodies. Not good. The longer the silence went on, the sicker he felt. Everything he had worked for had been snatched away in an instant. Patrick had been an amateur boxing champion in his teens and when he climbed into the professional ranks, he commanded a big following of Irish fans. He was tipped to become a middleweight champion when a detached retina brought a swift end to a promising career. No career meant no money. His nest egg dwindled away until he decided to use his remaining funds to buy a kilo of coke. He tripled his money and built up a reliable customer base and developed a trusting relationship with his suppliers. Things went well until he saw the opportunity to export across the Irish Sea. Moving drugs in bulk brought massive profits. It also brought massive risk. He made contacts and found backers. He had taken the step-up to the big league, made assurances, guarantees that the buyers were solid and could be trusted. The entire plan had disintegrated before his eyes. No million euros and no drugs. The delivery men and the buyers were incommunicado and that could mean only one of two things: Either they had conspired to rip him and his backers off, or the deal had been hit by another outfit. The second was the most likely, not that it mattered long term. If he couldn't produce the cash or the goods, he would be at the bottom of the Liffey very soon. His position was dire, the options limited. The backers had told him to be at the bridge where he would be contacted.

'Patrick, how's things?' A voice disturbed his thoughts. Patrick turned to see a man in his sixties approaching. He was powerfully built with a neck like an ox. His olive-green military jacket looked as old as he did, and his army boots were scuffed around the toes. A wool beanie hat covered his head, the exposed hair silvered by age. He didn't make eye contact as he sidled up next to him. Looking down at the muddy waters, he rubbed his hands together and blew into them to keep them warm. 'Are you having a bad day?' the old man asked chirpily.

'I've had better.'

'And I'm sure that you have had worse too, no doubt?'

'If I have, I can't recall it.'

'Think positively.'

'I am trying.'

'The General wants to know what you're going to do about his money, Patrick. He's very concerned that you might disappear and leave him with his dick hanging out in the cold.' He looked at him for the first time and smiled. 'You wouldn't be planning anything like that would you, Patrick?'

'No.'

'No plans to travel at all?' he said, frowning. 'That surprises me.'

Patrick shook his head and sighed. 'I won't be going anywhere without his say so. I wanted to see what he had to say before I do anything.'

'So, you have a plan?'

'Sort of.'

'Good,' he said patting him on the back. 'Positive attitude. That is what we want to see. What are you going to do?'

'I can't find out what happened by standing on this bridge talking to you.' Patrick sighed. 'I need to speak to the buyers before I can tell him anything and I don't think a telephone call will suffice. I need to look into their eyes when I talk to them.'

'Assuming they're alive, Patrick,' the old man said, turning towards him again. His eyes were sharp and alert, belying his age. 'My experience of these situations is that the people being robbed tend to die and the thieves disappear.'

'They always leave a trail,' Patrick said firmly. 'No one can sell a shipment that size without leaving a trail.'

'Who was your contact?'

'A guy from Liverpool called Gary Mason.'

'Do you know who is behind him?'

'No,' Patrick said, shaking his head. 'He fronts a big family. They won't be hard to find. He told me that they were big players in Liverpool.'

'He told you that, did he?'

'Yes.' Patrick frowned. 'Why?'

'Usually when someone tells you that he is a big player, he isn't.'

'I checked with some people in the city. They confirmed that Gary Mason is a known face.'

'A known face?'

'Yes.'

'Jürgen Klopp is a known face, but he wouldn't be any good at setting up a fucking drug deal, would he?'

'I was happy that they were reliable. They had the money. It should have been a quick deal, in and out.'

'Should have been.'

'I think someone hit the deal. Another outfit.'

'Maybe, or maybe they made it look like another outfit hit the deal.'

'Until I speak to them, I don't even know what actually happened. All I know is the trawler captain and the buyer are silent. Nothing from either.'

'It doesn't look good for you, lad.'

'I know that.'

'You know it will be on your head, don't you?'

'I know that too. All I want is the chance to get the money back.'

'I've been around people like this for longer than I care to remember. Even when the culprits are identified, it is very rare that a consignment is recovered intact.' Patrick nodded and looked back at the river. He felt his stomach tighten with fear. The chances of him surviving this were minimal. The old man or someone like him would be sent to put a bullet through his forehead. And that was only if they believed that he wasn't involved in the heist. If the General believed he had set the whole thing up, he would be nailed to the floor, tortured and dismembered until they were convinced that he wasn't, before his remains were burned in an oil drum. The old man studied Patrick in silence. His eyes seemed to bore into his mind. 'The fact that it is on the mainland makes things more complicated.'

'If you're trying to cheer me up, it isn't working.'

'I'm not here to cheer you up, Patrick,' the old man said, smiling. 'I'm here to decide if you are involved in it or not.'

'I am not involved,' Patrick said looking directly into the old man's eyes.

'Okay, let's say you're not. What then?'

'I need to try to get the money back. At least give me the chance to try.'

'Lucky for you, the General doesn't think that you're to blame and he sent me here to see for myself. I agree with him.' Patrick looked at him, eyebrows raised in surprise. 'He said he was tight with your old man.' Patrick nodded. He had never met the General and he didn't know anything about his father, but it explained why he wasn't dead already. 'He wants you to get the ferry over to Holyhead and find his goods or the money. You have one week, Patrick.'

'I'll go tonight,' Patrick agreed. The relief was enormous, a chance at least to redeem the deal. 'Tell him that I said thank you for the chance.'

'Two more things,' the old man said, pushing his hands deep into his jacket.

'What? Just name it and I'll do my best.'

'Your best better be good enough, lad.'

'It will be.'

'Okay. I think you're on the level. He wants his money and he wants the rats dead. If you can find out who did this then he wants them taken out of the game.'

'Fucking hell!' Patrick whistled and shook his head. 'Even if I find the product, that could be impossible. They won't be advertising the fact that they did it, will they? They could be in the wind by now.'

'I agree with you. It is a tough ask but they are his terms. Find the money and remove the rats from the equation.'

'Why is he so keen for them to be wiped out?'

'He can see the potential in what you were trying to do.'

'He does?'

'Drugs are our business nowadays. Times have changed. Dublin is becoming saturated with that shit. Every teenage wannabe thinks he's Scarface these days. We're taking a half a dozen punks out of business every weekend, but they're replaced by another half a dozen the week after. It is a relentless battle just to stay static. We can't win this battle.'

The old man shook his head. 'The little fuckers are everywhere, and the police are always one step behind. Exporting in bulk makes sense and the risks are lower. The General wants to move out of the retail sector. You showed him that it is possible even if you did fuck it up.'

'It should have been simple. At least that's what I thought,' Patrick said thoughtfully, lighting a cigarette. He inhaled deeply and let the smoke flow slowly from his lungs. 'It was a good idea in theory.'

'It still is,' the old man agreed. He paused. 'In theory that is. Now then, what you need to remember is that theories are what we have just before we get fucked over.'

'Not the best start was it.'

'Not at all but he realises the potential.'

'Good.'

'It can't be achieved while there is a rat's nest across the water. Someone opened their mouth and tipped off the wrong people. Finding them shouldn't be too hard. We speak to your buyers and find out who knew about it. We can narrow it down from there.'

'We?'

'Oh yes. The other thing is that I'm coming along with you. Just to make sure that you come back, of course.'

'Of course,' Patrick mumbled. 'And what do I call you?'

'Call me Henry,' he replied with a half-smile. 'We had better get a move on. We have a ferry to catch.'

CHAPTER 7

Braddick walked out of the lift at Canning Place. All leave had been cancelled and the Major Investigation Team was gearing up to full speed. Twenty extra detectives had been drafted in from across the city, bringing the squad to sixty. The Drug Squad were a few steps behind MIT, still reeling from the news that their DI had committed suicide, but they were about to be briefed on the case and brought up to speed. The atmosphere was frantic but subdued; losing one of their own had hit the force hard. It was business as usual, but laughter was at a minimum. He walked through the bustle and exchanged brief greetings with his people. The tension in the air was palpable. He opened the door and stepped into his office where the ACC was pacing up and down. Sitting in one of the chairs was a dark-haired female with sky-blue eyes; the kind of eyes you can fall into. He nodded hello, embarrassed by staring at them for a second too long. She smiled back and lit up the room. She was about to speak but the ACC put a halt to their introduction.

'At last, DI Braddick,' the officer said stiffly. 'You must be shattered after that trip. All the way back from a foreign country. How was the journey back from Anglesey?'

'Fine, sir.' Braddick shrugged, thinking that they had returned from Anglesey not Afghanistan. 'Any more information about DI Cain?'

'I'm afraid things have escalated. It's worse.'

'Worse?'

'It's a terrible shame. A bloody shambles,' the officer said, shaking his head. 'The fire brigade were called to her parent's home last night.'

'What,' Braddick asked confused. 'Why?'

'Gas explosion, we believe. Two bodies were recovered but they're too badly burnt to identify yet. We're waiting on a dental report from forensics. On the face of it, we have to assume that her parents are dead too.'

'No way is that a coincidence,' Braddick hissed. 'Fucking hell!' He pulled out his chair and sat down heavily on it. He looked at the woman and shook his head. 'Excuse my language. We haven't been introduced.'

'DI Joanne Jones, but most people call me, Jo,' she said, leaning over the desk to shake his hand. 'We met a few years back. I was undercover with the Matrix team.'

'Really,' Braddick said, frowning. He was sure that he would have remembered her. She was very unforgettable.

'I've brought DI Jones in from UC to front up the DS for the time being,' the ACC interrupted. 'In light of what has happened, I would suggest that you brief both units at the same time and then decide between yourselves which angles you will cover. I want both departments working on this. Put it to bed quickly. The press will be having a party.'

'No problem for me, sir.' Braddick sighed and half smiled at Jo. 'I'll be at least an hour catching up with where we are at. It would be a big help if you can ask your team what they have on the recent whereabouts of Gary Mason and the Farrell family.'

'I know Gary Mason and the Farrells,' Jo nodded.

'You do?'

'Yes. His brother runs security for most of the clubs in town. Big Ron Mason?'

'That is him. They seem to have gone off the radar lately.'

'I'm sure DS will have plenty of up to date info on him.'

'Excellent.'

'What about the Farrells?' Jo prompted him.

'We thought that they were out of business, but it appears we were wrong. Maybe your team and Matrix are aware of their movements over the last few months. MIT wouldn't necessarily hear about them unless they popped up on our radar,' Braddick said. Matrix worked serious organised crime and had undercover officers on the streets.

'If they have been dealing again, Matrix will know about it. I'll get on it straight away,' Jo said, writing down the names. 'I'm familiar with both families,' she added. Braddick looked confused. She smiled. 'From my time undercover.'

'Of course, you would be.' He searched the memory banks but still couldn't place her. 'There's no need to fill you in on them then?'

'None at all.'

'Sounds to me like you're already ahead of the game.'

'With the Farrells, yes. First class scumbags, the lot of them,' she said, smiling. 'Eddie junior was at the top of my 'absolute wanker' list before he disappeared.'

'Just ahead of his father,' Braddick agreed.

'The apple didn't fall far from the tree.'

'It rarely does in that business.'

'If you don't need me for anything, I'll get on, sir unless there is anything else?' she said, standing. Braddick glanced at her physique. She was attractive. There was something about the way she carried herself. Her long raven hair was immaculate, her clothes smart but understated. She had applied make-up that emphasised her beauty without being too obvious. She was a head-turner, no doubt about it. The ACC seemed to be distracted as she walked to the door. She turned and caught him staring at her behind. 'Was there anything else, sir?'

'No, no,' he stuttered and looked out of the window blushing. 'Best you dive in at the deep end and get on with it. I need a few words with DI Braddick anyway.'

'Shall we say an hour?' she said, turning to Braddick and looking at her watch.

'That's fine,' he said. She closed the door and left the scent of Chanel Chance behind. 'I think she'll fit right in."

'She will. There's no doubt about it.'

'You wanted to talk to me about something, sir?'

The Assistant Chief Constable walked to the window and looked down at the Albert Dock. He could see the huge Ferris wheel turning slowly, hundreds of shoppers milling about oblivious to how perilous the world could be. A Mersey ferry was leaving its berth, leaving a foamy wake on the slate grey water. 'I want to talk to you about Steff Cain,' he said, turning to face him. He seemed to be thinking carefully about what he was about to say. 'I feel somehow responsible.'

'Sir?'

'Eyewitnesses say that she stopped her car in the slow lane, turned off the engine, got out and climbed up the east side of the bridge and then simply threw herself off.' He shrugged. His expression showed disbelief. 'To an outsider, there would appear to be no question that it was suicide.'

'To an outsider, yes. I agree.'

'Can you see her doing that, I mean can you really see that happening?'

Braddick looked at his fingernails but didn't see them. His mind searched for answers that were not there.

'Maybe, if it was someone else,' he said, looking up. 'Who knows what goes through the mind of someone before they kill themselves. We can't put ourselves there.' Braddick paused. 'But Steff Cain?' he said, shaking his head. 'I don't see any situation that would make her take her life. She was solid, well balanced and tough as nails.'

'My thoughts exactly.'

'She had everything to live for.' The ACC nodded in agreement. 'When you add in the fact that her parents were killed in a gas explosion the night after she took her life, then the alarm bells ring in my head. She didn't do that of her own choice. Not a chance.'

'I know what I think happened.' The ACC turned back to the window. He was staring but not seeing anything except what was in his mind. 'I want to hear what you think?'

'I think someone told her to jump, threatened her family and left her with no option. If it were your kids or parents being threatened, what would you do?'

'I can't even think about it.' The ACC pinched the bridge of his nose and closed his eyes for a moment. 'I want to know who did this, DI Braddick,' the ACC said, sitting down opposite him. He looked haunted. 'I want the bastards screwed to the wall.'

'Is there something that you're not telling me?'

The ACC stared at Braddick for a long moment before speaking. 'She came to me last week and told me that she had an informer who was ready to testify. He was frightened but he wanted to turn evidence and go into protection. Cain was close to bringing him in.'

'An informer?'

'Yes. He was ready to turn evidence on his employers. The intel was excellent. Everything looked kosher.'

'And you think this is related?'

'I am certain that it is what caused this, absolutely certain. There is no other logical explanation except that she lost her mind and we both know that that didn't happen, don't we?'

'Yes.'

'Then it has to be to do with the informer.'

'Okay, I'm following you so far. Let's say it was to do with that, then who is the informer?' Braddick sat forward.

'She wouldn't give his name. She was going to bring him in next week. I do know that he was high level and could bring down the entire operation in the city and probably beyond. She said that it would have ramifications across the country.' He paused for a moment to let the information sink in. 'She said that it would be too big for us to handle and that the National Crime Agency would need to be informed. She was certain that they would take the case over.'

'Bloody hell! Who did he work for?'

'Viktor Karpov.'

'Are you fucking joking me?' Braddick stood up and put his hands flat on the desk. 'Cain had someone inside the Karpov operation?' he asked, shaking his head. Visions of his dead girlfriend drifted to him, her face blistered and burned, her eyes gone, replaced by maggot filled sockets. The woman he had loved was just another victim of the Karpov machine. A machine that crushed all in its path. She was the only witness to a shooting. Braddick had become infatuated with her and convinced her to go into protection and their relationship spiralled out of control. He had crossed the line and began a sexual relationship with her. The Karpovs found out where she was and wiped her from the face of the earth. That is what they did. He had been a fool to think that he could protect her.

'Oh my God,' Braddick whispered beneath his breath. His guts twisted, making him feel weak. 'If the Karpovs discovered that she had a mole in their operation then they would have wiped out her entire family before she had chance to take a statement from him. Do you have any idea what these people are capable of?'

'I'm aware of the Karpov family, DI Braddick,' the ACC said defensively, but he didn't sound convincing. 'And I warned her to be very careful.'

'Careful?' Braddick scoffed. 'Careful? For fuck's sake!'

'I don't appreciate your tone.'

'Stuff what you appreciate where the sun doesn't shine,' Braddick said quietly. 'You knew that she was playing with fire. The Karpovs are pure evil. She never stood a chance.'

'She could have come to me, asked for help.'

'What could you have done against that organisation?' Braddick snapped. 'Fucking Batman couldn't have helped her. As soon as that name was mentioned, she should have been taken out of the operation and the NCA should have been brought in immediately. She was fucked from the start. This is on you.'

'Don't you think I didn't discuss that with her?' The ACC blushed purple with anger and embarrassment. 'Do you really think I didn't insist on that?'

'You didn't insist hard enough from where I'm sitting.'

'She was adamant that the informer would only come in with her.'

'Then you should have let them go and whistle in the wind before you dangled her out there!' Braddick said, shaking his head in disbelief. 'Anyone else, maybe…but the Karpovs, no way. You should have brought the NCA in straight away.'

'Don't preach to me, Braddick,' the ACC said frowning. Deep creases furrowed his forehead. 'We discussed this for hours. She was adamant that the informer didn't trust any of the serious crime agencies. He told her that the Karpovs have NCA officers on their payroll. He told her that he would only deal with her. Nobody else. She weighed up the risks and demanded to be allowed to bring him in. It was that or lose him completely.'

Braddick mulled over what he had said. It made sense. Braddick had been in the NCA when Karin Range came forward as a witness to a murder. When the Karpovs found her, she was murdered. He knew that there were rats in the agency; someone had given her location to the Karpovs. He had spent a year trying to sniff them out and when he pointed the finger at one of his colleagues, he had been sent back to Merseyside as a detective inspector and told to shut his mouth. When rumours about his relationship with Karin began to circulate, he was given the option to request a transfer back to his force or face an investigation. He was lucky to have kept his job. The ACC was right; there were rats in the agency. There were rats everywhere. He sighed heavily and closed his eyes.

'It's just fucking wrong.' Braddick sighed. 'She was a diamond.'

'I am as devastated about what has happened as anyone in this fucking building,' the ACC snapped, his face blushing with patches of crimson. 'More so because this happened on my watch and she came to me with it. I wish she hadn't. I wish I had done something differently, but I didn't. I have to carry that with me. She wanted to see it through, and I let her do that. The Karpovs must have found out and targeted her and her family and there isn't a damn thing that I can do about it. If I could go back and change things, then I would but I can't.'

'The Karpovs are a fucking threshing machine. They smash everything in their path. Everything and everyone. She should have had every member of her family put into protection.'

'And who would have signed off on the cost of that?' The ACC shrugged and tilted his head. 'Exactly how long would we have had to protect them?' He shrugged again. 'A year, two years, ten years, come on, you tell me?'

Braddick knew that his superior was right. They would never have been safe. Not even if they locked up every man with the surname Karpov. Not ever. He walked to the window, puffed out his cheeks and blew the air out with a whistle. Across the road, the river trundled by on the way to the Irish Sea, never slowing, never stopping, relentless in its progress. Cain had tried to capture a monster. Taking out the Karpovs was like trying to change the direction of the river using a bucket. He felt sick to his core.

'Viktor Karpov might as well have pushed her off that bridge himself. It explains everything.' All the anger had gone from his voice. It was pointless being angry with the ACC. He was as helpless as Cain was against an outfit like the Karpovs. Braddick sighed. A thought occurred to him. 'Who else knew about this?'

'I am not a hundred percent sure. Obviously, myself and her DS and whoever was working the informer. I'm assuming it is an undercover officer. She was keeping the information tight for obvious reasons.'

'Not tight enough,' Braddick said, still staring at the river. 'Who's her DS?'

'He's new, transferred in from Coppice Hill last month, Mike Pilkington,' the ACC said matter of factly. 'I've told him to get himself in here pronto.' Braddick turned to look at him, a concerned expression on his face. The ACC read his mind. 'He has no wife, no children and no close relatives to speak of. I checked that straightaway.'

'Good.'

'I want you and DI Jones to debrief him and find out exactly what they had on the Karpovs and see if there is anything that we can rescue from this. We need to know if we have enough to bring in the NCA. As I said before, I want these bastards nailed to the wall, DI Braddick.' Braddick exhaled loudly and nodded.

'Of course.'

'You will have your hands full with this Holyhead business, but you will have whatever resources you need at your disposal. I will make sure of that. Get the bastards, Braddick!'

'Okay, I need her laptop and access to all her files,' Braddick said, sitting down. He picked up his pen and tapped it on the desk. Karin's face drifted to him again. Viktor Karpov had given the order.

He killed her and took her away from him. If their paths ever crossed, he didn't think he would be able to bring him in, not alive anyway. 'Once I have briefed the teams and spoken to Mike Pilkington, I'll call you with an update and what we need to progress, okay?'

'Good.' The ACC nodded and stood up. He walked to the door and reached for the handle. 'You know that there was nothing that I could do, don't you?' he said, opening the door and walking out without waiting for an answer.

Braddick thought about it briefly. 'There was nothing that anyone could have done and that is the fucking problem,' he mumbled to himself. He thought about Steff Cain and how frightened she must have been, how helpless and alone she must have felt. Just like Karin had, just like he did sometimes.

CHAPTER 8

Detective Sergeant Mike Pilkington took his money from the cash machine and stuffed it into his brown leather wallet with shaking hands. Cash was king when you had to keep a low profile and he had the feeling that he would have to. His head was in a spin. He checked behind him, left and right before sliding the wallet into his dark trousers. Zipping up his black bubble coat, he headed down the street, keeping his head down and his eyes focused on anyone in close proximity. The news of his DI chucking herself off a bridge had come as a hammer blow. It was completely unbelievable. She was so solid and sharp. He was devastated. His hands were still shaking as he felt for his car keys. A bottle of whisky and a sleepless night had done nothing to improve his mood. Various scenarios ran through his head as he had tossed and turned but none of them added up. Steff Cain wasn't the type to quit anything, especially life. She had shown no signs of depression, in fact she was hyper.

The Drug Squad had been more successful over the previous twelve months than it had since its conception in 2005. Most people put that down to her. She had a knack with people. Her detectives were motivated and prepared to go the extra mile to get a result. The overtime bill was down as the team didn't grab at every half an hour they could, and the creative accounting of hours worked had stopped. Arrests were up, complaints were down, and she was being tipped for the top. DI Steff Cain was a shining light in the force. He had only been there a month, but she had made sure that he fitted in right away. She had taken to him immediately and as her DS, she had shared confidential information with him from day one. She was the best DI that he had worked with.

When the ACC contacted him with the news about her parents, he knew that she had been pushed from the bridge, not physically but pushed, nonetheless. The bastards had got to her some way, probably through her family. Family was always a person's weak point. She was a talented police officer surrounded by other talented police officers, but she was also a woman, a sister, a daughter and an aunt. The badge would protect you to a certain degree but not from those who didn't respect it. He knew that the Karpovs had a hand in what she did. He just knew it. They chewed people up and spat them out. His DI would have been an easy target. In isolation, away from the job, they were all vulnerable. It was a fact of life. He had considered his safety before but not with the same concern. Many of the men he had arrested over the years had threatened his life and he had always taken it with a pinch of salt.

Not this time. This time, the threats were real. Cain first and then her parents. The alarms were sounding. It hadn't crossed his mind that he might be in danger until the ACC told him to leave home as usual, no overnight case, and make his way to headquarters immediately. Then it hit home. They could come after me. They probably will come after me. It was all speculation, but it was educated speculation. The ACC was playing safe, obviously. He was playing it down. There was no evidence that the DI was under duress when she jumped and the gas explosion could have been a sick twist of fate, a coincidence. It could have been. He didn't believe it was a coincidence, but the alternative was unthinkable. No one wanted to think that a detective could be targeted and terminated by the bad guys. The bad guys weren't that powerful. They would not dare to assassinate a police officer and her family. No one could think that they were untouchable like that. They couldn't be because if they were, what was the point in it all? They could never win against that kind of mentality. People who fear nothing, respect nothing and do not value the lives of others, were undefeatable, surely? He was determined that they could be defeated. Determined but frightened.

    Mike turned away from the cash machine and walked towards the car park, at the end of the parade of shops. There was a bookie, a chip shop, a café, two charity shops and a bakery where everything was a pound. The smell of baking pastry was normally irresistible to him but today he couldn't think about eating. He couldn't think about much except Steff Cain. A dark cloud had descended around him. He felt vulnerable. His confidence as a detective had been shattered. Two men stumbled out of the bookmakers, shouting obscenities. They were arguing with the manager who had bundled them through the door. One of them was drunk, the other paralytic. The manger warned them not to come back until they had sobered up and then slammed the door. They turned on each other, each blaming the other for their expulsion. One threw a punch, missed completely and toppled over. His companion saw the opportunity and tried to kick him in the head, but he missed completely too, span around in a circle and landed on his backside. He staggered to his feet and relented. He tried to help his friend to his feet suggesting that they should go to the pub to sort things out. Mike avoided them and walked on, his thoughts with Steff Cain and the organisation that had assassinated her. That is what they had done. No doubt about it. He checked his mobile for messages. The screen was blank. He slid it back into his pocket and walked on. A car door slammed, and he turned on his heels. A woman ran from a taxi towards the shops, a toddler ran at her side to keep up. The beeping of a zebra crossing, normally an innocent sound, drilled into his brain. Every noise made his heart skip a beat. His nerves were frayed. He checked his watch and walked on quickly, weaving through the shoppers. Fish and chip wrappers blew in circles around a litterbin; the paving stones were spotted with chewing gum. A black taxi pulled to a halt next to him, its passengers climbed out and stared at him. Mike stopped for a moment, afraid before realising that they were looking beyond him. They walked by on their way to the shops. He may as well have been invisible, everyone around him going about their business. No one saw him because no one cared. Life in the big city raced on, oblivious to his grief. He took a deep breath and tried to compose himself. He knew that he was in shock, but he also knew that he had to pull himself together and get on with it.

When he reached the end of the parade of shops, a delivery van mounted the pavement, ignoring the double yellow lines. The engine roared and the brakes squealed. For a moment, Mike thought it was going to hit him. He jumped back out of the way, banging into a woman with a pushchair.

'Watch where you are going, knob-head!' the woman shouted.

'I'm very sorry,' he replied, shaken.

She glared at him as she walked on. His nerves were shredded. The driver of the van jumped out, slammed the door and headed into the bakery unaffected by the comments disgruntled passers-by made about his driving. Mike thought about pulling him, showing him his ID card and giving him a bollocking but decided against it. In the big scheme of things, it mattered not one bit. He walked around the back of the van to cross the road, checking that his car was where he had parked it. It was there and there was no one suspicious hanging around. The lights at the junction changed and the traffic roared by. He poked his head around the van to check for a break in the traffic and a motorcyclist whizzed by, inches from his face. Mike stepped back, his heart pumping rapidly before risking another peek. He heard the van driver opening his door, starting the engine and slamming it closed. Mike was about to step away from the van when he felt a hard shove in the small of his back. He reached out to stop his fall but grabbed nothing but fresh air. As he stumbled from behind the van, into the oncoming traffic, he briefly noted the number of the double-decker bus that knocked him onto the asphalt before running over him, crushing his skull like a balloon full of rice pudding.

CHAPTER 9

Braddick looked around the room at a sea of faces, some familiar, others not. Familiar or not, he knew that he was briefing the best detectives that their force had. He had undone the top button of his dark blue shirt, loosened his tie. The digital screens behind him showed images from the crime scene at Holyhead. DI Joanne Jones was stood to his right, at the edge of the bank of screens. Her presence had caused quite a stir, especially amongst the male detectives. She showed no sign of nerves and carried herself with a confident gait that few at her rank achieved.

'I want to break this down into definitive sections so that each team can focus on one aspect of the case. We will put the pieces back together at our four o'clock briefings,' he paused, watching the nodding heads, his team listening to every word. They were coiled like springs, waiting to be released on the case. 'Firstly, Malcolm, you are on witness statements and communicating the information from forensics to both departments.'

'Guv.'

'Carol, I want you on house to house coordinating with uniform. Someone must have seen our witness and someone in the Mason clan knows who he is. Shake their cages and get someone to talk.'

'Yes, Guv.'

'We have a minimum of two dead, possibly eight more. I want to start with the victims we know about first. Let's look at the importers.' The screens changed to show six faces of various ages. Fishermen who crossed the Irish Sea with best intentions. 'We have two bodies. This one is Linus Murphy.' The image of Linus appeared. His tortured corpse hanging upside down. The warning carved into his chest was black and scabbed. 'North Wales Police are communicating with Dublin for now. That may change as we progress. Linus Murphy had been a trawler man since leaving school. He had no criminal record. The other five ID's found at the scene belong to individuals who have never been charged or convicted of anything worse than a parking ticket. The trawler belongs to Murphy and up until yesterday, it was a perfectly legitimate fishing vessel. Holyhead port authorities have no record of it ever docking in the harbour before yesterday. They didn't fish that area.' Braddick nodded to one of his constables. 'Simon, I want you to chase up NWP and follow up anything that you're not happy with directly with Dublin.'

'Guv.'

'We still don't know who Patrick Finnen is,' Braddick said, pointing to the bloody inscription on Murphy's chest. 'Go direct to Dublin for information about him.' Simon nodded and made a note.

'We are working on the premise that he is the money behind the shipment. If this is his real name, they will have come across him before. There's no doubt about it.' He gestured to Jo to take over.

'For those of you who don't know me, I'm DI Joanne Jones. Call me, Jo. I recognise a lot of you from my time in Matrix although you probably won't recognise me.' She paused while a few eyebrows were raised. 'I was known as Lilly during my time with Matrix.'

'Lilly?' someone gasped. A murmur spread through the room, some expletives, some surprised laughter. 'Fucking hell!' someone said a little too loudly. Braddick stared at her, open mouthed. He remembered Lilly. The image of a ravaged junkie, greasy hair, sunken eyes and blackened teeth appeared in his mind. He had met her, years before but didn't know she was a UC. Lilly had been the most productive UC officer since Matrix had been conceived. Braddick had interviewed her as Lilly and never once suspected that she was a UC.

'It's amazing what can be done with contact lenses and false teeth,' she said, smiling thinly. The room fell silent. Lilly was held up as the icon that perspective UC's should aspire to be. The fact that she had been a successful undercover explained why she had been shoehorned into the top job with the Drug Squad. 'Let's get on.' She waited until she had their complete attention. The screen showed a well-built male in his fifties. 'This is Gary Mason,' she said, turning to the image of the second victim. 'We think Mason was the buyer. NWP found another three sets of ID belonging to, Frank Farrell, Brian Farrell and Jimmy Farrell, all cousins of the infamous Eddie Farrell who disappeared with his son, Eddie junior a while back.' A ripple of derisory comments broke the silence and she waited for it to die down before continuing. 'Our sources reckon that some of the Eddie Farrell estate has been liquefied, giving Gary Mason and Farrell's cousins a bankroll. It would appear that they invested it in drugs. We are working on the premise that they set up a deal with an outfit from Dublin. Unfortunately for them, someone else knew about it and hit the handover before stringing them up from the rafters.' She paused. 'We have to assume that they are dead. We also have another player and it is imperative that we identify him. The man who made this nine, nine, nine call.' She played the call to the room. 'We are working on the premise that he is part of the Mason clan and that he is alive. He is the only witness we have, and we need to find him as a matter of urgency. DC Barnes and her team are knocking on doors as we speak but so far, the family are not talking.'

'Why Dublin and Holyhead?' a DC asked, his hand half raised.

'Excuse me?'

'I mean why import from Dublin to there?'

'Four hundred miles of unprotected coastline.' Jo shrugged. 'North Wales is a smuggler's paradise. The coastline is impossible to police and once on land, the roads are quiet, and you can be in any major city in a couple of hours.'

'Why would the Farrells change suppliers?' another officer asked. 'They've been selling gear for years. Why risk a new route.'

'You're assuming that it is a new route,' Jo said flatly. 'We can't assume anything at this point. Eddie Farrell could have been importing there for years, we don't know anything for sure. However, my guess is that when Eddie Farrell vanished, his contacts would have thought that he had been assassinated or that he had cut and run, either way no one would trust the family. I think they liquidated his assets and looked to set up a supply line for themselves, new or not, we don't know yet.'

'But can we be sure that someone ripped them off?' an officer asked. 'It could have been an inside job.'

'This wasn't just a robbery,' Braddick interrupted. All eyes turned to him. 'Look at the overwhelming force that was used. Eight men missing presumed dead,' he paused to let it sink in. 'They moved in with enough firepower to subdue ten men instantly.'

'Military backgrounds?'

'Almost certainly,' Braddick nodded. 'They moved with stealth and had the firepower to overpower the men without them having a chance to escape or fight back. They could have taken the money and the drugs without firing a single shot and left everyone alive.' The nodding heads told him that the majority agreed with him. 'This wasn't about money. The men have vanished, but they purposely left their ID's for us to find and process. They have left the families unsure what happened to their loved ones and eight of them have no way of knowing if they are alive or dead. This was about fear. It is about striking terror into the minds of anyone thinking of setting up as a rival outfit. There are only two, maybe three outfits capable of this.'

'The Turks.'

'Possibly.'

'The Latvians.'

'Two years ago, maybe but not anymore.'

'That leaves the Russians.'

'That would be my guess,' Braddick agreed.

'That narrows it down to the Karpovs, the Vashechkins and the Kuznets,' Jo said, looking at Braddick. Braddick frowned a little. He hadn't heard of the latter families. She looked at the room and nodded. 'Yes, you might be surprised to know that we have three soviet outfits operating in the city now. You DS detectives will be aware of them, but they may not have popped up on the MIT radar yet. The Karpovs you are all familiar with, the others are established in London and the south coast and they are creeping north with frightening success. Any one of these three outfits could have pulled this off.' Braddick nodded, impressed. 'Obviously, we know that the Farrells acted as muscle for the Karpovs, so they have to be favourites for this. I'm putting two DS teams on each outfit to see if anyone is in possession of a new delivery. When new gear arrives in the city, it creates a buzz, good if it is quality and bad if it is crap. Once we identify who has new product, we can follow the drugs up the chain.'

'Is there any news from the divers, Guv?'

Braddick shook his head. 'They have searched the harbour and found nothing. Wherever they are, they are not in the water.' He changed the images again and the bridges across the Menai Straits appeared. 'I want a team on the camera footage from both bridges. We're looking for at least three vehicles, probably more, vans, people carriers or similar. They will have crossed onto the island and left within four hours tops,' he pointed to a team to his right. They nodded enthusiastically. 'If you can find the vehicles, it will take weeks off this investigation.'

'Guv.'

'I want round the clock obs on this man,' Jo said changing the images. The picture of an eighteen stone brute appeared. His bushy black beard was streaked with silver; wavy hair gelled back from a protruding forehead. 'Some of you will be familiar with Big Ron Mason, Gary Mason's brother,' she said, pausing to gauge the reaction. Half the room knew him. 'For those of you who don't know him, Big Ron was Eddie Farrell's cousin. They didn't like each other but Ron did a lot of Farrell's wet work.' Braddick watched the faces around the room. Her terminology belonged to someone who took torture and murder as simply part of everyday life. 'If anyone was going to step up into Farrell's shoes, Big Ron is the man.' The nodding heads told Braddick that the teams were following her in total agreement. 'If our witness made it off the island alive, then he will be going to see Big Ron at some point.' She turned to one of her detectives, who was sat near the front. 'Donna, I want you and your team on the family's *Facebook* and *Twitter* accounts. It is a big family, lots of cousins, uncles, aunties; someone will be chatting online about Gary Mason's death. Three of the Farrells are still missing, guaranteed social media will be buzzing about it. Look out for any other names being mentioned. I think we can find out who our witness is.'

'Guv.'

Jo looked at Braddick and stepped back signalling that her input was exhausted. He noticed the ACC entering the office to his right. He looked ashen and somewhat panicked. His eyes were fixed on Jo. She noticed his manner and walked around the edge of the room to reach him without disturbing the briefing.

'Where are we with the Ford Focus?' Braddick asked Ade Burns. His DS held up a piece of paper.

'The insurance goes back to a limited company based in Litherland. No tax returns have ever been filed at Company's House and it is listed as 'no longer trading'. Dead end, Guv. The address is a piece of waste ground.'

'What about the shotgun?'

'The serial number has been ground off, no prints or DNA.'

'I want a team to go back to each of the Farrell and Mason families and put the pressure on. They are all related. Someone knows who our witness is,' Braddick said, clapping his hands. 'Everyone knows what they are doing. Keep me updated. If we find the witness and the vehicles used by the hijackers, we can have this wrapped up quickly.' He watched the ACC and Jo going into his office. The door closed behind them. He had the sinking feeling that something bad had happened.

'Have you got a minute, Guv?' Ade said, approaching. Braddick wanted to hear what was going on in the office. Ade sensed his mood. 'Just a quick one. It's important.'

'Of course,' Braddick said, apologetically. 'What is it?'

'One of the DC's from Vice was talking earlier.' Ade lowered his voice. 'He has got tickets for a charity gig at St George's Hall tomorrow night. Something to do with raising money for Alderhey Hospital.'

'And?' Braddick asked, watching the office door.

'One of the main sponsors for the night is City Break Hotels.'

'I'm not following here, Ade.'

'The City Break chain was bought out last year, remember.'

'Of course, I do,' Braddick said, nodding. The light bulb in his mind snapped on. 'The Karpovs bought them out with their umbrella company, right?'

'Right,' Ade said, taking his arm, guiding him away from prying ears. 'This DC reckons that Yuri Karpov was at last year's event. I know we can't lift him for anything, but I thought…'

'Get me those tickets, Ade,' Braddick said, patting him on the back. 'I think we should go and spoil his evening, don't you?'

'My thoughts exactly, Guv.'

Braddick grinned at the thought and headed to his office. He opened the door without knocking. The ACC was standing next to the window, staring over the river. Jo was perched on the desk, telephone in hand. She looked at Braddick and shook her head.

'What?' Braddick asked, closing the door behind him.

'It's Mike Pilkington,' she said.

'What?' Braddick sighed. He tensed, waiting for the blow.

'He was run over by a bus forty-five minutes ago.'

CHAPTER 10

Ronny Mason walked out of Chester station and wrapped his coat tightly against the wind and rain. He looked around nervously. His eyes fell on a bar directly opposite, The Town Crier and the urge to drink himself into oblivion was overwhelming. He pulled his hood up over his short, dark hair and stepped towards a zebra crossing. A horn beeped across the road and he watched as a young woman ran to meet her lift. Her boyfriend picked her up and swung her around, their laughter infectious. Their embrace made him jealous. He longed for the touch of a fulltime lover, someone who genuinely wanted to spend time with him. Being secretly gay was just another cross that he had to carry. He was surrounded by homophobic misogynous thugs. Women were 'pussy' rather than people, their reproductive systems far more valuable than their personalities. Gay men were faggots, queers, arse bandits, and worse. He had heard it all his life. Coming out in the Mason-Farrell clan was not an option. They all thought he was quiet, a shy boy who couldn't approach girls. He couldn't tell them otherwise. His sex life was limited to just one man and a few quick fumbles arranged online. He wanted to settle with an older man, someone who would look after him. Maybe it was a father figure he craved because his own father showed him no emotions but disappointment and anger. He wanted the relationship to be stable, his affection reciprocated. He hadn't found exactly what he was looking for. Most of the men he met casually used him, abused him and then disappeared before he could get dressed and ask for a number. The sordid encounters only added to his sense of being useless and unlikeable. There had only been one regular man and he picked him up and dropped him whenever he felt the urge. Ronny liked him. He liked him a lot and so he ran to him like a puppy dog whenever he called, hoping that one day it might be more than just sex. Whatever developed from the relationship, he could never share it with his family. Never.

The wind cut through him as he waited for the lights to change. A line of black cabs peeled away from the rank as passengers climbed in and headed off to their destinations; hotels, restaurants, fun places to be with friends and loved ones. Places he wouldn't be going to anytime soon.

The phone call home hadn't gone well. His father didn't speak to him but one of his cronies had growled some instructions to him and then hung up after giving him a bollocking for calling the landline. How could calling home be wrong for fuck's sake? He couldn't do anything right as far as they were concerned. No doubt, he would be blamed for the fuck up. His father would find a way of twisting events so that he felt responsible. He always did. Ronny anticipated a fat lip at least. Big Ron was quick to dole out his own version of justice whether it was just or not. Ronny had the features of a boxer despite never having stepped between the ropes. His father had shaped his face with his fists. Ronny dreamed of punching him back one day, although he knew that he didn't have the strength or the gall to actually do it. He had seen Big Ron demolish multiple opponents in nightclubs, their blows bounced off his head like it was a bowling ball. One unfortunate reveller had hit him from behind with a bar stool. The look of horror on his face when Big Ron turned around and smiled was priceless. He was found in a skip in an alleyway, bleeding from every orifice, a chair leg stuck up his rectum. Only the swift action of the paramedics saved his life. Tackling Big Ron was beyond most mortals.

'Ronny!' a voice called from his left. He looked around and saw a Lexus parked on double yellows. The driver was familiar, one of his father's doormen, a lump called Rickets because of his bowlegs.

'Get in,' he ordered angrily. His black face was pitted, a permanent scowl fixed to it. Rickets was always angry about something and nothing. Ronny swallowed hard and ran to the passenger door. He reached for the handle, but it was locked. 'Back seat, knob-head!' Rickets growled and gestured with his thumb. Ronny opened the back door and climbed in. The car was warm and a welcome relief from the elements, despite the hostile atmosphere. 'Put your belt on,' Rickets mumbled as he put the vehicle into first and sped away so fast that the wheels squealed. A black cab sounded its horn loudly as he cut across its path. 'Fuck you!' Rickets shouted as he headed towards the city centre. 'Fucking taxi drivers,' he snarled. 'Cunts the lot of them. They think they own the road.' Ronny nodded in agreement, thinking that Rickets was the only cunt on the road at that moment.

Four hundred metres on, as they approached a roundabout, the Lexus swerved to a violent stop next to the kerb. Ronny was confused until he saw a dark figure approach the car from a doorway. The huge figure was dressed in a short black jacket, gloves and a hat pulled down to his eyes. The passenger door opened, and Big Ron climbed in, making the car rock. Rickets waited for the door to close before speeding off again. The silence was deafening.

'All right, Dad?' Ronny said nervously. 'Thanks for picking…'

'Shut up!' Big Ron said, turning around as far as his bulk would allow him. 'You had better tell me what happened, and it had better be good.'

Ronny didn't think it would be good whatever he said. It never was.

CHAPTER 11

Ieuan Jones walked into the Edinburgh Castle and stamped the rain from his boots on the mat. The bar was to his left, lounge to his right. He opened the door to the bar and stepped inside. The odours of stale ale, damp and chip fat drifted to him. He remembered how it used to be. Images of a packed pub, cigarette smoke hanging heavily in the air like a pungent mist, pool balls cracking against each other and laughter everywhere, came to him from his distant memory. It had been a busy drinking hole twenty years ago. They were all busy back then and he missed those days. His local was the centre of the community, the social hub where people met and talked. No one stared at their phones mid conversation in those days. The town was busy back then. The fishing industry was booming. A fleet of forty trawlers had been devastated by quotas from Brussels. The main employer, an aluminium plant had pulled out of the town and the local economy slumped. When the big supermarkets moved onto the island, the small businesses on the high street were forced out. The town centre suffered a fatal body blow as the revenue that was once spent there, which went directly back into the local economy, went into the coffers of the retail giants. They sucked the town dry and sent the profits to the capital. The knock-on effect was that the pubs died too. No one had the money to drink in the pubs as often as they had. Alcohol was cheaper in the supermarkets. The smoking ban was the final nail in the coffin. Ieuan, once a successful landlord himself, bailed out with most of the other publicans. There were days he missed the social life, a staple that he yearned for. The days when the Holyhead pubs were busy were long gone.

He took off his woolly hat and ordered a pint of bitter from a frosty faced barmaid, said hello to some of the locals in his mother tongue and then headed over to two men who were sitting near the window. One of them he knew, the other was a stranger. They had positioned themselves as far away from the other punters as they could. Henry hadn't changed since their last meeting many years before. His khaki jacket looked a little more frayed at the cuffs, but it was the same one that he had always worn, an anchor to his paramilitary past that he couldn't let go of. The stranger was younger, dressed in jeans and a blue parka. His hair was neat and dark, grey flecks above the ears. He shook hands with Henry, ignoring Patrick. There was no warmth in the welcome.

'This is my friend Patrick,' Henry said coldly.

'Let me tell you, I haven't come here to meet new friends. What do you want, Henry?'

'There's no need to be rude, Ieuan.' Ieuan stroked his dark bristles with his right hand and glanced at Patrick. He nodded a silent hello. Patrick smiled and removed his coat. His denim shirt was rolled up at the sleeves.

'I haven't got time for niceties,' Ieuan said flatly.

'Fair enough,' Henry said, smiling. 'It is nice to see you again, though. You look well.'

'What the fuck do you want?' Ieuan asked, taking a long swig of his pint. His brown eyes bored into Henry. 'I told you we were done years ago.'

'Get straight to the point, why don't you,' Henry chuckled. He seemed to be enjoying the standoff. 'You never did beat around the bush. Ieuan used to work with us a long time ago, didn't you, Ieuan?'

'Yes, and it cost me five years of my life,' Ieuan snapped. 'Where were you and the General then?' he asked calmly. He stared at Henry and took another drink; froth lined his upper lip. 'Let's not pretend we're friends, Henry. You're lucky that I'm here at all. Now what the fuck do you want?'

'Don't be like that. You know why we did what we did. That was the way things had to be done. You knew that. Get caught and you're on your own. That was the way it was. I was gutted when I heard that you had been sent down, but I could hardly send a letter could I?'

'Have you come to apologise?' Ieuan scoffed. 'Because if you have, you can shove your apology up your arsehole.'

'No apology. They were the rules that we played by and you knew that.'

'You changed the rules to suit yourselves, Henry. They always seemed to be weighted in your favour, eh?'

'There's no point in raking over old ground. We'll never agree, will we?'

'Not in a million years.'

'I'll keep this as brief as I can. There was an incident in the harbour here yesterday,' Henry said, looking around to make sure no one was listening. A handful of locals were gathered around a pool table at the far end of the bar. Two men were throwing darts and chatting in Welsh. 'We want to know what you know about it. That's all. I simply want to know what you have heard.'

'What is it to you what happened here?' Ieuan smirked. 'I thought your interest here was finished a long time ago?'

'There was a deal arranged and it didn't go to plan. Let's just say that we have a vested interest in it.'

'Oh dear, that sounds expensive. How much of an interest?'

'A substantial amount.'

'Did someone fuck you over, Henry?'

Henry sipped his beer and tilted his head. He shrugged and smiled. 'You could say that, I suppose.'

'I figured that out when you called,' Ieuan said, nodding. His white moustache was developing with every sip of his pint. 'It isn't like you to let a deal go south. Are you getting sloppy in your old age?'

'These things happen from time to time. It can't be helped sometimes. Things go wrong.'

'They do. The trouble is the game has changed. There's a lot of foreign talent around nowadays and they play by different rules, Henry,' Ieuan said, draining his pint. There was amusement in his eyes. 'We used to live and let live as long as it didn't encroach on our business, but these guys want what you have too. People like you and me and the

General, we don't belong in it anymore. We're obsolete. We're dinosaurs. These new players will chew you up and spit you out in fucking bubbles,' he said with a chuckle. 'They are a different breed of predator nowadays, although I think you have just found that out the hard way, eh, Henry?'

'Oh, don't underestimate the power of experience. There's still life in these old dogs yet.' Henry signalled to the barmaid for another round. She smiled briefly and then tutted, mumbling to herself about whether his legs had fallen off. 'These new outfits are all machineguns and bullets. They don't have the brains that they were born with. They haven't considered the repercussions of their actions. That is a huge mistake.'

'You're fucking deluded, Henry.'

'Maybe I am but I have a job to do and I'll do it. I'm sure you still have all your contacts. What have you heard?'

'I heard that someone got toasted in the old fish factory. Two dead and eight missing,' Ieuan shrugged.

'Eight?' Henry and Patrick exchanged concerned glances.

'That's what I heard. Two dead and eight missing. Do you still feel confident, Henry?' Ieuan laughed sourly. 'Any outfit that can carry out that kind of operation is one that you should steer clear of.'

'They had the element of surprise. The fish factory is an ideal place for an exchange, but it is also the ideal place for an ambush,' Henry said glancing at Patrick. His eyes added, 'You didn't do your homework, lad.'

'Let me tell you about the fish factory. It should have been demolished years ago, but it is a listed building, you know.' Ieuan leaned forward, elbows on the table, chin on his fists. 'I worked there as a teenager; you know. It was good money in those days,' he said, glancing at Patrick. Patrick listened politely. 'We used to come in here on payday and play three card brag. You could lose your wages and your friends in half an hour. I've seen grown men leaving here in tears, dreading telling the wife that they had lost their money at the pub. Used to be packed in here in those days.' Henry smiled thinly allowing him to reminisce. Ieuan swigged his pint, realising that he was rambling. 'Once the fishing quotas came in, the fleet disappeared. Anyway, I am going off the subject.' He sat back and looked around. 'I have heard that a dragger crew from Dublin are missing, the skipper strung up with a message carved into his chest. It was a message to a man called Patrick Finnen. It told him to stay in Dublin. Heavy duty stuff, that, eh Patrick?' he said, looking at Patrick for the first time. 'Would that be a coincidence that you have the same name or are you Patrick Finnen, eh?' he said, smiling coldly.

'No coincidence. I am Patrick Finnen.'

'Are you the same Patrick Finnen that used to be a boxer?'

'I did. Eye damage ended me.'

'Shame. I watched some of your fights. You could have gone all the way.'

'So, I've been told.'

'Let me tell you something, Patrick. This is a fight you won't win. Stay in Dublin, they said, eh?' he said, leaning closer. 'You should have listened, son. You are chasing a dragon and you're going to get burnt. Leave it alone or you will end up in a box. If they find your body, that is.' Patrick held his gaze and sipped his beer. There was a painful silence.

'What are the local plod saying?' Henry asked. They sat back for a moment as the barmaid brought fresh pints. Beer slopped onto the table, but she made no apologies. Patrick paid her and told her to keep the change.

'Diolch,' Ieuan thanked her.

'Well? What are they saying?' Henry prompted.

'I've heard different things, but the upshot is that they are handing it all over to the coppers from Liverpool.'

'Why?'

'The dragger crew are Dublin's problem and the other corpse, and his mates are from Liverpool. My source said that they couldn't get rid of it quickly enough. Can't say as I blame them. Looks like a right mess to me. You would be well advised to stay the fuck away from it. Take your losses and let them kill each other. The outfit that hit your deal are professionals, probably ex-military.'

'There's no way they could have been hit by a local firm?' Henry asked.

'From here on the island?' Ieuan nearly choked on his beer. He wiped his mouth with the back of his hand. 'You're fucking kidding me, right?' he laughed.

'I'm asking the question, that's all.' Henry raised his eyebrows. 'I have to cover all the bases. I heard the town has its fair share of dealers.'

'Different league, Henry, different league altogether.' Ieuan shook his head and smiled. 'Two or three main players at most with half a dozen wannabies each working for them selling twenty quid deals in the pubs. Don't get me wrong, they all think that they're the Welsh Pablo Escobar but look around you. The pubs are fucking dying. You're talking amateurs and professionals. Whoever hit that deal was major league. You need to look further afield than the island.'

'Okay. I appreciate your honesty. I had to explore the possibility.'

'I don't envy you. It is almost sad that you're chasing this. This will be the end of you. My guess is you're on the way to Liverpool, eh, Henry?' he asked with a wink. 'Now that place is a jungle. There are some big players there. Were your buyers from there?'

'Do they have any leads?' Henry asked, ignoring the question even though the answer was obvious.

'I've heard that a call was made to the emergency services,' Ieuan said quietly. 'I heard that they think there is a witness. The caller was a Scouser.'

'But he hasn't been picked up?'

'No sign of him.' He drained his pint and stood up. 'Now you know what I know. Good luck with your search because you're going to need it and God help you if you find whoever took your stuff. You two are way out of your depth.'

'Thanks for your help,' Patrick said, standing. He offered his hand. Ieuan looked at him and hesitated before shaking it. 'Take my advice, son, fuck off home on the first ferry back to Dublin. My guess is you're the fall guy for this fuck up.' He gestured towards Henry with his head. 'Don't be taken in by this man. This man is not your friend. Henry is nobody's friend, are you, Henry?' Henry looked at his pint and shifted uncomfortably. 'Do you know what this man used to do?' No one answered. 'I reckon he's put more men in the ground than you've seen summers but hear me when I say that whoever took your shipment is far more frightening than old Henry here, eh, Henry?'

'I appreciate your time,' Henry said with a nod. His eyes stared coldly into Ieuan. The amusement in his eyes had gone, replaced by ice.

'You appreciate no one's time, especially mine. Now fuck off and don't call me again,' Ieuan said, staring back. They locked eyes for a second and then he turned and walked out of the door. The two Irishmen sat in silence and finished their drinks, each locked in their own thoughts.

CHAPTER 12

Ronny felt his mouth drying up as he tried to pick the right words. His father was glaring at him, whisky on his breath, loathing and disappointment in his eyes. He was used to seeing disappointment in his eyes. It was part of growing up as Big Ron's son. His mind raced through what had happened. There was no point in dressing things up. Big Ron could tell when he was lying, and anyway, it wasn't his fault. He knew that it wasn't, yet he couldn't help but feel the blame.

'From the beginning,' Big Ron growled. 'Don't miss anything out!'

'Our Gary dropped me off on a road near the harbour. There were some steps that went up to a monument on top of a cliff. It looks over the harbour and the train station. He told me to go up there and keep a lookout. He said to ring him if I saw the police or anyone else coming,' Ronny said, avoiding eye contact. 'I did everything that he said. I did exactly what he said, Dad.'

'Okay, okay. Then what happened?'

'I saw them driving into the warehouse and then I couldn't see them anymore. I thought I saw them moving near the harbour, but I couldn't tell if it was them or not.' Ronny thought about it. He had thought about it all night. With hindsight, they might have been there waiting to ambush them, but he didn't want to tell his father that. 'Then a black people carrier turned up. I watched it driving along the road and as soon as it turned towards the warehouse, I called Gary, just like he said. The road was about half a mile long so they would have had loads of time to be ready, but they didn't answer the fucking phone!'

'What type of vehicle was it?'

'Toyota,' Ronny lied. He didn't know but admitting that would be a mistake. 'Definitely a Toyota.'

'Did you get the reg number?'

'No. I couldn't see the plate because of the angle,' he lied again.

'Idiot.'

'Don't call me that.' Ronny began to get agitated. The pressure was getting to him. 'I did everything that he said, Dad, everything. It wasn't my fault.'

'I'll be the judge of that. What did you hear on the phone?'

'Nothing.'

'What do mean, nothing?' Big Ron snapped. 'Did it ring?'

'Yes.'

'Then that isn't nothing is it?'

'No,' Ronny stammered. 'I meant they didn't answer. It went to answering machine over and over. I must have called twenty times, honest I did. The signal kept dropping.'

'Go on.'

'I saw them get out. They had guns. Like machineguns but shorter. I looked through the binoculars and saw a flash. Someone fell down holding their leg. I think it was our Gary, but I can't be sure.'

'How many were there?'

'Five in that car but then another one came along, but it didn't come down the road. I mean I didn't see it go down the road, but it might have done. I called the police then so I might have missed it turning in.'

'Did it or didn't it?'

'I don't think so, Dad, but I'm not sure. Why does it matter anyway?'

Big Ron swiped his huge hand across Ronny's face, the knuckles bruising the cheek immediately. 'You need to be fucking sure, idiot!' He raised his hand again, but Ronny moved backwards as far as he could.

'I'm fucking sick of you calling me that. I didn't arrange this fuck up, our Gary did. Is he an idiot too?'

Big Ron lunged over the seat and grabbed him around the throat. His hands closed tightly around his neck, squeezing his windpipe closed. Ronny began to gasp for breath, eyes bulging from his head, hot tears spilling down his cheeks. 'Don't you talk about him like that. You had one job to do, lookout! How can you not know if the second car drove down the road or not?'

'You're going to strangle him,' Rickets said matter of factly. He looked in the rear-view mirror as Ronny's face began to go purple. 'Better let go, Ron or you'll kill him. You'll never know what happened.'

'No one would miss the fucking idiot!' Big Ron said, releasing him. Ronny curled up on the back seat, panting for breath. 'Get up!' Ronny pushed himself upright, tears stained his cheeks. 'Now think! How many men got out of the second car?'

Ronny gasped for air and swallowed painfully. 'Five,' he muttered. He wasn't sure but he daren't say that. 'There were five more. I don't see why it matters. It doesn't change anything, does it?'

'It matters.'

'Why?'

'Because if I know how many men they have at their disposal, I can narrow down which outfit it is.'

'Oh, I see.'

'Now, what happened when the second vehicle turned up?'

'I was watching it through the binoculars. Then I called the police. Then I looked again. When I looked through the binoculars again, one of them was looking straight at me through his binoculars. He pointed at me and they all looked up at me. I panicked.'

'Then what?'

Ronny paused. He looked out of the window and tears flowed freely. 'That's when I ran. I didn't know what else to do.'

There was an uncomfortable silence. 'I'm going to crucify the bastards!' Big Ron slapped the dashboard. 'They have no idea who they are fucking with. What did they look like?' Big Ron asked angrily.

'Who?'

'The fuckers that took my gear and killed my brother, who do you think?'

'They were all big guys, dressed in black, some in combats. They all had cropped hair, some skinned completely. Most of them had sunglasses on.'

'Is that the best that you can do?'

'I don't know what you mean?'

'Have you ever seen any of them before?'

'No.'

'Not in town or at any of the clubs?' Big Ron frowned, glaring into his eyes. 'Think hard. Could you have seen them before?' Ronny shook his head adamantly.

'No, definitely not.'

'Did any of them stand out, tattoos on the hands or neck, anything out of the ordinary?'

'No.' Ronny had no idea. He hadn't looked for anything like that.

'Where is the mobile?'

'What?'

'The fucking mobile that you called the police with!'

'Oh,' Ronny reached into his pocket. 'Here.'

'Wipe it clean and throw it through the window,' Big Ron snapped. Ronny wiped the phone with his jacket, lowered the window and chucked it, watching as it hit the road at eighty miles an hour and disintegrated. 'We need to get him to the farmhouse. If the police get hold of this fucking idiot and question him, we're all fucked!'

'Stop calling me that!' Ronny snapped like a petulant child. 'I wouldn't say anything to the filth. I am not a grass. It wasn't my fault. I am not an idiot!'

Big Ron raised his hand and Ronny cowered against the back door. 'You're right. You're beyond idiocy. I don't even know the word for how fucking stupid you are.'

Ronny closed his eyes and dreamed about running away.

CHAPTER 13

Braddick walked around the desk and sat in his chair. Anger boiled in his guts. The ACC had his forehead against the glass, its coolness soothing. His eyes were closed, his thoughts spinning around in his mind. Jo was on the telephone talking to the uniformed officers at the scene. She instructed them to collect all the CCTV footage from the area where Mike Pilkington had died. They listened in silence until she was finished.

'Apparently, he stumbled under a bus. How the fuck do you stumble under a bus,' she said, shaking her head. 'Witnesses said he just fell forward.'

'How many witnesses are there?' Braddick asked.

'Two and the bus driver.'

'Two?' the ACC snapped. 'That is one of the busiest intersections in the area. There must be more witnesses than that. Surely someone saw something.'

'You know what it is like getting people to come forward. Nobody wants to get involved.' Jo shrugged.

'Did the driver see anything untoward?'

'They had to sedate her but before she broke down, she said that he stumbled out from behind a van. She had no chance to stop. She's been taken to the Royal.' Jo pushed her hair behind her ears. It settled like dark silk below her shoulders. 'He has a receipt from a cash machine in his pocket. His car is parked across the road. They have secured it and are waiting for a flatbed to take it to forensics. Once we have the CCTV, we'll have a better idea of what happened.'

'Do you think he was pushed?' the ACC asked.

Braddick and Jo exchanged glances and they both nodded.

'Yes.'

'Definitely.'

'This is madness,' the ACC muttered. 'These people are out of control. Who do these people think they are?'

'They are virtually untouchable,' Jo said flatly. The ACC looked at her angrily. She shrugged. 'We lock one of them up and another one replaces him. One of them gets shot and his place is filled before the body is cold. They have a never-ending supply of soldiers. As long as there is cash, they have recruits queuing up. Any one of them will put a bullet in their rivals without blinking. Their recruits are better trained with weapons than we are. We're fighting a foe that we can't kill. It just regenerates itself. It is sad but true.'

'They are not untouchable. I don't agree,' the ACC muttered. He shook his head defiantly. 'Not one bit.'

'I do,' Braddick sighed. 'Jo is right. If we find footage of someone pushing Pilkington under a bus, who do you think it will be?' he asked turning his palms to the ceiling. 'Viktor Karpov?' He frowned.

'Yuri Karpov?' No one replied. 'It won't be any of the top echelon. It will be one of their thugs, who doesn't give a fuck if he goes to jail or not because the Karpovs will look after his family in Russia either way.' The ACC sat down heavily on a chair. His body seemed to deflate. He put his head into his hands. 'These people have nothing at home and so they have nothing to lose. We can't touch the Karpovs unless we can find out who Cain's informer is.'

'And how do you suggest we do that?' the ACC asked, sitting upright.

'Cain and Pilkington, have it documented somewhere,' Jo said. 'We just need to find out where.'

'We need his car keys,' Braddick said, sitting forward.

'What?' the ACC asked.

'We need his keys,' he repeated. 'We haven't found Cain's laptop, yet have we?'

'No.' The ACC frowned. 'It wasn't in her car or her flat and her desk has nothing in it that would help.'

'They could have been through her things before we even knew that she was dead,' Jo added. 'We need to search Mike Pilkington's car and home before anyone else gets there,' she said, reading Braddick's mind. Braddick nodded that he was about to say the same thing.

'We can't just search his place. We don't know that a crime has been committed,' the ACC said, shaking his head. 'I mean I know how it looks but we don't know for sure. I don't think we could get a warrant. The family could sue the pants off us.'

'The only two people who know about the identity of the informer are dead. Now that tells me that the Karpovs don't know what information they had or who it was from. If they find out before we do, the source will disappear permanently. You want to know who took out our people, don't you?' Braddick reasoned.

'Of course, I do.'

'Then forget we ever had this conversation,' Braddick said, looking at Jo. She nodded and looked at the ACC.

'I don't…'

'We get the keys and search Pilkington's place and leave it as we found it. No warrant, no lawsuit, no more bad guys being one step ahead all the fucking time,' Jo said calmly. 'We can be there and back in an hour.' The ACC thought about her words. He turned back to the window and shook his head. Braddick waited for his response.

'Of course, I can't sanction anything illegal. You know that. When an officer is killed in the line of duty, emotions run high and mistakes can be made. If someone searched his house with best intentions to catch his killers then that would be an understandable mistake, don't you think?'

'Emotions run high, just like you said,' Braddick said, nodding.

'Mistakes can be made. We're only human,' Jo added.

'I think you both know what you are doing.' The ACC flushed red, uncomfortable with his choices. 'Very good. You appear to have everything in hand,' he said with a nod. He walked to the door and opened it. 'I'll leave you to it, carry on. Keep me posted.' The door closed and Braddick stood up.

'I think we have just had a green light?'

'That's the way I read it.'

'Listen, if Cain had an informer coming in,' Jo said, turning towards him. 'Then she must have had a link between her and them. There's no way an informer would be communicating directly with a DI. Not at first.' She shook her head thoughtfully. 'That would be way too risky.'

'You're right. There must be an undercover working on this but who is it?' he said. 'How are you doing with your officers in Matrix?'

'I have arranged calls and meetings today with everyone that I can contact at the moment,' Joanne said. 'Every DS in Matrix is bringing me a status report on where their UC's are and what they are working on although I have a feeling that whoever Cain had on the job was reporting to her and Pilkington directly. I'll know where everyone is within the hour.'

'With Cain and Pilkington dead, that means there could be a UC out there in the wind.'

'If communication is broken, there's an emergency protocol for Matrix UC's but it changes every week. Once I know where they all are and what they are working on, I'll be able to communicate with them.'

'How?'

'They use a specified location that changes,' she shrugged. 'I've never needed to use it before, but it was designed for situations like this.'

'All that time on the streets as Lilly and you never lost contact?'

'Not once,' she said with a shake of her head. 'I was lucky. I know some UC's that did but it was mostly for operational reasons when they did. They did it on purpose if someone was sniffing around getting suspicious. Some of them went off the grid for weeks.'

'That makes sense,' Braddick agreed. He looked at his watch. 'We need to find this informer quickly. I don't think we have much time.'

'Me neither.'

'The Karpovs may already know who the informer is.'

'I have thought about that,' Jo agreed. 'It might have been the leak that led them to Cain in the first place.'

'Maybe,' Braddick grimaced. 'Let's take a drive and see what we can find at Mike Pilkington's place.'

'I'll arrange to pick up the keys from the mortuary,' she said, picking up the phone. She dialled the mortuary and asked to speak to the property clerk. After a ten-minute search of Pilkington's belongings, she put down the phone, frustrated. 'Guess what?'

'No keys?'

'No keys.'

'His car was across the road?'

'Yep.'

'No fucking keys.'

'No fucking keys.'

'Someone stole his keys.'

'Yep.'

'Just get his address,' Braddick said, struggling into his leather. 'We don't have time to mess about and we don't need keys anyway. I'm guessing whoever took them will have opened the door already.'

CHAPTER 14

George picked his way through the disused offices, once the headquarters of a large photograph developing company. They once had branches on every high street, charging a fortune for developing people's blurry memories. Decades ago, they were a brand name, but the photographic arm had gone into liquidation with the arrival of digital cameras. He accidently kicked a rusty cola can and it clattered across the dusty concrete, settling next to a rotting desk that stood alone in a space the size of a football pitch. He stopped and listened as the noise echoed across the vast office. His nerves were shot. He looked around and wondered what it would have been like to work there. He could only imagine what it would have been like years earlier as business began to decline, each new mobile phone camera better than the last, albums replaced with internet sites. They must have seen their decline coming a mile away, like photocopying shops and launderettes. They were all defunct and obsolete. He looked around and imagined it full of desks and full of people. The workforce must have been plagued by uncertainty as to how they would pay the mortgage. Tranche after tranche of redundancies would have whittled down the workforce month after month until the huge office was almost empty.

He chuckled at the image of one last employee sat at the single remaining desk that was in front of him, waiting for the phone to ring.

A clatter from his right made his heart jump. It was pounding in his chest. He held his breath and ducked low behind the desk, the only shelter in the vast building. His nerves were on edge. He had called his handlers a dozen times in the last forty-eight hours and no one had shown up, their mobiles switching straight to voice mail. He couldn't leave a message. It was against protocol. He had used a different call box each time and cursed when the answering services kicked in and the phones swallowed his money. There had been problems before but the lack of communication for such an extended period was very unusual. He sensed that something was amiss. Things with the informer were coming to a head, which made it all the more unusual for contact to be broken. Cain had been so on the ball all the way through that he couldn't understand the silence now. Being undercover was a lonely job anyway but he suddenly felt vulnerable. He had never felt so exposed before. Communication was his only link to reality. Now that it was gone, he craved normality.

He peered beneath the desk but couldn't see anything but litter and weeds. Electric cables hung from the ceiling where scavengers had salvaged light fittings, smoke alarms and vent covers. A pigeon took off and clattered against a grimy window at the far side of the building and he breathed a sigh of relief. The panicked bird tried to fly through the glass over and over until it landed exhausted on the window ledge.

George stood up and flicked his finger at the frightened bird, angry with himself for being so jumpy. He adjusted his filthy raincoat and walked on, searching for the stairwell. The only stairwell that was still intact. This was the default meeting place. If things went wrong and contact was broken, he was to head to the third floor and find the canteen. A communication would be left there every week. It was the last resort before email or telephone contact could be used. Undercover officers could never carry mobiles or smart devices. They were too easy to trace and as a lot of their work was illegal, it was forbidden. Setting up a drug deal was entrapment and social media left evidence that could allow criminals to walk away from charges. That said, he wished he could just text Cain. His choices had been narrowed down to one. It was a simple protocol that he had never envisaged using. Emergency protocol. 'You will probably never need to use it, but we need it in place just in case.' He could still hear his first handler saying it. That was three years ago when his real life had disintegrated before his eyes. He had found out that his wife was shagging another detective while he was on nightshifts and things went from bad to worse. When it all came out, it seemed that everyone at the station knew, except him of course. The detective involved was a popular man, captain of the rugby team and everyone's best mate. Betrayal hurt more than anything. It was beyond pain. He was devastated. The trust had gone at home and at work. He didn't trust his wife and he didn't trust his colleagues. Every time he pulled a nightshift or overtime, he couldn't concentrate. His mind was full of distrust, images of his wife giving her attentions to another man haunted him. He could see her doing things for that man, that she hadn't given to him for years. Things that they enjoyed when it all began, a different lifetime ago.

It was too late to apologise. The damage was done. When he pulled a nightshift, he would call her repeatedly, shouting at her if she didn't answer immediately. His accusations were cruel and relentless. In the end, he drove her away, forgiveness an easy concept but difficult to put into practice. When she left, he volunteered for UC work and embraced the loneliness completely. He reinvented himself as George, a homeless junkie and small-time dealer. His information had brought down more dealers and pimps than he could remember. None of them ever suspected scruffy old George of ratting them out. George was away with the fairies, or so they thought.

He crossed the desolate office space and spotted the door to the stairwell. It had been wedged open. The door was supposed to be padlocked, the key hidden beneath a floor tile. The tile would be marked with a square scratched into the corner. George tiptoed towards the doorway and identified the tile, slipping the blade of his penknife underneath the corner. He lifted the tile and looked beneath. The key was there. Whoever opened the door didn't know about the key. That was a good thing, wasn't it? It could be homeless people looking for a dry spot to sleep or it could have been metal scavengers looking to strip the upper floors. He relaxed a little and looked at the floor in front of the doorway. There was a clear pathway leading from the east side of the building to the door and beyond towards the stairwell. It was a pathway trampled by multiple sets of boots, probably scavengers looking for copper. He approached the doorway and checked the frame. It was intact apart from a set of screw holes where the padlock fastening had been. The holes were clean, wood coloured as if the screws had been removed recently. He stepped inside and checked the corridor to his right. The debris on the floor was undisturbed. It led away into the bowels of the building and into total darkness. The stairwell was in front of him. The dust on the stairs had been walked on, multiple times, by multiple sets of feet. George thought there was an imbalance in the number of prints going up and down but didn't think it was important.

George decided to proceed with caution. He pushed the door closed behind him and looked around. Picking up an empty cola bottle and an old lager tin, he stood them behind the door to alert him if anyone followed. The building was vast and empty, but it was better to be safe than dead. He turned and headed for the stairwell, hugging the wall and peering up into the gloomy void as far as he could. Listening intently, he climbed the first three steps. Water was dripping from somewhere higher up. Dust and grit crunched beneath his feet. As he reached the first landing, he ducked and checked the next elevation. It was clear. He picked up the pace, confidence returning with each step. An old photocopier, the size of a small saloon car, lay tipped on its side, draped with a spider's gossamer blanket. It blinked in the shafts of light as he navigated his way around it. A three-legged chair was balanced on the first step of the next flight, gossamer webs strung between the legs. A giant house spider the width of his hand sat in the centre of the web, waiting and watching. Its body seemed to pulse as he neared. A shiver ran down his spine. Eight eyes twinkled in a shaft of light. They appeared to follow him.

He skirted around it and took the stairs two at a time, always looking up for signs of danger. As he reached the third floor, he stopped dead in his tracks. The footprints were much more defined now. The dust on the floor was dry and thick and held its shape. He could clearly make out prints which led down the corridor. They didn't go any higher up the stairs. Whoever had climbed the stairs had gone no further than the third floor. Was that a coincidence? He stopped and pondered his next move.

George crouched down and listened. The sound of water dripping was relentless and seemed to echo through the building. He listened; his breath caught in his chest. Thump, thump, thump, the blood pulsed through his ears. His intuition told him something wasn't right. It was rarely wrong, honed by his years on the streets. He couldn't hear anything untoward, yet he sensed the presence of others. The skin on the back of his neck prickled as if a cold breath had touched him. Something told him to turn and run. *Run. Run now.* He stopped and waited. Having slept rough in unsecure places, his hearing became acute, warning him of danger approaching even while he dozed, deep sleep a luxury that he seldom achieved. Someone was nearby. Someone bad. He could sense evil.

George saw a sign on the wall, dust obscured the letters, but he could just about make out the word 'canteen'. He stayed low and close to the wall and moved to his right. The doorways that he passed were open. Some were blocked with rubble, others with doors hanging cracked and broken. The rooms behind them were dark and dank, the air rank with decay. The further he crept, the darker the corridor became. Even the light didn't want to go there. *Run, George, his mind whispered. Something bad is going to happen, you know it is. Run.*

He saw the gent's toilets opposite him, the ladies next to it. The footprints turned left and disappeared through a set of double doors that were still intact. A sign above said it was the 'staff canteen'. George stopped and listened at the door, ear to the wood. Water dripping, blood pulsing through his head, and something else. Something bad. Something familiar but warped. He couldn't put his finger on it. Wheezing, sighing, rasping breath maybe? Animal or human? Weak and feeble, suffering or dying. Was it animal? He couldn't tell. George decided that he wasn't going through the doors. *Follow your instincts, George. They have kept you alive so far.* He couldn't bring himself to walk through the doors. He would be walking in blind and he didn't know what was on the other side. Something was there, he could sense that. *Something bad. Very bad.*

It may have been paranoia, but he wasn't prepared to take the chance. He moved on, looking for another way into the canteen. The corridor was littered with bricks and air-conditioning tubing. Breeze blocks lay in the darkness, waiting to trip any intruders. The obstacles seemed to be guarding the building's salvageable elements from thieves. George walked on, feeling his way carefully, not wanting to alert anyone to his presence by falling over. The dirt beneath his boots crunched, hardly audible yet deafening to him in the blackness. His stomach knotted at every sound.

The corridor turned right, the darkness deepening. He paused to allow his eyes to adjust. Double fire doors blocked the path. He reached them and pushed with both hands. They rattled but wouldn't give. He felt down and touched thick chains threaded through the handles. His fingers felt a rusty metal padlock. The way was blocked. Even the scavengers hadn't penetrated the building this far. George sighed and turned to retrace his steps. He stumbled on a brick and lurched forward. His arms shot out to soften his fall and he scraped the palms of his hands painfully on a breeze block. He swore beneath his breath and froze to the spot. The noise echoed down the corridor. The sound of rats scurrying in the darkness came from the anterooms. He could hear their claws scratching at the floorboards as they scarpered for cover. A high-pitched squeak came from the canteen, then a mewing sound like a cat with a fur ball in its throat. Animal or human? They had heard his fall, no doubt about it. *Run, George. Run for your life.*

Muffled sounds of distress drifted along the corridor. Different sounds, different tones. There were several. They seemed to be coming in unison. George reached the canteen and placed his ear to the door again and listened. The muffled sounds of distress were louder, more urgent. He had a choice to make. Investigate or run. *Run. Run away.* George looked around and found a piece of metal on the floor. It wasn't very substantial, but it was better than nothing. He waited and listened again. The noises were quieting but were still there. He took a deep breath and pushed one of the doors open, stepping back as it swung closed again. He waited for whatever was inside to come out, but nothing happened. The mewing sounds became louder. Some were high pitched, some deep and rasping.

He pushed the door open again, peering inside as it closed slowly. He tried to see where the sound was coming from. Inside was dark, almost black. He picked up a brick and pushed the door again, ramming the brick against it to keep it open. The dim light from the corridor seeped in but didn't penetrate far enough for him to see. He repeated the process with the second door and hid behind the frame. No gunshot came, no ambush, only the sounds of rasping breath and muffled cries. He looked inside and saw silhouettes. The silhouettes of people. The noises became louder and more agitated. He could smell sweat, urine, and excrement, and something else. The metallic odour of blood.

George stepped inside and put his back against the wall, sliding along it, he made his way around the room until he reached the windows. Thick drapes fashioned from tarpaulin had been nailed over them. The stench of damp and dust hung to the material. He grabbed one corner and pulled hard, ripping the dusty material easily. Light filtered in through the tear. He pulled again, harder this time and watery daylight flooded in. George looked around and he couldn't believe his eyes.

CHAPTER 15

Braddick pulled the Evoque to a halt and looked at Mike Pilkington's house. He raised his eyebrows and exchanged a surprise glance with Jo. It was a three-bedroom detached on a new development, three storeys high. The curtains were closed downstairs but there were no lights on. A well-manicured lawn surrounded the property, split by a driveway that led to a double garage. The neighbouring properties were well kept with high end vehicles parked on the drives.

'Nice place,' she muttered opening the passenger door. 'Lottery win or rich parents?'

'I hope so. Either that or he's a whiz at poker.'

'If I was that good at poker, I wouldn't be working, would you?'

'What and miss all this fun?' he grinned. 'You can't be serious.'

They climbed out of the vehicle and walked up the gravel driveway. The front door was closed and locked, no signs of any disturbance. Braddick lifted the letterbox and peered through. The hallway was bright, painted white with sepia prints on the walls. The staircase was on the left, two doors opposite it. The kitchen was directly in front of him. He could see unopened mail on the microwave. All seemed quiet, normal, and undisturbed. It was the image of modern suburbia, except Mike Pilkington didn't have the wife, dog and two children. The nuclear family didn't always fit hand in hand with the job. Some officers made it work but the divorce rate across the force was ridiculous. If potential husbands and wives were made aware of the figures, they would never consider marrying a police officer. Maybe Pilkington was gay? Braddick didn't know and didn't care about his sexuality but something wasn't right.

'Let's go around the back,' Braddick said closing the flap and stepping back from the door. As he did so, a shadow moved at the top of the stairs. Then another. Shadows. He stepped aside quickly and pulled Jo with him. 'Did you see that?'

'I saw it,' she whispered, pulling her mobile from her fur lined jacket. 'Now a crime has been committed. I'll call an Armed Response Unit.'

'You stay here and watch the front door. I'll take the back,' Braddick said jogging around the corner.

'Don't go in there, Braddick!' Jo whispered after him. He didn't hear her, and she didn't think that he would listen even he had.

He skirted the double garage and followed a paved path towards the back garden. A high ornamental brick wall and wrought iron gate blocked his way. He took a deep breath and launched himself at the wall, stepping halfway up with one foot while reaching for the top with his hands. His fingers grasped rough brickwork and his feet kicked at the bricks, trying to gain purchase to push him up and over the wall. He threw his left arm over, gripping the top and locked his elbow. His chest impacted against the bricks, winding him and for a moment, he thought he was going to fall. He was about to let go when he felt hands beneath his boots, supporting him, pushing him upwards and over.

'Armed units are on their way!' Jo called to him as he dropped on the other side. He landed heavily, twisting his left ankle and cursed beneath his breath. The garden was enclosed by a wooden fence, lined with conifer trees. A birdbath held pride of place in the centre of a striped lawn. He jogged to the corner of the house and peered around it. A large rectangular conservatory covered most of the rear elevation. He could see that the conservatory door was ajar. Braddick crept below the kitchen window. He reached the other side and looked inside. The kitchen was black and silver with an island at the centre, white marble tiles covered the floor. Muddy footprints led from the conservatory, across the tiles and into the living room. He kept low as he ran to the open conservatory door and crept inside. The footprints were still wet, literally minutes old. Braddick grimaced and swore when he realised there were two sets. That changed things dramatically. He paused for a second and weighed up the options. Confrontation was not an option. He was outnumbered and the chances were that they would be armed. The Armed Response Units would be on their way. That would tilt things in his favour. Until then, he just had to contain the situation. Keeping them inside was the key.

He took another quick appraisal of the layout. The kitchen was to his left. He crept to the doorway and peered around the frame. It was empty. He tiptoed through it and made for the hallway. Pausing to think, he moved for the front door, keeping an eye on the doorways to his left and the stairs to his right. There were muffled voices and the sounds of things being dropped on the floor upstairs. He couldn't decipher what they were saying but he was sure they were speaking Russian. He listened and guessed they were on the third floor. The front door was closed and locked with a Yale, which could be opened from the inside. He crept towards it and fastened the bolts top and bottom and then fastened the security chain. They could be undone just as easily but it would slow down their exit if they tried to leave through the front door. With the front door locked, he peered up the stairs and moved swiftly down the hallway and then stepped into the living room. The room was a long rectangular shape with a door that led into the conservatory at the far end. There were three units to his right, all their drawers had been opened and rifled through. The cupboards beneath them were in the same state, doors open and contents all over the floor. He slid along the wall to the conservatory and closed the door quietly. The key was in the door, so he locked it and snapped the key off in the lock before heading back into the kitchen. Voices and heavy footsteps drifted to him from the top floor. He heard them coming down, their boots heavy on the stairs. There wasn't time to run through the kitchen and conservatory into the garden. He would be trapped if he did. The ornamental wall had been too high the first time he had tried. Looking around in a panic, he closed the kitchen door and jammed a dining chair beneath the handle. The dining table was made from wood. It looked heavy. Braddick pushed it towards the door and tipped it up against the door before sprinting to the garage. He knew the chair wouldn't hold for long. The garage door opened, and he stepped inside, reaching for the light switch. He could hear the sound of approaching sirens and the screech of tyres. Footsteps clattered down the bottom set of stairs and angry voices came from the hallway. He heard the front door being rattled.

Braddick looked around the garage. One bay held a quad bike, the other an old MGB. On his left was a well-equipped tool bench and he ran to it, searching for a weapon. He selected a rubber handled claw hammer and held it tightly in his right hand. The voices from the house had become hushed and panicked. He could hear them rattling the conservatory door, trying to escape through the back of the house. His Russian wasn't good, but he figured that they weren't happy. Braddick knew that he had to get out before they tested the garage door. He had no way of locking it or blocking it from his side.

Braddick looked along the walls near the adjoining door and saw a bank of switches. Two of them controlled the lights. None of them were labelled. He decided to press them all and see what happened. The sound of breaking glass from the house made him stop and listen. He flicked the switches. Raised voices came from inside and more voices came from outside. He could hear orders being shouted from the back garden. The sound of an electric motor kicked in and both garage doors began to open. More breaking glass came from inside. A cry of pain pierced the air. Tendrils of tear gas began to drift under the door. He reached for an oily rag and put it over his nose and mouth. The sound of men coughing, and spluttering came from the hallway. The garage doors were half a metre open and rising slowly. He thought about crawling under them. He heard the handle of the connecting door rattle and saw it turning downwards. It would be open in a second. He looked at the distance that he needed to cover to crawl under the exterior doors. It was too far. He was caught like a rabbit in the headlights of an oncoming car as the handle turned and the connecting door burst open.

CHAPTER 16

George looked at the bizarre scene with his mouth open. He didn't know what to do first. His brain couldn't comprehend what his eyes were seeing. The sounds of distress had become deafening, making the situation more confusing. There was no volume button to turn off the sound of suffering. He was completely dumbfounded. Confusion was joined quickly by ice cold terror. Who had done this and why? More to the point, were they still here?

His legs went weak. He leant against the window and thought about what to do. Their eyes begged for help, but he couldn't move. His muscles were frozen with fear. To rush in now was not an option, no matter how desperate they looked. He looked from face to face as his mind raced. Five pairs of eyes, badly battered and bruised, stared back at him, pleading for help. Tears ran down their cheeks. Their faces were black, blue and purple, split and swollen. Tape covered their lips. They were seated at a round table which was bolted to the canteen floor. Their hands were bound with thick gaffer tape and nylon rope. He could see stainless steel nails protruding from their skin, glinting in the light, the shafts encrusted with blood. Someone had bound them, beaten them and then nailed their arms to the table. That was a task that one man couldn't complete alone. It would take many men. He thought about the footsteps coming up the stairs. Multiple prints had gone up but not so many went down. This explained it.

'Calm down, calm down. I'll get help for you,' George said, approaching the table. They became more frantic as he neared. 'I said calm down!' he shouted this time. The injured men became quieter, their muffled cries replaced by sobbing. 'I'm going to get you help,' he said, looking at each one in turn. 'But you have to be patient. I can't get those nails out without hurting you. If I try and release you, you will bleed to death. You need the fire brigade here and paramedics on standby. Do you understand?'

Some of the sobbing became more intense. They tried to talk but their pleas were garbled noises. A mobile phone bleeped, and his attention was drawn to a handset, which had been placed in the centre of the table. The screen illuminated and flashed. George looked around nervously.

'Does that phone belong to any of you?'

The men shook their heads, their eyes terrified.

'Does it belong to whoever did this to you?'

They all nodded.

'Are the men who did this still here?'

They shook their heads, eyes still pleading for help.

George picked up the mobile. It showed an MMS notification. He opened the file and stared at the image. The photograph of a man battered and bleeding appeared. There was no message and the face wasn't familiar. The sender's number had been withheld. Whoever had sent it was making a point although he didn't know what it was. He made up his mind what to do. George scrolled back and opened the phone app. He dialled nine-nine-nine and explained the situation as best he could. The operators and police switchboard were very sceptical about what he told them. When they asked for his name, he hung up, but he knew they would be on their way. His story may sound farfetched, but they had to respond. George looked at the handset and decided to hang onto the mobile for a while. Under normal circumstances he wouldn't but things were far from normal. 'Help is coming. They are on their way. Keep calm and you'll be out of here soon.'

He walked over to the kitchen area, which had been stripped bare of the equipment that once serviced hundreds of employees every day. The first responders would be fifteen minutes at his best estimate. He had told them that there could be armed men in the building. That would add another twenty minutes minimum while they summoned Armed Response Units to declare it safe for the emergency services to enter. He looked around the bare walls until he saw what he was looking for. The outline of a tub sink system was etched into the brick, the stainless sinks removed decades ago. A single pipe protruded from the wall; its end capped off with a brass plug. He searched around until he found a discarded fast food cup. George unfolded his penknife and popped the plug from the pipe. Brown water gushed from the end and he allowed it to spray onto the floor until it was clearer before filling the cup. The pressure dropped dramatically, and the water was no more than a drip before he had it three quarters full. He slipped the knife back into his pocket and went back to the hapless men.

'The police are on the way and I can't be here when they arrive,' he said, peeling the tape from the face of the nearest man. 'This will hurt,' he warned. The man cried out as he ripped the tape from his mouth. Tears of pain, frustration and joy ran down his cheeks. George put the dusty paper cup to his lips. 'Just a sip, no more. Too much will make you ill. It will taste rusty but it's better than nothing, eh?'

'Thank you,' the man said. He sipped the water and closed his swollen eyes. 'God bless you,' he croaked. George noted the Irish lilt.

'Irish?' George asked.

'Dublin.'

'All of you?'

'Aye.'

George looked at the men closest to him. Beneath the table he saw their rubber boots. Five men, all Irish, all wearing rubber boots. He couldn't work out what had happened. What had he stumbled into? Was it a coincidence that these men were there?

'What are you doing here?' George asked, removing the tape from a second man. He gave him a sip of water and moved onto the third and fourth. They exchanged furtive glances, their eyes filled with fear and pain. No one wanted to speak. 'Don't all answer at once,' he said sarcastically, giving the fifth man water. 'Was the question too difficult?' No one replied. 'Shall I ask a simpler one?'

Silence.

'I could call 999 and tell them it was a hoax?'

'No, no, don't do that, mister. We're just scared and in pain.'

'I get that. What are you doing here, though?' George asked sternly. The more he thought about it, the more convinced he was that this could not be a coincidence.

'We are fishermen. Our skipper lied to us. We were tricked into sailing on a smuggling trip that went wrong,' the first man muttered. George heard the first siren approaching. The five injured men looked towards the window instinctively. 'Oh, thank the Lord,' the fisherman muttered.

'Where did it happen, here in Liverpool?'

'No. We sailed from Dublin to Holyhead. That's where they jumped us.'

'What happened?'

'We were jumped on the dock by Russians. At least we think they were Russians. They had machineguns. There was nothing we could do.'

'Russians?' George asked, reaching for the mobile phone that they had left behind. 'Why would they bring you all the way here?'

'Fuck knows why,' the fisherman answered hoarsely.

'Russians with machineguns?'

'Aye, they killed our skipper.' The man was at the edge of breaking. 'They strung us up like pigs in a slaughterhouse. Asking what we knew…' he began to sob, biting his swollen lips. 'We didn't know nothing. Only our skipper knew…'

'Sounds like you had a lucky escape,' George said. He saw the shock and contempt in their eyes.

'Lucky?' One of them gasped. 'They nailed us to a fucking table, mister!'

'If they thought you knew anything, you would be where your skipper is, believe me. It might not feel like it right now, but you had a lucky escape.'

'Forgive me if I don't feel that lucky,' the man replied sourly. 'I don't feel a little bit fucking lucky.'

'You are lucky to be alive and you're lucky that I came along when I did,' he said. He stopped and thought. 'Did they say why they brought you here?' He looked at the image that had been sent to the mobile. Who was that sent by and why? Another siren approached joined quickly by another. The men shook their heads. George took a quick peek out of the doorway. The corridors were empty and dark. 'Help is here, good luck to you.' George ran to window and looked through the grimy glass. The first responders had arrived but were keeping a safe distance until the armed units arrived. It would give him enough time to escape without being seen. He couldn't risk being taken in. It could compromise his status. George turned to leave when something shiny caught his eye. He walked towards the serving hatch that separated the kitchen from the canteen. Fixed to the wall was a Panasonic wireless camera. He frowned and looked into it for a moment. The mobile phone buzzed in his hand and another image appeared. This time the photograph was of George, looking straight into the camera.

CHAPTER 17

Braddick stepped back as the door burst open. He could hear voices shouting. Gas swept through the air, blinding and choking him. Everything moved in slow motion. The door swung violently towards him. It was only his speed and agility that stopped it wiping him out. More shouting came from inside the house. More breaking glass. Cursing in foreign tongues. Coughing and retching. He lost his balance for a moment and nearly went down. His vision was blurred, the gas stung his eyes. He tried not to breath too deeply.

'Armed police!'

'Drop the weapon!'

A figure crashed through the doorway. He was a big man with cropped blond hair, one hand covered his nose and mouth. He stopped when he saw Braddick and raised a weapon. Their eyes met and froze. Tears streamed down his cheeks as they stared at each other for a long second. Braddick was staring down the barrel of a Glock-17. He heard more shouting and three shots rang out. Someone cried in pain and fell heavily but the man in front of him remained standing. He waved the pistol in his face and shouted words that he didn't understand. His voice was thick and guttural. The garage doors clicked open fully and

Braddick heard more orders shouted. This time in English from the front of the house. Black clad figures moved in his peripheral vision. They entered the garage in formation, their movements well-rehearsed, smooth and silent.

'Armed police! Drop the weapon!'

From the corner of his eye, he saw more of the dark clad figures approaching from the driveway, weapons raised, pointing his way. The man hesitated and then turned his weapon at the armed policemen. Braddick saw his chance and raised the hammer instinctively. He brought it down in a vicious arc, the head impacting with the man's wrist. The dense steel shattered the bones as if they were porcelain. The man screamed and dropped to his knees. The weapon clattered across the concrete and he was swamped in seconds by the ARU. They cuffed him and bundled him away.

'Are you okay, sir?' one of the officers asked, handing him a breathing mask. 'The air will clear in a few minutes.'

'Yes, I'm fine,' Braddick said, putting the mask on. His eyes were still streaming. He headed outside into the fresh air to clear his lungs of the stinging gas. 'Make sure that he is searched before he gets to the station. We're looking for anything that holds data, memory stick, MP3, mobile phones, etcetera,' Braddick ordered with a nod. 'The other one?' he asked, gesturing towards the house.

'He tried to break out of the rear, sir.' The officer shrugged. 'He wouldn't relinquish his weapon. He took two in the chest.'

'We were worried about you,' Jo said, approaching the garage. She waited for the air to clear and studied the building. 'Did you see anything useful in there?'

'I'm fine, don't worry,' Braddick said dryly. 'But thanks for asking.'

Jo frowned and walked into the garage unaware of Braddick's sarcasm. She looked around the old MG and then walked over to the quad. 'Expensive toys,' she said, looking at the mileage. 'This is new.'

'Probably cost less than the average woman's shoe collection.'

'Depends where you shop. Let's take a look inside,' she said, ignoring his sarcasm once again. 'I want to know what they were after.' She stepped through the connecting doorway into the hall. Braddick followed her and glanced at the body of the dead Russian. He didn't appear to be carrying anything. 'Has he been searched?' Jo asked.

'Nothing on him,' a uniformed officer answered.

'They ransacked the place downstairs,' Braddick said, looking inside the living room. 'What do you think they were looking for?'

'The identity of the informer,' she shrugged. He didn't respond. 'Is that what you think?'

'I don't know what to think.' Braddick walked to the bottom of the stairs, his face blank. There were a thousand possibilities to consider. He needed most of them ruled out so that they could concentrate on a much smaller number of scenarios. 'Let's get this place secured and a full search team in here. Put two teams from MIT on it and let CSI do a sweep.'

'CSI?' she asked, frowning.

'You never know what they might come up with,' he said, thinking. 'A random print, DNA hit, who knows?'

'Do you think he was bent?'

'I don't want to think anything like that yet.' Braddick shrugged. 'Pilkington was living way beyond his means.'

'If Cain and Pilkington do have an informer inside the Karpov operation, the identity of that person would be very valuable,' she said, looking at a pile of his correspondence that had been scattered on the floor.

'So would the identity of the UC.'

'Where would they have kept that?'

'If it was me, I would have it stashed on my phone or laptop where no one would see it and if they did, they wouldn't know what it meant,' Braddick said. He stared at a sixty-inch curved screen. 'If there is something here it is not in plain sight, it's hidden where a couple of Russian thugs wouldn't find it.'

'Or us,' she added, her phone under her chin.

'Or us,' he agreed.

'Search team is on the way.' She covered the microphone as she spoke to him. He nodded and walked into the kitchen. It was the only part of the house that hadn't been ransacked. He thought about his kitchen drawers and his parent's kitchen drawers. They were full of good stuff. Valuable stuff that they might need one day. Emergency stuff. Secret stuff. He was about to look through them when Jo called his name. She sounded excited. 'Braddick, you have to hear this.'

'What?'

'ARU, fire and ambulance have been called to a derelict building near Edge Lane,' she said, her eyes wider than usual. Braddick waited for her to explain. 'There are five Irishmen nailed to a table on the third floor. They are claiming to be fishermen from Dublin.'

'Fucking hell!' Braddick said, shaking his head. He took a deep breath and frowned. 'Are they going to make it?'

'Yes.' she nodded. 'They're in a bad way but alive.'

'We need to talk to them, pronto,' he said. 'Let's get to the Royal before it turns into a circus.'

CHAPTER 18

Patrick Finnen stepped into a phone box on Lord Street and dialled the number again. It rang three times and switched to answering machine, again. This time, he left a different message. A message Henry had told him to leave. The receiver may not be sure what it meant but he had a good idea that they would get the gist of it. It was a 'get in touch or else' type of message. Subtle but threatening. Patrick could see that there was more to Henry than first met the eye. Ieuan Jones had called him a hit man, as near as damn it. A hit man or enforcer, there was no difference. They hurt people, frightened people, interrogated and tortured people and ultimately, murdered people. Henry hid it well. Beneath the jovial Irishman was a stone-cold killer. Patrick had encountered a few men like Henry along the way. Men who had been sucked into the troubles, joined the paramilitaries as young men and learned how to kill and terrorise. When the troubles faded, the organisations on both sides didn't disband, they just stepped into the shadows and changed focus. They policed their own areas and moved into the supply chain, squeezing everyone else out by using their well-honed skills to persuade. Men like Henry were dangerous. Patrick was glad that he was on his side, but he was very wary too. If they failed in their mission, Patrick was under no illusions that Henry would be the man to kill him. Henry was a killer, full stop.

They had separated and agreed to meet in Flanagan's Apple, an Irish pub on Mathew Street. Henry reckoned that he needed to buy some supplies and meet up with some of his old contacts, who drank in that area. The area was rife with tourists on a Beatle quest, easy to con and easy to rob. He had planned to go and check the place out, ask a few questions and get a lead on Gary Mason and his cronies. Patrick hung up the phone and opened the door. A gale was blowing off the river, turning Lord Street into an icy wind tunnel. He pulled up the hood of his parka and jogged across the road past McDonalds, towards Mathew Street. The streets were busy, tourists and shoppers mingling, moving from shop to shop, pub to pub. He heard half a dozen different languages being spoken and he didn't recognise any of them.

Patrick could tell that Flanagan's was busy from the outside. He could hear the racket inside as he approached. He climbed three steps to reach the bar door and stepped into the warmth. Food and ale aromas hit him. The sound of a band drifted up from the cellar downstairs, mingling with the clinking of plates coming from the restaurant upstairs. The low ceilings seemed to amplify the noise. It was noisy, almost uncomfortably loud but laughter and conversation filled the air. The floorboards were stained dark brown like the oak beams on the ceiling. He pushed through the crowd to the bar and ordered a Guinness, surprised by the price compared to home. Beer in Dublin was ridiculously priced. Then he tasted it. He frowned, disappointed with the comparative flavour. It just wasn't quite the same. The smell of pastry and garlic reached him, making him realise how hungry he was. He looked at the faces that lined the bar. There was no sign of Henry. Patrick turned around and shouldered his way through the crowd. He scanned the booths looking for him. After making a full circuit of the bar, he headed downstairs to the cellar where the band was playing. The familiar tones of the pennywhistle and a fiddle drifted to him. A singer with a harsh Belfast tone boomed out his version of 'Dirty Old Town'. The sound of conversation seemed to be louder downstairs as the punters competed with the music. He looked around and spotted Henry in a booth with two men. He saw Patrick and beckoned him over. His face smiled but his eyes drilled into his head, looking for a sign of betrayal. Henry didn't trust Patrick any more than Patrick trusted him.

'This is my friend, Patrick.' Henry introduced him. Patrick smiled, Ieuan's words echoed around his mind. *This man is not your friend, Henry is nobody's friend.* The men stood and shook hands enthusiastically. 'This is Clint, and this is Graham. They're old colleagues of ours,' he explained. 'They worked for us many moons ago.'

'All right, Patrick!' The men nodded and grinned. 'You're the boxer, aren't you?'

'I was, yes.' Patrick blushed. They were like bookends, pugilist's noses and cropped receding hairlines. Their Adidas tracksuits were identical, one blue, the other black. Patrick had the impression that they were in awe of himself and Henry. 'It seems like a long time ago now.'

'We used to watch you every time you fought, didn't we, Clint?'

'We did, mate. That fight against the Mexican, Morrales. That was class. Absolute class.'

'It was class.'

'Thank you,' Patrick said, embarrassed.

'We did a bit of boxing when we were younger, didn't we, Clint?' Graham nudged his friend and grinned.

'We did. Schoolboys and the amateur ranks,' Clint said, grinning proudly too. 'We did all right too. Won a few area trophies, didn't we?'

'We did.'

'We were not in your league obviously. All respect to you. Nice to meet you, Patrick.'

'Fucking buzzing to meet you, Patrick. Can we get you a pint?'

'And you, Henry, you'll have another won't you?'

'I'm all right for now.' Henry smiled. His glass was full.

'I've just bought this one. I'm all right thanks. It's nice to meet you too,' Patrick said, raising his glass. He sat down and decided to stay quiet and let Henry do the talking.

'The lads were just telling me about your friend, Gary Mason and his family.' Henry took the lead. The two men grinned and nodded enthusiastically. 'It seems that he's well known around town. Patrick said that he was well known, didn't you, Patrick.' Henry nudged him in the ribs. Patrick looked at him, unsure if he was taking the piss or not. 'Well known, you said. You got that right.'

'Do you know him well?' Patrick asked, taking a drink of his pint. He could feel Henry's eyes on him.

'Yes, we know Gary. We know everyone around town, don't we, Clint? 'Graham said, nudging Clint. They laughed and swigged their beer. 'There's no one in town that we don't know. Unless we don't want to know them!'

'Well, put it this way, we know everyone who is worth knowing, eh?' The two men laughed in unison. 'We don't waste time with nobodies!' They looked at the Irishmen to see if they were as impressed as they were with themselves.

'So, you do know Gary Mason?' Patrick repeated flatly. He wasn't in the mood for joviality and the double act were irritating him. The men stopped smiling. They looked at him, offended. 'Do you know him well or do you just know of him?'

'Yes, like I said, we know him,' Clint answered, sullenly. He sipped his pint and remained tight lipped. Henry stared at him, making him feel uncomfortable. He wiped his mouth and cleared his throat before speaking. 'We've known the Masons since we were schoolboys. Reputations start early in this city and the Masons have a reputation. They've been around forever.'

'What can you tell us about Gary?' Henry asked, nudging Patrick to be quiet. He could see that he was running low on patience but annoying friends who had information, wasn't good. Not if he wanted to learn anything.

'Depends on what it is worth.'

'We could make it worth your while.' He shot Patrick a scolding glance. Patrick reached into his pocket and passed a rolled up fifty-pound note to Clint. 'How is that for beginners?' Henry smiled thinly.

'That's more like it,' Clint grinned. 'What do you want to know about the Masons.'

'Whatever you can tell us.'

'They're a big family. They've been in the mix since they left school. Their fingers are in every pie in town, if you know what I mean.'

'Really?'

'Really. This time last year, the Masons were thought of as lapdogs to the Farrells. They were working with the big boys, but they weren't as big as the Farrells were. Things have changed though. We've been hearing a few bits and pieces the last few months haven't we, Graham?'

'We have, mate.'

'Like what?' Henry encouraged him. He was lost already but he didn't want to interrupt them when they were on a roll.

'Wait a minute, why are we talking about the Farrells?' Patrick wasn't so patient. 'Who the fuck are the Farrells?'

'They are cousins with the Masons,' Graham explained. 'Their cousins were another rung up the ladder. The Masons have always been around but the Farrells made it to the top of the tree.'

'They were major league. Their cousins were Eddie Farrell and his sons,' Clint lowered his voice. 'Have you heard of them?'

'No,' Henry glanced at Patrick and they both shook their heads. 'The name Farrell doesn't mean anything to us. Should it?'

'Probably not in Dublin. Eddie senior was a sharp young man growing up, always looking for a scam. He made a lot of money quickly, drugs and prostitutes mostly. I remember he had a Corvette before he was twenty. He was hard as nails but sharp with it, you know what I mean?'

'I know what you're saying.'

'He was a millionaire before he was thirty, always one step ahead of the law and two steps ahead of the competition. His legitimate businesses made as much money as his bent ones. His sons joined him when they left school and they did very well for years. The Farrells were established and untouchable until the foreign outfits started moving in.'

'Foreign muscle?'

'About fifteen years ago it all changed.' Clint leaned forward and lowered his voice. 'Turks, Latvians, Estonians, Albanians, you fucking name somewhere and they had a crew here. It was like the fucking United Nations here, wasn't it, Graham?'

'It was unbelievable, mate. It was like the Wild West here on a Saturday night. Places were getting shot up every week. Eddie Farrell was clinging on by the skin of his teeth.'

'Then the Russians arrived and crushed the fucking lot of them. They identified that the Farrells were the main competition in town and that they could keep all the other wannabies in their place. So, the Farrells went into business with a bigger mob.'

'The Russian mob,' Graham reinforced the point, just in case it wasn't clear enough. 'Heavy shit, mate.'

'They made a deal and became the muscle for a Russian outfit called the Karpovs.' He paused. 'You must have heard of them?'

'We have heard of them although they don't have a foothold where we are yet,' Henry said. He looked at Patrick with a concerned expression. Patrick's heart sank at the name. The fact that an established Russian mob had been mentioned shook his confidence. 'They're a competent outfit then, the Karpovs?'

'Competent?' Clint chuckled and nudged his friend again. 'Are the Karpovs competent, Graham?'

'Very fucking competent, mate.' Graham said, staring straight into Patrick's eyes. 'They are one fucked up bunch of psychos, mate. I think you probably have to skin one of your own kids and eat it to get into that mob, you know what I mean?'

'We know what you mean.' Henry smirked. He could see that the colour had drained from Patrick's face. The chance of rescuing something from the deal was slipping away. 'So, the Karpovs were behind this Farrell family?'

'Big time, mate,' Clint said nodding. He leaned forward again, his voice a whisper. 'Eddie Farrell didn't take a shit without telling the Karpovs what colour it was. You know what I mean?'

'I know what you mean.' Henry chuckled. 'So, the Farrells were up there with the big boys?'

'They were up there all right. Top of the tree for years they were until someone killed Eddie's son.'

'Really?' Henry pretended to be interested. He could feel Patrick shifting in his seat. He wanted to know about Gary Mason and Clint was going all around the houses. 'Someone killed his son?'

'Yes, really. They caved his head in with a brick.'

'A brick?' Henry nudged Patrick. 'Would you believe that, Patrick?'

'You couldn't make it up, could you?' Patrick muttered sarcastically. He smiled to feign interest.

'A brick across the head. Killed him instantly. A fourteen-year-old kid did it.'

'Fourteen years old, no way!'

'Yes way, mate,' Clint said, seriously. 'Eddie lost the plot apparently. He caused havoc trying to get to the kid who killed his son and the Karpovs kicked off because of all the attention he was bringing down on them. The story goes that they fell out with the Russians and then vanished. One day they were there and the next, vamoosh!'

'Vanished?' Patrick muttered. 'What do you mean they vanished?'

'Disappeared, mate!' Clint scoffed.

'No one disappears. What happened?'

'No one knows for sure.'

'There must be rumours.'

'Plenty of rumours, aren't there, Graham?' Clint chuckled.

'There are plenty of rumours, mate.' Graham agreed.

'Could you share some of them with us?' Patrick asked flatly, tiring of the men's incessant chat. They glared at him. 'If you don't mind that is.'

'No, we don't mind,' Clint said, pretending not to be offended. He sipped his beer and made them wait a few seconds. He leaned close again, his voice hushed. 'A couple of the doormen on one of Karpov's nightclubs reckon they were given an early bath.' He winked.

'Early bath,' Graham repeated and winked too.

'You know what I mean?' Clint tapped his nose with his index finger. 'Feeding the fishes.'

'Finding Nemo,' Graham added.

'Playing submarine commanders…'

'Snorkelling with his boots on.'

'Okay, okay. We get it,' Henry said, holding up his hand. Clint looked disappointed. 'Which nightclubs do the Karpovs run?'

'What?' Clint frowned.

'You said that the doormen on their clubs were talking about what happened to the Farrells,' Henry said. 'Which nightclubs are theirs?'

'Liquid and Gold,' Clint grunted.

Patrick made a note of the names on his phone. 'This is all very interesting but where does Gary Mason come into this story?'

'I was just telling you the history behind it or it won't make sense,' Clint said sulkily. He shifted in his seat and looked around to make sure no one was prying. 'When the Farrells were with the Russians, they were bossing everything, Big Ron Mason was their attack dog. He was the real teeth behind the operation. Anytime there was friction between the Farrells or the Karpovs and anyone else in town, you could put money on it that Big Ron had sorted it.'

'They're cousins, you know, the Farrells and the Masons,' Graham added, knowingly.

'Yes, you said,' Patrick smiled thinly. 'Several times.'

'Okay, mate,' Graham snapped. 'There's no need to be an arse. We don't need to tell you fuck all, you know?'

Clint and Graham looked at Patrick, angrily. Henry turned to him and shook his head. 'Do you want to hear this or not?' he said calmly but his face was stern. 'If you don't want to listen, fuck off to the bar and get another round.'

'I didn't mean any offense,' Patrick said, swallowing his beer. 'It's been a long week. I'm just tetchy.'

'No problem,' Clint half smiled. 'Anyway, I was saying that the Masons did the wet work for Eddie Farrell and the Karpovs. You know what I mean?'

'Yes. We know what you mean.'

'Big Ron was their enforcer. No one fucks with Big Ron.'

'Big Ron is one fucking mean man, isn't he, Graham?'

'He's a very bad man.' Graham agreed. 'Some of the stuff that I've heard about him would make your toes curl…'

'Hold on, hold on!' Henry held up his hand. 'And where exactly does Gary Mason fit in?' Henry frowned, confused by this new name. 'I'm struggling to keep up here,' he joked. 'We have the Farrells, the Karpovs and now Big Ron Mason. Tell me who Gary is, please.'

'Big Ron's little brother.' Clint shrugged as if it was obvious. He smiled. 'He is a fucking Muppet.'

'A fucking Muppet?' Henry glanced at Patrick. Patrick hadn't done his homework. Gary Mason was not at the top of the tree. 'We thought he was in charge, didn't we, Patrick?'

Patrick nodded, tight lipped, blushing slightly. The two men looked at each other and laughed. Henry didn't see the funny side. They saw his expression and stopped laughing, quickly.

'He couldn't run a raffle. Gary Mason is in charge of fuck all,' Graham said, looking from Henry to Patrick. 'Is he, Clint?'

'He's in charge of fuck all, mate.'

'Big Ron fronts the Masons. He always has. If it wasn't for the Karpovs, Big Ron would have been top dog years ago. The Karpovs backed Eddie Farrell and that is the only reason Big Ron was kept inline. He would have eaten Eddie Farrell for breakfast and shat him out at lunchtime.'

'Big Ron is the man in charge, proper nutcase, mind you.'

'So, Gary Mason was second in command?'

'Yes. That's what we said.'

'And you reckon that the Masons have stepped into this guy, Eddie Farrell's shoes?' Henry asked.

'Pretty much.' Clint nodded. 'Rumour has it that the Farrells left a lot of money behind. Eddie was a millionaire several times over, wasn't he, Graham?'

'Several times.'

'Of course, his sons should have inherited the estate but one was dead and the other vanished along with Eddie. We heard the property and businesses went into probate because he is missing, not dead. The thing is there were plenty of cash rich income streams and we heard Big Ron snapped them up before any of the Farrells could get their greasy paws on them. Plus, he liquidated some properties that

Eddie had stashed away in a shell company. We heard that Big Ron has found a lot of Eddie Farrell's money. Money that the law or his cousins can't touch. They probably didn't even know it was there. Farrell was minted.'

'Fucking minted, mate.'

'Drug dealers tend to be,' Patrick grunted.

'Well you're not a very good drug dealer then,' Clint joked. 'You don't look minted to me. Maybe he's a shit drug dealer, eh, Graham?'

'Yes, shit drug dealer,' they laughed. Patrick grinned and drank from his pint. There was no point in getting into a war of words with them. They seemed harmless enough if not a little annoying.

'Funny,' Henry laughed with them. 'You were saying…about Farrell's money.'

'When they disappeared, the estate was huge. The Masons got their hands on a wedge of money, didn't they, Graham?'

'That's what we heard. Since then, they have been strutting around town like Johnny Bigspuds. Especially Gary Mason. He's a prick.'

'Say we wanted to talk to him. Where would we be likely to find Big Ron?' Henry asked casually.

'He runs security for most of the city centre pubs. He's always around somewhere checking on things, but he tends to be in Rotter's at the end of the night. He actually owns that one. Rumours have it that he's trying buy a few more. We heard he's using Farrell's money to buy up whatever he can.'

'You said it was called Rotter's?'

'Yes. It's the big club beneath the tower,' Clint explained. 'Why all the questions about Ron Mason?' Clint asked. Henry shot him a glance; his lips narrowed. 'I thought it was Gary that you were interested in.' Henry stared at him in silence. 'Okay, okay. Just asking, that's all. If you don't ask the question, you never get the answer, eh, Graham?'

'Is right, mate.' Graham frowned. 'Come on, spill the beans. What has Gary Mason done to attract your attention from all the way over in Dublin?'

'You haven't heard, have you?' Patrick asked quietly.

'Heard what?' Clint grinned.

'Gary Mason is dead. They had a deal hijacked and Gary was killed.'

'Fuck off,' Clint said shocked. 'Gary Mason is dead?'

'Yes.'

'I don't believe it.'

'Is this true, Henry?'

'I'm afraid so.'

'Someone had Big Ron off and killed his brother?' Clint said, nudging his pal. 'We're not having that, are we, Graham? That is fucking unbelievable.'

'Un-be-fucking-lievable.'

'We would have heard about it. Surely, we would have heard about it.'

'I'm telling you, they got jumped.' Patrick lent forward. 'They strung Gary Mason up and beat him to death.'

'Who did?' Clint asked. His voice almost a whisper.

'We don't know.' Henry smiled. 'Yet. That is why we are here. To find out.'

'Where did this happen?'

'Holyhead.'

'North Wales, Holyhead?'

'Yes.'

'Holyhead where the ferries go to Ireland?'

'The same.'

'So that is why you two are here?'

'Yes.'

'No way. They killed Gary Mason?' Clint whistled through his teeth. 'That is not sinking in at all.'

'Well, it is true.'

'Murdered during a drug deal? I'm assuming it was a drug deal?'

'It was.'

'So, what happened?'

'We're not sure. All we know is that the deal was hijacked, Gary was murdered, and Frank, Brian and Jimmy Farrell are all still missing.'

'No fucking way! The Farrells were there too?' Clint hissed; a narrow smile touched his lips. He looked at Henry for confirmation. Henry nodded that it was true. 'We had heard rumours that the Masons were gearing up, but we had no idea that they were bringing the Farrells back into the game. Gary Mason set this up?'

'He did, with Patrick here.' Henry nodded. 'And whoever whacked him stole our property. Obviously, we want our money back.'

'Ah, now it makes sense,' Clint said, tapping his nose again. 'Now I can see why you have been wheeled out of retirement, Henry. You must have been retired?'

'You never really retire. Not in my game. You just don't get your hands dirty as often.'

'I'm shocked. This is bad news for you but not bad news for everyone.'

'What do you mean?' Patrick frowned.

'There will be a lot of people who won't be sorry to see the back of Gary Mason and a few of the Farrells. That will be a massive blow for Big Ron. I didn't like his brother, but they were tight. Losing Gary will weaken his position. Some people will be happy about that. It is always good when the competition is weakened. He will be on the warpath.' Clint sat back and looked at Graham. 'Go and get a round in and get chasers too. I think we should raise a glass to poor old Gary. Will you have a whisky with us?'

'Go on.' Henry nodded.

'Scotch for me,' Patrick said. Graham stood up and walked off to the bar. He hitched up his tracksuit pants to cover his designer boxer shorts.

'I knew there was a reason why you were asking all these questions about the Masons, but I didn't realise it was so big. Now I get it.' He shook his head. 'Did you lose anyone?'

'The captain of the dragger.'

'Dragger?'

'A trawler. We sent some product over the water by boat.'

'And someone found out about it.'

'Obviously. We need to find out who that was,' Henry said. Graham returned to the table with a tray. He placed the four pints in front of them and then put the whisky next to them. 'Absent friends,' Henry said, raising his glass. They clinked glasses and swallowed the burning liquid.

'I can't believe that someone fucked you and the Masons over, and I can't believe they have kept that quiet,' Graham said, emptying his shot.

'The Masons and the Farrells must have closed ranks and kept the news quiet for now,' Patrick explained. 'It is not good for business. It will be all over the newspapers and the television no doubt.'

'So, who the fuck did this?' Clint turned to Graham.

'More to the point, who could do that?' Graham asked. 'There are not many outfits with the balls to pull that off.'

'And that is why I asked you to meet us,' Henry said. 'Not just for old time's sake. We need your help.'

'I'm not sure that we want to get involved, to be honest, Henry,' Clint said, shaking his head. 'Asking questions around here can make you dead.'

'Dead as a dodo,' Graham agreed.

'Come on, lads. It is no big deal for you. It was a simple transaction that was hijacked. These things happen but we have a considerable investment in it.' Henry shrugged. 'We're here to recover our goods or the money but to do that, we need to know what happened. You can help us there. No one needs to know that you have helped us. You can trust me, you know that.'

'We trust you, Henry. It isn't you that I'm worried about. No offence.'

'None taken. All we're asking is that you help us find out who hit the deal. Once we know, you won't hear from us again.'

'Do you think it might be an inside job?' Graham guessed. 'Because the Farrells are missing. Do you think they turned on the Masons, whacked Gary Mason and fucked off with your stuff?'

'Maybe but I doubt it. Do you think that could have happened?'

'No way. I can't see the Farrells turning on Big Ron and killing his brother,' Clint said, shaking his head. 'That would be suicide. He would demolish them one by one. They wouldn't dare. Like I said earlier, the only reason the Farrells stayed on top was because of Eddie's deal with the Karpovs. With them gone, Ron is the man.' Clint whistled through his teeth again and sat back. He steepled his fingers and looked at Henry. 'Whoever did this is on top. This is beyond most outfits. What are your instincts telling you happened?'

'We don't know. That is the point. We're not ruling anything out yet.' He paused. 'We can't afford to get this wrong.'

'Whoever hit you doesn't give a fuck about you or the Masons and that narrows it down for you.'

'I know who my money is on,' Graham said with a nod. 'An outfit who thinks they can do what they want, when they want to, and they think that because they can.'

'No one can take our product without facing consequences from our end. No matter who they are,' Henry said, pointing a finger. The corner of his eyes twitched, anger building. 'We still have a sting in our tails.'

'I bet you do, Henry.'

'We do. That's why I'm here.'

'What went missing, Henry?' Clint asked seriously. 'Drugs or money?'

'Both.'

'You were importing?' Clint said, shaking his head.

'It was a new enterprise.'

'What was it?'

'Zombie.'

'Fucking hell.' Clint whistled again. 'That stuff is like fucking gold dust. No wonder you got hit. Everyone wants to sell that shit. The punters can't get enough of it. Not many people can get their hands on it and when they do, it doesn't last long.'

'I need to know if anyone locally starts selling it,' Henry said quietly. 'I'll look after you. You know that.'

'We'll keep our ears to the ground.'

'Good. Who is competent enough to hit the Masons?' Henry asked.

'Competent. That word again,' Clint chuckled. 'Competent like the Karpovs?'

'Exactly.'

'There aren't many outfits up to a job like this. I would put money on it being them. I just can't see anyone else risking it.'

'If it was them, we'll find out in the end.' Henry shrugged. 'That is what we're here to find out.'

'That is heavy shit, Henry,' Graham said, sitting back. 'If the Karpovs hit the Masons and killed Gary, you should leave it to Big Ron. Let him deal with it. Does he know who hit them?'

'We don't know. They're not talking to us,' Patrick interrupted. 'They are in the same position as we are. They don't know what happened either so they don't know who they can trust. They will suspect we did it.'

'Fair comment,' Clint agreed.

'Like I said earlier, we have a considerable investment to protect,' Henry said quietly. 'I'd appreciate it if you can put the feelers out.'

'We will. Asking questions about the Karpovs can be expensive, Henry.'

'Whatever it takes.'

'You need to tread carefully. Some investments you win and some you lose,' Graham said, draining his pint. 'I'd be tempted to cut my loses on this one. If you grab the tail of that particular dog it will bite you on the arse. I wouldn't be messing with that lot.'

'If it was your money, you might have the privilege to walk away,' Patrick interrupted. 'I don't.'

'Oh dear,' Clint said, smiling sourly. 'You did the deal off your own back, eh, Patrick?' Patrick nodded, almost imperceptibly. 'And someone leaked the site of the drop and they pulled your pants down.' Clint shook his head. 'Now you have Henry and his bosses on your case.'

'Something like that.'

'I don't envy you right now,' Graham chuckled.

'I remember a few boys back in the old days that fucked up. Henry's bosses aren't very tolerant.' He smiled thinly as he spoke and nudged Graham. Graham grinned. 'That didn't end well for them, eh, Henry?' Henry stared blankly at them. 'They were found nailed to the floorboards in a derelict squat in Bootle. No one knew who had done it, did they, Henry?'

'You're up to your neck in shite on this one, Patrick,' Graham added.

'I know that. Whatever happens, I need to be able to explain myself.' Patrick shrugged. 'It will be what it will be.'

'One thing is for sure,' Graham said, lowering his tone. 'The Masons have got a rat in their nest. I'll bet it was one of the Farrells that blabbed about the deal to the Karpovs.'

'What makes you think that?'

'It just makes sense to me. I've heard that some of the Farrells are pissed off that Big Ron has stepped up and taken over the business but none of them have got the balls to challenge him. Leaking the time and place of a big deal would be worth a lot of coin and it would be one in the eye for Big Ron.'

'That makes sense.' Patrick said thoughtfully.

'Fuck yes!' Graham chuckled. 'Think about it. The Farrells were puppets for the Russians for years. They worked closely together. It makes sense that some of them made friends and are still in contact with them. Just because Eddie lost the plot and pissed them off doesn't mean everyone fell out with them, does it?'

Patrick shook his head. 'No. It makes sense, I suppose.'

'Even if you find out it is the Karpovs that hijacked the deal, what are you going to do about it, Henry?' Clint asked seriously.

'Now we know who is in charge of the Mason's operation, we're going to speak to him. Then we need to find out who crashed the party.'

'And then what?' Clint chuckled. He looked from one to the other. 'Say you find out that the Karpovs are responsible, you can't just ask for your gear back.'

'Why not,' Henry smiled coldly. 'They stole it. We want it back.'

'Because they are huge, Henry,' Clint said, spreading his arms wide. 'Aren't they, Graham?'

'FM's, mate.'

'FM's?' Patrick asked.

'Fucking massive.'

'And nasty, Henry. These fuckers will go after your family if they can't get you. They have no scruples. This is not like the old days. You're out of your league here.'

'Don't underestimate us,' Henry said, lowering his voice. 'We brought plenty of big players to their knees, remember?'

Clint and Graham looked at each other and nodded. 'Fair comment,' Clint muttered. 'No one fucked with you lot in the old days, Henry but these guys are hardcore. They are the big boys in the yard now.'

'Oh, I get that. These guys are bullies stealing dinner money from the smaller kids at school.' Henry grinned but his eyes were cold. 'Most bullies don't like it when the little kid turns around and gives him a bloody nose, but it happens.'

'Are you going to give the bully a bloody nose, Henry?' Graham chuckled.

'We'll give him a bloody nose to think about first.' Henry finished his drink. His face turned to stone. He pointed his finger in Graham's face. 'We'll give him a bloody nose and then we'll kick his fucking teeth down his throat.' Clint's mouth fell open, but he didn't speak. Graham looked shocked by his sudden aggression. 'One way or the other, we want our property back, don't we, Patrick?' Patrick nodded, although he wasn't sure what Henry had in mind. The look in his eyes told him that things were about to get a little crazy. 'Talking of which, is the stuff we left behind safe?'

'Of course, it is,' Clint nodded nervously. He reached into his pocket and put a key and a business card onto the table. 'The address for the storage unit is on the card. All your stuff is in there.'

'Good man.' Henry smiled and raised his glass. They all clinked glasses and finished their drinks. 'How well do you know Ron Mason?'

'Like I said, we go way back. We're not bosom buddies but we've done a few bits and pieces for him over the years.'

'He's not talking to us. We need him to talk to us. I want you to set up a meeting for us,' Henry said with a smile. Clint looked nervous. Graham looked very uncomfortable. 'Is that a problem?'

'No,' Clint said. 'It's no problem.'

'Good,' Henry said, sitting back. He seemed to relax. 'Let's talk no more about it for now. I want to get drunk.' He threw another fifty-pound note onto the table. 'Get another round in, Graham.'

'I'll come with you,' Clint said, pocketing the money. 'I need a piss.' The two men stood up and walked to the bar.

'What is in that storage locker?' Patrick asked when they were out of earshot.

'Persuasion.'

'Persuasion?'

'Aye,' Henry said with a nod. 'We're going to need all the persuasion that we can find to get anything out of this deal. Trust me, Patrick. I know what I'm doing.' Patrick finished his pint and looked at the band. He didn't trust Henry one little bit.

CHAPTER 19

SIX HOURS LATER

Big Ron Mason listened to the news on the television. It was the third time that he had watched the loop on Sky News. He emptied his bottle of Jack Daniels and grimaced as the burning liquid swilled around his mouth, numbing his tongue. He was trying to numb his brain with alcohol, but it wasn't working. His brother, Gary, had been a pain in the arse growing up but he loved him, nonetheless. They were best friends. Gary had been his number two since they were in school. He thought back to an incident with the Kio brothers when he was fourteen and Gary was thirteen. The three of them had waited for Ron near the gates after school one day, following an argument that had occurred at break time. Ron didn't like Degsy Kio and Degsy didn't like Ron. Their mutual dislike had been simmering for months and it was only a matter of time until it spilled over into violence. Testosterone filled their veins; spots covered their faces. They were turning into young men and aggression coursed through them. Degsy and Ron were both feared and respected, but they needed to sort out the pecking order.

Degsy was the same age as Ron, the middle Kio was a year older and the eldest had left school the year before. Degsy would wind Ron up in school but when it came to it, he knew Ron was too much to handle on his own. Ron was big for his age even then, but he was outnumbered, and the odds were stacked against him massively. Degsy had called him out to settle things after school but Ron knew that if his brothers were there, they wouldn't stand there and watch him be beaten. They would join in. It would be three onto one, no matter what the outcome. He knew he was in for a hiding at best, but pride wouldn't let him run. Ron was scared but hid it well. Rumours about the Kio family had circulated the estate for years. They were all trouble and fought as a pack. The elder Kio had been to Borstal for stabbing another kid the year before. Rumours said that he always carried a blade and that he wasn't scared to use it.

When the bell rang that afternoon, Ron saw them waiting near the gates; a crowd of onlookers was gathering in anticipation of seeing someone get a good hiding. The Kio brothers were strutting around like peacocks, absolutely convinced that there was only one outcome. What they didn't anticipate was Gary Mason getting involved in proceedings. Gary had heard the rumours in school that the Kio brothers would be waiting for Ron after school. When school let out, he ran as fast as he could to catch up with his big brother.

'What are we going to do, Ron?' Gary had asked nervously. 'Degsy's older brother is mad. I've heard that he carries a knife.'

Ron had felt his heart swell with pride. His younger brother had said 'we' and 'us' without a thought for his own welfare. He was ready to fight next to his brother, shoulder to shoulder without question. His loyalty was unconditional. It was unconditional that day and every day after that. They became inseparable.

'Go for their eyes and their bollocks, kiddo,' Ron had replied. *'And if you get close, bite them hard and don't let go.'*

When they got to the gates, the crowd parted and formed a circle. The Masons dropped their bags, rolled up their sleeves and removed their ties. They smiled at each other and ran full pelt at the Kio brothers. They were fearless even then. The Kio brothers were surprised by their ferocity. They had the better of them at first, but Gary and Ron were powerful and resilient. No matter how many punches they took, they kept coming. Gary did as his brother had told him. He scratched Degsy's left eye, nearly blinding him and when they came close together, wrestling, Gary sank his teeth into his cheek, biting down hard. Degsy had screamed like a girl which drove the Masons on to new heights. With their noses bleeding, they fought until the Kio brothers were battered and exhausted. They capitulated and begged for them to stop. Ron and Gary weren't for stopping. They continued to flail, punches and kicks landed from all angles. Ron had the older brother by the hair, pulling his head down, he kicked him in the face repeatedly until his trainers were soaked in blood. Eventually the Kio brothers broke away and ran. The Masons laughed, hugged each other and then chased them until they were exhausted. When they stopped to catch their breath, the Masons attacked again. The eldest Kio left missing an earlobe, crying like a baby and the Mason brothers never had any trouble again. Not unless they went looking for it. As they grew up, they were best men at each other's weddings, god fathers to each other's kids and a shoulder to cry on when their marriages collapsed. He would miss Gary badly.

As Ron watched the news report again, a tear filled his left eye, anger boiled in his guts. Images of the harbour at Holyhead flickered across the screen, followed by head shots of Linus Murphy and his brother, Gary Mason. His stomach knotted. He watched as photographs of the Irish fishermen flickered by and then they panned to the Royal, where they had been taken following their discovery. An Irish detective did a thirty second interview about how relieved they were to have found them alive. His cousins, the Farrells, were still listed as missing. He dialled nine-zero-one on his throwaway mobile and listened to another voicemail from the suppliers. The Irish accent grated on his nerves. They were becoming impatient. The last message was threatening. He knew that he needed to talk to them, but he wanted to be sure that they hadn't set him up first. A call from a casual acquaintance called Clint had further reassured him. Watching the news had convinced him that they were victims too. His main mobile rang, Rickets was calling from the Royal.

'Rickets?' Big Ron answered. 'What have you heard?'

'There are police all over the place, Ron. I spoke to one of the nurses,' Rickets said. His voice sounded like he had swallowed gravel. 'The Irishmen are telling people that the men who took them were Russians.'

'You're sure?'

'All five are saying the same thing.'

'What about my cousins?'

'Not good news, Ron.'

'Go on.'

'They said that they were already dead or dying when they got off the trawler, but they have no idea what they did with the bodies.'

'Bastards,' Ron muttered. His huge fist tightened around the handset, threatening to crush it. 'I'm going to send them home in envelopes. They will be sorry that they were born. What about the zombie?'

'No one has heard anything about the gear, Ron,' Rickets warned. 'It would be better to wait for it to surface before we go steaming into the wrong crew.'

'What are you saying?'

'We need to wait.'

'Not a fucking chance, Rickets!' Ron growled. 'They will break it up and start selling it. I want the shipment intact. The Irishmen will want their money. I'm not paying for half a load. We're going to hit them first and hit them hard. I want them reeling to the point where they don't know what fucking day it is. We've got to go in hard.'

'How do you know who to hit though, Ron?' Rickets asked carefully. 'We have to be sure. There are couple of Russian outfits around nowadays. It's not just the Karpovs anymore. We need to narrow it down. We have to be sure, Ron.'

'How do you propose to do that?'

'Let's ask one of them.'

'Good idea.' Ron smiled. He stood up and walked to the table where a new bottle of JD was waiting. 'Bring one to the farm and let's talk to him. Do it tonight.'

'It's too dangerous bringing them to the farm, Ron,' Rickets warned. 'The police will be all over this and they're looking for us. I'll improvise.'

'Just find out who killed my brother.'

'I'm on it, Ron. Trust me.'

'Call me when you know something.'

Young Ronny listened to the conversation from the doorway. His hands were shaking. He felt like a fool. All their assurances had meant nothing. They had said that nothing bad would happen. His father was grieving for his brother. He was hiding it but he knew that he was. His thirst for Jack Daniels wasn't helping. It would fuel his anger. It always did. The police would want to talk to his father, and they would want to talk to him too and they would get them eventually.

His father was angrier than he had ever seen him and that was saying something. Big Ron was always angry. It was just a matter of time before he exploded. Ronny felt like he was inside a pressure cooker. The urge to open the front door and run across the fields was overwhelming. The atmosphere was oppressive. The farmhouse was like a cage. He didn't want to be there, but he could hardly complain. His room was like a cell. It was cold and damp and the single bed stunk of sweat and urine. Whoever had slept there before him, had poor personal hygiene. He was hungry too, but the kitchen was filthy and the cupboards were empty, the shelves spotted with mouse droppings. He hadn't been in the cellar. The door was always padlocked. He had heard what went on down there. Rickets would tease him with horror stories when he was drunk. He knew that the stories were embellished but the dark truth ran beneath them. The people they took down there didn't come up in one piece. He knew what his father, Rickets and the others did to people down there. They extracted information and then made them easy to dispose of. Anyone that crossed the firm was dealt with. Having heard Big Ron on the phone, he had a feeling that it would become operational again very soon.

CHAPTER 20

George knew that he had been compromised but he didn't know who by. There was no other explanation for what he had stumbled across at the Kodak building. Five Irishmen nailed to a table in the exact place where he was supposed to leave an emergency communiqué, was not a coincidence. It was not just the same building; it was the exact place. The canteen. Somehow, they knew that he would show up there eventually and now they had him on camera. That meant that their knowledge of UC protocol was in-depth and current. He had to assume that the first picture was an undercover who had been tortured for the protocol. George didn't know him but then he didn't know any of the other UC officers. He also had to assume that if they wanted the protocol, then they knew that Cain had stopped communicating. How could they know that?

It narrowed down who he could trust to no one. George had ripped the camera from the wall and stuffed it into his pocket along with the mobile phone and took them with him. They had gone to a lot of trouble to compromise him and find out his identity. He was convinced that they would follow him from the derelict office block. They would be watching. The emergency services were parked to the north, so he headed to the south side of the building and checked around. Dense overgrowth bordered the abandoned building. There were a hundred places to hide and wait. They could be hiding anywhere. He took a deep breath and climbed through a broken window. The rain soaked him as he walked across the blistered car park, weeds as tall as he was pierced the asphalt. He stumbled over an abandoned pram and headed for a gap in the bushes, keeping his eyes on the shadows. The undergrowth was muddy and fallen branches cracked loudly as he clawed his way through the foliage. The leaves were saturated, rainwater dripped on his skin, trickling down his neck, sending cold shivers down his spine. He felt fear tickling his mind. Someone had set a trap to identify him and he had walked into it with his eyes wide shut. They had a picture of him, and they had let him know that they had it. His instinct told him to step out of the dark world of undercover work back into the light immediately, but his conscience wouldn't let him. There were things he had to sort before that could happen. He needed to shake them off long enough to tidy things up. Any traces of his life as George had to be erased before he could surface. They were toying with him, but he wasn't going to play their game. The Irishmen had said that they were taken there by Russians. It had to be the Karpovs. There could not be any other explanation. They were onto him and now they knew what he looked like. He would clean up and then get out.

The sound of sirens blaring came to him. They were entering the building from the other side. He could simply walk around the corner and identify himself to an armed officer and get escorted back into the real world. If he did that, the informer would vanish. All the months of hard work and persuasion would have been for nothing. He couldn't bring himself to give up on that. A mole in the Karpov empire was priceless. The opportunity to bring them down was within their grasp. It was there for the taking. He knew Cain would play things by the book and bring in the NCA as soon as the informer had been brought in. The NCA would put him into the protection program and they would never see them again, but the information gleaned from him could bring the Karpovs down. It could achieve more than any police force in Western Europe, Eastern Europe or the Soviet Block had. The Karpovs had run riot over the law for too long to let them off the hook now. He had to try to wrap things up before he went back in.

Climbing the boundary wall, he landed on the pavement next to the main road into town. The light was fading. The traffic was heavy, headlights glinted off the surface water. He waited for a break in the traffic, crossed the first carriageway and then studied the bushes where he had come from. No one had followed. He crossed the second carriageway, weaving through the vehicles and headed to a crowded bus stop. The rain poured harder, soaking the people not covered by the shelter. He mingled between them, watching to see if anyone followed from the bushes. There was no sign of anyone tailing him. That meant nothing. They may just be very good at it. He couldn't be complacent. Not now. Hidden by the miserable commuters, he slipped through a gap in the railings and jogged across a children's playground, checking behind him every fifty metres or so. No one followed. At the other side of the park, he crossed the road and jumped onto a bus headed for the city centre. The windows were steamed up with condensation. He sat on the back seat and closed his eyes, planning his next move.

When the bus stopped at the station, he opened the emergency exit at the rear of the vehicle and jumped down onto the crowded pavement. He could hear the driver cursing him as the alarm rang but he ignored him and slipped into the throng of shoppers. After circling the bus station, he checked behind him and then disappeared into the crowds that were heading towards the shopping centre. He walked around the block for ten minutes and then ducked into Primark and headed for the lift. He stayed in it until it reached the top floor and then made for the changing rooms that were nearest to the fire escape, grabbing a pair of jeans, a coat and hat as he went. A security guard stood chatting to a pretty brunette. He was too distracted to notice George as he slipped into the male changing rooms and swapped clothes. He removed the security tags from his new outfit and then took out his lighter, setting fire to his old trousers before he left the booth. As he crossed the shop towards the fire escape, he heard voices shouting, a scream and the sound of panic. The fire alarms began to ring, and an automated voice ordered everyone to leave the building via the nearest exit. The stairwell was crammed within minutes and he allowed the crowd to carry him down the stairs and onto the access road at the back of the building.

He turned left and walked up to Hardman Street before crossing Lord Street to the St John's precinct. There he ran up an escalator that led into the centre and then waited near the balcony, watching the crowds go by, searching for a face he had seen before. People flocked to and fro, white, black, yellow, mixed race, fat, thin, tall and short. He waited until he was convinced that he hadn't seen any of them before. Convinced that he wasn't being followed, he headed back down the escalator and walked for a hundred yards, then he turned sharply and headed back up the escalator and repeated the process. Despite his caution, he knew his spell undercover was over. There was no option now.

George walked into Wilkos and bought a padded envelope and a pen. He ripped the packaging open and addressed it. His time was limited. He had decided to do what needed to be done and then go into the station the following day. It would be an end to his stint as George, but he could always reinvent himself somewhere else, a different city maybe. The priority now was warning their informer that they were in danger. He moved to the stairs and ran down them, taking them two at a time. There was a post box on the ground floor. He pumped coins into the machine and stuck the stamps onto the package. Taking another look around, George posted the padded envelope and checked around again to make sure that no one had seen him. The camera and mobile phone from the derelict offices were in the envelope, which was addressed to the senior Detective Inspector of the Drug Squad. He wasn't sure what they could pull from them, but it was better than carrying them around. There was nothing more to do for an hour or so. He had to keep on the move until then.

Hunger hit him like a sledgehammer. Things had been so out of control that he hadn't had time to eat. He pulled up the zip on his new jacket and headed towards his favourite chip shop, the Lobster Pot. His mouth was watering at the thought of fish, chips and mushy peas. As he crossed the road, two figures moved from the shadows. One female and one male. They spoke briefly and then followed him.

CHAPTER 21

MIT

Braddick nodded a silent hello to the armed officer on guard. He stepped inside and looked down at the man in the bed. His face was bruised and swollen, black and blue with contusions, his arms bandaged from the wrist to the elbow. The smell of disinfectant was overpowering. A nurse added notes to his file and half smiled at him as he approached the bed.

'Not too long,' she said as she straightened her hair self-consciously and turned to leave. 'He's in a lot of pain and might drift in and out.'

'Okay, thank you,' Braddick said smiling as she left. The door closed silently behind her. 'I'M DI Braddick,' he said introducing himself. 'You're Peter Collins?'

'Aye,' the fisherman answered, his voice thick with phlegm and congealed blood.

'What can you tell us about who did this to you?'

'Only what I have said already,' he muttered. 'It all happened so fast. One minute we were tying up the boat, the next we were being held up by Russians with guns.'

'How do you know that they were Russians?' Braddick asked. The fisherman frowned. 'I mean how can you be sure they weren't Eastern European for instance?'

'One of the lads told me,' he stammered. 'When they were moving us. He said they were Russians.'

'So, you can't be sure yourself?'

'Not really.'

'They questioned you?'

'That is not how I would describe it.'

'Sorry. They wanted information.'

'Yes.'

'What did they ask you?'

'They wanted to know what we knew about the drugs,' he said quietly. Braddick remained silent to let him expand. 'If we knew who had supplied them. They kept asking who had given them to Linus. We didn't know anything. None of us knew anything about it. Linus stitched us up good and proper.'

'You must have known something was going on.'

'What do you mean?'

'I mean you must have realised that it wasn't a normal fishing trip.'

'I didn't know anything about it.'

'I checked the nets,' Braddick said. 'They were dry. You must have thought it was odd not dropping the nets.' The fisherman shrugged; pain creased his face. 'Linus is dead, staying quiet won't bring him back.'

'The fish were already onboard when we sailed. The load was already crated and iced.'

'You must have thought that was odd.'

'Linus told us he had made a deal with some of the bigger trawler captains. He said he was buying everything over quota to save them dropping them back in the sea.'

'Go on.'

'He said he could double what he had paid by selling it on the black market to wholesalers in the UK. All we had to do was sail to Holyhead, unload, and sail back. He said it was easy money. Fishing without the hard graft. None of us knew what was in those crates. If we had, we would have told the Russians when they tortured us, believe me we would.' He gestured to his arms and began to sob. Tears ran from his eyes. 'They did me last. I had to watch them nail my pals to the table, knowing it would be my turn soon. They beat us senseless and nailed us to a table for fuck's sake!' His voice quivered. 'If I had known anything about the drugs, I would have told them.'

'I believe you.' Braddick nodded. 'Take it easy. The last thing I want to do is upset you, but we need to know what happened.' The fisherman closed his eyes and bit his bottom lip. 'Tell me how they moved you.'

'What do you mean?'

'When they moved you from the dock,' Braddick said calmly. 'Can you remember what vehicle they took you in?'

'No,' he said, his eyes still closed. 'I was blindfolded. I didn't see a thing. I think I passed out for a long time. I don't know any more than I have said already. I just want to go home.' He heard the door open and Jo appeared in the doorway.

'Did you see any vehicles?' Braddick pressed. 'Think hard.'

'I remember a white van, that's all.'

'You didn't see anything else?'

'No.'

'You didn't see the Russians arrive?'

'No. They must have been there already. I have no idea what they put us in, but I can tell you it was quiet.'

'Quiet how?'

'Just quiet. The floor was metal, I remember that, and I heard doors slamming like on a van but when we were moving, it was quiet.'

'I don't understand what you mean.'

'The engine sound was muffled. Maybe I imagined it. I was out of it.'

Braddick looked at Jo and she shrugged. 'The doctors said that your families are on their way. Once you're on the mend, they'll release you. So long as what you're telling us is true of course.'

'It is the truth,' he snapped. 'Linus used us. The silly old bastard nearly got us all killed. He lied to us. It is his fault that we are here.' The door opened and the nurse walked in.

'I think that is enough for today,' she said smiling. 'Peter will be exhausted from the meds. He needs to sleep.'

'We're about done,' Braddick said, turning for the door. 'Just one more thing.' He glanced back at the patient.

'What?'

'The man who found you and called it in, what was he doing there?'

'He was just a tramp looking for somewhere dry to sleep, I guess. I think he was on the run from you lot. He definitely didn't want to be there when the police arrived.'

'Have a safe journey home.' Braddick smiled. The fisherman nodded and closed his eyes again. Braddick and Jo stepped into the corridor and shut the door behind them. 'What about the others?' he asked Jo.

'I talked to two of them. The others are out of the game for now.' She shrugged. 'Same story from both. I think they are telling the truth.'

'Me too,' Braddick said thoughtfully. 'Do you know what I can't understand?'

'Why they let them live,' Jo said flatly.

'Exactly. It doesn't make sense.'

'Maybe they were happy that the fishermen didn't know anything about the shipment. Linus did and they killed him.'

'I get that,' Braddick said, shaking his head. 'But why bring them all the way back here?'

'To send a message that this is their turf,' Jo tutted. 'The usual testosterone fuelled bullshit.'

'I'm not convinced.' Braddick shook his head. He pushed his hands deep into his pockets. 'I get the feeling that we're missing something.' He took out his mobile and dialled the station. It answered almost immediately. 'Any joy with the cameras from the bridges?'

'We're ploughing through the footage, Guv,' the detective said enthusiastically. 'Two container ferries and one passenger ferry docked during the timescale we're looking at. Over two hundred vehicles landed. We've asked the ferry companies for their records to eliminate registration plates, but it is going to take some time.'

'What about Ron Mason?'

'Still no joy. He's gone to ground. If anything comes in, I'll call you straightaway.'

'Good man,' Braddick sighed. 'Keep on it.'

'Yes, Guv.' Braddick was about to hang up. 'There is one thing though.'

'Please give me some good news.'

'There's a parcel on your desk, Guv,' the detective said, lowering his voice. 'One of the post room boys said the handwriting looks like DI Cain's.'

'Go and open the parcel,' Braddick said. He felt is heart quicken. The sounds of the office crackled on the line for a minute.

'Are you still there, Guv?'

'Yes.'

'It's a laptop,' the detective said excitedly. 'DI Cain's laptop.'

'Get it to the tech boys immediately,' Braddick said. 'Tell them that I want everything that she did on that laptop for the last two weeks and then work backwards and tell them I want it yesterday.'

'Yes, Guv.' The line went dead. Jo raised her eyebrows in question.

'What was that?'

'Steff Cain posted her laptop to me,' he said, turning to face Jo.

'Fucking hell,' she whistled. 'It will have all the UC information on it. I'll head to the tech lab and see you at the station later,' she said, heading for the lifts.

'Keep me in the loop.' Braddick nodded and looked at his phone again. He dialled the DS in charge of the search team at Mike Pilkington's house. The feeling that they were missing something was eating away at him from the inside out.

CHAPTER 22

Rickets pulled the Audi to a halt on a double yellow line. He turned off the lights but kept the radio on low and the heater on high. The street was cobbled and narrow, neon signs flashed on both sides. It was dark and raining and the pavements were empty. The late night revellers wouldn't appear until after midnight. The other side of town was always busier early on. He watched the door of the nightclub halfway down the road. The sign above it read 'Liquid' in blue neon. He remembered it had been called at least a dozen different names during his lifetime. It was a downstairs basement club with a narrow staircase leading to it. The dance floor was huge. A bar a hundred metres long served cocktails, shots and beer to six hundred punters at any one time while the doormen monitored the dealers. Coke, Ketamine, and ecstasy were sold to fuel the dancers, the club taking the lion's share of the profits. Unauthorised dealers were hammered, robbed, and ejected in brutal fashion to deter others. The club had changed hands many times as waves of foreign muscle washed over the city. Italians, Poles, Chinese, Pakistani and Turks had run the place, each outfit stronger and more violent than the last. The Karpovs ousted the Turks from the city two years earlier and their grip on the drug supply was cemented. They controlled the big venues and crushed anyone trying to take a bite of the action. Their tactics were appalling. Nothing and no one were untouchable. Property, vehicles, pets, elderly relations and children were all fair game. Cross them and they would hurt you and those you care about. The hardest men in the city had their weak points and if they tangled with the Karpovs, they would find them and exploit them. It didn't matter how tough they were, how good a fighter they were, they could all be broken. No one wanted to risk feeling the wrath of the Russian organisation, which led to a status quo in the city. There was a fragile peace, begrudgingly or not, everyone knew where they stood. Alliances had been formed over the years although they rarely lasted long and usually ended violently. The Karpovs always came out on top. Rickets knew a couple of their doormen. He had met them when Eddie Farrell was providing muscle to them. He was hoping that he could find one of them tonight.

After forty minutes of mind-numbing boredom, a figure emerged from Liquid. The man looked up and down the street and lit a cigarette. He turned up the collar of his coat and stepped into the rain, heading in the opposite direction. Rickets started the engine and followed slowly, edging over the cobbles, keeping close to the kerb. The man reached the end of the street and crossed the road, turning left onto an unlit section of road. Bin bags and cardboard boxes were piled up against the walls, sodden and rotting. Rainwater poured from the drainpipes, flooding the gutters. Rickets put the vehicle into second and picked up speed. He reached the end of the street and followed the man, picking up speed again. He sounded the horn and waved as he drove by. The man waved although he looked confused about who he was waving at. Rickets braked and indicated left, pulling up to the pavement a few yards ahead of him. He wound down the passenger window as the man approached.

'Leonid,' he called through the window. The man stopped and bent to look inside the vehicle. Water dripped from the end of his nose. 'It's me, Rickets. We worked at Revolution together.'

'Oh, yes! Hello, Rickets.' The man recognised him and smiled. 'What brings you down this end of town?'

'I came to see an old mate,' Rickets lied. 'Do you want a lift. Jump in, its pissing down.'

'That would be great,' Leonid said, opening the door. He climbed in and the car rocked with his weight. 'This weather is shit. It rains in the summer. It rains in the winter. It is always fucking raining,' Leonid moaned. Rickets could smell vodka on his breath, his words slurred slightly. 'I am going to the petrol station on the dock road for some cigarettes. I should have bought some on my way to work but I didn't have time. You know how it is.'

'No problem,' Rickets said, checking the rear-view mirror. He pulled away and accelerated hard. Leonid was still struggling into the seatbelt. The Audi lurched forward at speed; the engine roaring.

'Are you in a hurry,' Leonid joked, nervously.

'No hurry,' Rickets said, slamming on the brakes hard. Leonid was propelled forward, his head hit the windscreen, stunning him. Rickets grabbed the back of his coat and pulled him backwards before smashing his forehead into the dashboard. A gash had opened above his nose. Rickets pulled him up and then rammed his face against the dashboard again and again. Two teeth clattered off the stereo. The Russian's body went limp, but he thrust his head against the dash once more for safety's sake. There was an audible crack as his nose bone splintered. Rickets checked his mirrors and the street ahead. The road was deserted. He popped the boot and climbed out into the rain. Leonid was a big man, but Rickets was powerful. He dragged him around the car and bundled him into the boot, fastening his wrists and ankles with cable ties. Slamming the boot closed, he rubbed his hands together against the cold and blew into them. His breath made a plume of mist and he shivered as he climbed back into the driver's seat.

'This is not the weather for digging holes in the woods,' he muttered to himself as he started the Audi and headed out of the city.

CHAPTER 23

MIKE PILKINGTON'S HOUSE

Yellow tape flapped in the breeze. Uniformed officers huddled in groups, stamping their feet against the cold. Inside, white clad figures moved quietly through the house. Yellow markers were spotted about the ground floor where the ARU had brought down the intruder. The smell of blood, urine and excrement lingered in the hallway. DS Ade Burns made his way through the garage, stopping to look at the MG. It was mint for its age. He inspected the tool bench, impressed, his fingers touching the cold steel. They were all high-quality pieces. He figured the entire set would cost over five hundred pounds; the kind of tools professionals used. They were way too pricey just to use for an hour on a Sunday. He wondered what a Drug Squad detective would be doing with tools like that. There weren't enough hours in the day to eat and sleep properly never mind finding time to rebuild an old classic car. The garage was spotless. Someone spent a lot of time in there. He didn't know Mike Pilkington well, but he didn't come across as a petrol head. Ade took a last look around and decided that there was more to Pilkington than first appeared.

He stepped into the hallway and looked into the kitchen. A CSI was painstakingly searching through the cupboards and drawers. The units were new and bespoke. He reckoned the tiles cost a month's salary at least. His ex-wife had wanted something similar. The arguments had gone on for months. The silly bitch had always wanted whatever he couldn't afford. Kitchens, bathrooms, designer shoes, holidays, the list was endless. Whatever they had was never good enough. She always wanted one better. He frowned at the memories and shook his head. Thinking about her pissed him off. Letting her piss him off, pissed him off even more. He pushed the thoughts from his mind and scanned the kitchen again. Ade didn't disturb the technician while he worked. He walked down the hallway and peered into the lounge. A female CSI looked up from a pile of unopened mail.

'Hello, Ade,' she said with a nod. There was no warmth in her eyes. 'What are you doing here?'

'Oh, you know, fighting crime, defending the weak and vulnerable, striking fear into the hearts of criminals everywhere and nailing parking tickets to as many windscreens as I can along the way.'

'What, did you get a promotion?' she said sarcastically. 'They don't let you give out parking tickets yet, do they?'

'I might be doing just that if they make the corruption charges stick. I've been caught stealing toilet rolls from the station.' He winked. She laughed sourly and shook her head. 'Have you found anything exciting?'

'We're not sure yet, nothing too unexpected.' She sounded guarded. 'We're running some checks.'

'Oh, that sounds very mysterious.' Ade frowned. 'What type of checks?'

'The usual,' she said, blushing a little. 'Electoral role, mobile phone records for the address. You know how it goes.'

Ade nodded and walked into the room. He pretended to be taking a cursory inspection. As she processed the mail, he glanced over her shoulder. She had sorted it into two piles. One pile was addressed to Mike Pilkington, the other to Michael David Pilkington. It explained why they were running basic checks on the occupancy. As far as the force was concerned, Pilkington was a bachelor living alone. Ade looked at the furniture. One armchair was worn, the arms showed signs of regular use. The material was marked where the sweat of the owner's hands had stained it. The rest of the suite was pristine. Ade could tell only one person used the suite.

'I'm going to take a look upstairs,' Ade said, glancing at the CSI. She looked up and nodded, thin lipped. 'I'll catch you later.'

He stepped into the hallway and headed for the stairs. The beige carpet was thick, no signs of being worn by foot traffic. A plug-in air freshener exuded the smell of pine. It didn't have the feel of a house occupied by a single male. The first floor was well lit. Tasteful black and white prints were mounted on the walls. He could see into the bathroom. The toilet and shower were visible from the stairs. White marble tiles covered the floor. As he reached the landing, a colleague stepped out of the main bedroom. He seemed surprised to see Ade.

'All right, Ade,' he said, greeting him.

'Hiya.'

'Terrible business,' he muttered and shook his head. 'I liked Steff Cain.'

'She was a good copper,' Ade agreed.

'I didn't really know Mike Pilkington, but I wouldn't mind five minutes with the bastards who took them out.'

'Me and you both, mate.' Ade nodded.

'What brings you here?'

'I was on my way back from the scene. I just wanted a look around myself. I'm trying to get a feel for it. You know what I mean.'

'Knock yourself out, Ade,' he said, patting him on the shoulder. 'We're nearly done on the top floor. We'll do the garage and garden tomorrow when we have daylight.'

'Cheers,' Ade said, stepping into the bedroom. A huge bed dominated the room. The bedding was slate grey and neatly made. He opened the wardrobe door and scanned the contents. All the items were the same size. His clothes were all designer labels. The suits were mostly Hugo Boss. Ade didn't have a clue how much a Hugo Boss suit would cost but he guessed that anyone who owned more than one earned a substantial amount more than he did. He walked to the bed and opened the drawer of the bedside cabinet. Indigestion tablets, ibuprofen, condoms, blackberry flavoured lube and a six-inch sheath knife. It could have been for protection, or it could have been a kink. He frowned and closed the drawer, opening the next one down. Socks. The third drawer down held boxer shorts and vests. Everything was well ironed and neatly folded away. He ran his fingers underneath the clothing but found nothing but wood.

'What are you looking for?' A female voice made him jump. He blushed a little and grinned. 'I don't think you should be poking around in here. Not until we're finished anyway.'

'Old habits die hard,' he mumbled. 'I can't help having a look myself.'

'I get that,' she said flatly. 'But what are you looking for?'

'I was trying to work out who lives here.' Ade shrugged. 'I didn't know Mike well. Just trying to get to know him. You know what I mean?'

'Yes.' She nodded. Her face remained deadpan. 'Please don't touch anything.' Ade held up his hands in surrender. 'I need to dust in here so if you don't mind…'

'No problem,' Ade said, heading for the door. She stepped aside to let him pass and looked uncomfortable as he brushed his groin against her, 'accidently'. 'I'll let you get on. I need to get back to the station anyway. I'll see you again sometime,' he muttered as he headed for the stairs. She didn't answer. The atmosphere between them had been strained since he had bumped into her in town a few months earlier. She had looked amazing in a little black dress and he was very pissed. After declaring his undying love for her and trying to stick his tongue down her throat, she had told him to fuck off and they hadn't talked since. Embarrassing as it was, she needed to get over herself. If you squeeze yourself into a tight dress and wiggle your arse, men will try it on. That was why she had put it on in the first place, wasn't it? Dress up, put on makeup, perfume, try to look as fuckable as possible and then call him a pervert for trying. Ade didn't understand what her problem was. He didn't understand any of them really. He felt pissed off again as he reached the bottom of the stairs and headed back into the living room. The CSI had bagged the mail and labelled each packet. He could see the top document was a bank statement in the name of Michael David Pilkington. There was over thirty thousand in the account. Regular payments were paid in every month. He wanted to open the packet and study the documents, but he knew that he would have to wait for forensics to finish their work. Whatever Mike Pilkington had to hide would be revealed soon enough. All he could hope was that there was something there to make him look like he was dirty. It would cause a shitstorm but so what? All it took was one bent copper and the Internal Corruption Unit would descend on the entire division. Corrupt coppers attracted attention that no one in the force wanted. Corruption had a smell to it that drifted through the entire station, pervading every nook and cranny, infecting everything that it touched. No one was beyond scrutiny. Fingers would be pointed; whispers would be heard from behind every door. Everyone would be scrutinised. Accusations would be thrown, and some would stick like shit to a blanket. The blame didn't always fall at the right feet.

Ade left the room and walked down the hallway. The CSI in the kitchen saw him and nodded hello. He stepped into the garage and closed the connecting door behind him. One of the garage doors was fully open, the other half closed. He ducked low to see if the uniformed officers outside were nearby. They were out of sight for now. Ade walked to the MG and opened the passenger door. He leaned in and popped open the glove box. It was empty. Ade reached inside his jacket and removed a Makarov pistol that was wrapped in cling film. He checked outside again and then unwrapped the plastic, placing the gun into the glove box. The wind howled and brought a fresh deluge with it. He closed the flap and shut the door quietly before walking out of the garage, pulling his coat tightly around him against the rain.

CHAPTER 24

George licked the plastic tray and savoured the saltiness. The traces of vinegar danced on his tongue. He was full but a little disappointed to have finished his fish and chips. He tossed the wrappers into a bin and wiped his greasy hands on his trousers. The rain was still bouncing off the pavements and the crowds were thinning out. The shops were closing, and the nightlife hadn't begun yet. He looked around and pulled up his hood and headed for the river, taking the long way around. The naked statue outside Lewis's looked down on him as he walked towards Chinatown. He would cut through along the cobbled streets to reach the red-light district around Jamaica Street. There, he could leave a message with a prostitute who called herself Candy. Finding her would be easy enough. She always worked the same pitch. If she wasn't there, then she would be servicing a client somewhere and that didn't take very long. She didn't move far from her pitch, choosing to use the alleyways nearby as her stage. If the client had a vehicle, then it was a bonus. At least she could stay warm and dry while she performed. Ade had left messages with her before. One of her bosses was the link to the Karpovs.

George walked through Chinatown, the aromas teasing his senses. He was glad he had eaten. Taxis rattled past spraying rainwater in their wake. They swooped towards the pavement, picking up and dropping off diners. He grinned as a couple sprinted past him, bent double against the rain as if stooping would keep them dry. They ran, laughing into a restaurant and his grin disappeared. Memories of an old life haunted him. A life when he lived and loved like 'normal' people, before the job swallowed him up and drove his wife into another man's bed. The restaurant door closed, the slam like an icy dagger through his guts. Even his fondest memories of her didn't make him happy. They gave him no solace from the loneliness. Seeing couples being happy made him incredibly sad. He was bitter and almost begrudged their happiness.

George picked up the pace and weaved through a beige brick housing estate. The Bridgewater Street buildings loomed in the distance, empty and derelict. Once mills and warehouses, they were a rotting reminder of the port's distant past. The area was known as the Baltic Triangle. It had undergone a dramatic facelift as Liverpool reinvented itself. Redevelopment had brought investors to the area and the police had tried to clean it up, moving the sex industry to other parts of the city. Candy and a few other diehards weren't for moving, no matter how many times they were lifted and moved on. She would wait half an hour and go right back to her spot next to the seven-storey mills.

As George arrived, he could see that Candy wasn't there. Someone was. A streetlight cast a watery yellow light over the area beneath it. He could see the skinny female form of one of Candy's workmates. She called herself Zara, or Kara or Tara or something similar. Her real name was Norma. She had only been on the scene a few months. George liked her. He liked most of them, if the truth be told. Most of them were simply trying to keep their heads above water. They weren't cut out for fulltime employment. Most couldn't fill out an application form. There was the odd one who was smart and chose to work the streets because it paid better than Tesco did but on the whole, the majority had no other option. Addiction was an expensive illness. He realised the potential of making friends with them and he had befriended as many working girls as he could, buying them coffee and cigarettes, sometimes giving them money if they were short of a fix. Most of them were addicts and addicts were a great source of information. He had lost count of how many dealers he had fingered to the Drug Squad off the back of listening to their chitchat. They gravitated towards him because he was like them, on the streets, grafting for a living in the gutters, outcasts shunned by society. Zara saw him coming and lit a cigarette, blowing the smoke at him as he neared.

'Fucking hell,' she said rolling her eyes skywards. She stuck her tongue out.

'I wouldn't put that back in your mouth,' George said, shaking his head.

'Look what the wind has blown in. Fancy a blow job, mister?'

'Will you take your teeth out?'

'Cheeky bastard.' She frowned but her eyes smiled. 'That will be a tenner more.'

'I can't afford you.'

'Damn right you can't.'

'How's business?' George grinned.

'What the fuck do you care?' she said, looking him up and down. She sneered at him and then a smile lit up her face. Opening her arms, she hugged him. 'Only joking, gorgeous George,' she said. 'How are you?'

'I'm okay.' He squeezed her and picked her up, turning her around in a spin. 'How's my favourite tart?'

'Hey, you cheeky bugger!' She laughed.

'Where's your sidekick?' he asked, putting her down.

'Why do you always ask about her?'

'She's cheaper than you.'

'You get what you pay for,' she giggled. 'She is blowing some guy in the mill. She hates going in there, but this fucking weather is killing us.'

'It is killing me too. How long has she been gone?'

'Too long,' she said, turning towards the derelict mill. 'You could have brought me a coffee.'

'Sorry. I'll bring you one tomorrow.'

The sound of wood creaking came from above. George looked up into the darkness. Raindrops spiralled down on his face, glinting in the streetlight. He heard a thump and a moan coming from the upper floors. A shadow appeared far above him. It hurtled towards him, gaining shape and colour as it entered the circle of yellow light. He grabbed Zara's arm and pulled her backwards. They fell as one and landed sitting in a deep puddle. The object hit the floor. A sickening splat echoed up the street, sounding like a thick steak being slapped on a wooden table and he found himself staring at a red leather handbag.

'Jesus, I'm soaked!' George gasped. 'I nearly shit myself.'

'You arse! My knickers are soaked.'

'What knickers?'

'Shut up, you imbecile.' Tara looked at the bag. 'That is Candy's bag.'

'Well, it didn't fall itself. How do we get into the mill?' George said standing. He pulled Zara to her feet. 'She must be in trouble.'

'My arse is soaking wet!' Zara brushed at her behind. George picked up the bag. His fingers felt a sticky liquid on it. He looked at it under the yellow light. It was covered in dark smudges. He stared at his hands and sniffed his fingertips. 'What the fuck is that?' she asked.

'Blood.'

'Fucking hell!'

'How do I get in there?'

'Round the back, come on!' Zara ran towards the corner. 'I'll show you. Follow me.'

George took off after her. She moved quickly for a woman in heels. The sound of her shoes clicking on the pavement echoed down the street. She veered left and disappeared through a wooden hoarding. The gap was narrow, the edges sharp. George followed her and scraped his face. He felt a trickle of blood run down his cheek. On the other side was rubble strewn waste ground. He had to pick his footing carefully, his progress slowed dramatically. Zara was twenty metres ahead of him as they approached the looming structure and he could no longer see her. The sound of her footsteps echoed from the darkness and he could smell her perfume on the breeze. He focused on where his feet were landing and followed as fast as he could.

'Hurry up!' she shouted as she disappeared through a gaping black hole in the brickwork. A metal window cover creaked as she moved it. He heard it clang as it fell back into place. 'Candy, where are you?' He heard her calling.

He reached the window and pulled at the metal sheet. It didn't budge. Moving it to the left, it groaned against the bricks. The metal bit into the soft flesh of his palms. A gap opened but it wasn't wide enough to climb through. He pulled the sheet to the right and it swung open. The dank air inside was repulsive. It stopped him in his tracks for a moment. The darkness took on a different grade, deeper, almost liquid. He could barely see his hand in front of him. Zara's footsteps had slowed but he could hear them to his right. He moved that way and picked up a rectangle of light ahead. She was using her mobile as a torch.

'Candy!' she shouted. A muffled cry came from above. Dust and grit fell from the floorboards above, showering him. He closed his eyes and rubbed at them with the back of his hands. 'She's upstairs,' Zara hissed. 'Hurry up for fuck's sake!'

George caught up and stopped next to her. 'Show me the way,' he said panting. She took off and he followed blindly, trusting her knowledge of the traps and falls inside the mill.

'Up here,' she called as they approached a dilapidated staircase. 'Stay against the wall!' The light from her phone illuminated a few metres ahead of them. 'Candy!' Cobwebs glistened like silver curtains at the top of the stairs. Dust floated like snowflakes towards them. Zara reached the top and darted to her left. George reached the landing and caught his right foot on the last step. He tripped and staggered a few paces, trying desperately to stay upright. 'Candy!' He heard her shout from behind him. Her phone glowed. 'Hurry up, George! What the fuck is wrong with you?'

'There's nothing wrong with me, I just can't fucking see in the dark,' he gasped.

'Candy!' Zara stopped and waited for a sound. 'Where are you?'

They crept forward using the phone to light their way. The sound of scurrying vermin came from all around, left, right, front and behind. George listened intently, trying to block the sound of the rats out. He waited for a more significant noise to guide them. 'Candy!' he called.

'Candy!' Zara called.

'Where would she normally go?'

'What do you mean?'

'With a punter,' George explained. 'Where would she take them in here?'

'No more than ten yards from the entrance.'

'What was she doing up here then?'

'Fuck knows.'

'Candy!' he called again.

Footsteps above. Thump, thump, thump, thump. Left to right above him. Dust and dirt rained down again.

'Upstairs!' she said, grabbing his hand. 'Come on!'

They ran to the next staircase and navigated it slowly. Steps were missing here and there. The darkness seemed to intensify, reaching out to swallow them up. They reached the top hand in hand and she shone the torch around. The floorboards to their left were missing, only the beams remained.

'Candy,' George called. His voice echoed from the walls and came back to them. 'Where the fuck is she?'

'I'm here.'

George turned around quickly.

'Are you okay?' He reached out and placed his hands on her shoulders. She looked at him with a narrow smile on her face. 'We were worried about you.'

Candy's hand flashed in front of his face. He felt a stinging sensation along his neck. She stepped back as arterial spray jetted from his throat. He instinctively put his hands to his neck to try to stop his life force from spilling out, but the pressure was too powerful. He dropped to his knees as his blood sprayed between his fingers. Zara laughed behind him. Darkness began to descend, and her face began to fade. Candy stared at him, emotionless. Her lips moved, '*Die you fucking grass,*' she said as he died.

CHAPTER 25

BIG RON

The sign on the gate read, 'Mason Brothers Security'. Patrick pressed the buzzer and waited. Moody clouds were gathering again, threatening to release their load on the already saturated city. It had been a busy morning. Thanks to Clint, Ron Mason had finally made contact and offered a sit-down meeting to discuss the heist. Henry had insisted that they meet immediately and then he had gone walkabouts, missing for three hours. When he had returned, they rushed across the city to where Ron Mason ran his security business. Big Ron knew that the police would be watching his premises and had smuggled himself in the back way. The industrial unit was a fortress, metal shutters on the windows and razor wire atop the fences. The Irishmen waited for the gates to open and drove into the car park slowly. As they pulled to a halt in a bay marked 'customers', the gates closed behind them. Patrick switched off the engine and opened the door.

'Let's get this thing sorted,' Patrick sighed.

Henry put his hand on his arm and stopped him from climbing out.

'Don't say anything in there unless I ask you a question. I want you to let me do all the talking, understand?'

'Are you kidding me?' Patrick frowned. 'I am not a snot-nosed teenager, Henry. I set up this deal.'

'You did set it UP, but you didn't do your homework and when you didn't do your homework, then you fucked up this deal, Patrick. You arranged a deal with your fingers crossed and your head stuck up your arse,' Henry said staring into his eyes. 'That is not the same thing as setting up a deal at all. Either keep quiet or stay in the car.'

'This guy is in the same position as us,' Patrick protested. 'We were all fucked over by the same people. It is my neck on the line. I want to...'

'Shut the fuck up!' Henry snapped. 'We don't have time for you to whinge. What you want is irrelevant.' Henry raised his index finger. 'Our objective has changed. The General has been very specific about what we are here to achieve. I am not here to make friends. I am here to collect payment and nothing else.'

'I don't understand. I thought we...'

'Don't think, Patrick. It's dangerous. Look where it got us the last time.' Henry opened his door and climbed out. 'For your own sake, do as I ask or stay in the car. 'Patrick followed him reluctantly and slammed the driver's door shut. CCTV cameras turned and followed them. The warehouse door opened, and Rickets appeared, scowling. Another two men lurked behind him, threatening and intimidating. Henry looked from one to other, defiantly. 'I'm guessing you're the monkeys. Where is the organ grinder?' He grinned. 'Take me to your leader.'

'Funny fucker, eh?' Rickets smiled coldly and gestured with his head. They stepped inside and followed him. The warehouse was cold. A dozen vans bearing the company logo stood idle. Men in security uniforms were coming and going. Engines were started and exhaust fumes tainted the air. Jet sprays hissed as some of the fleet was being cleaned. Rickets led them down a long corridor to a door marked 'office'. He knocked twice and opened it, stepping back to let the Irishmen in. Big Ron Mason sat behind his desk, standing as they walked in. He nodded and offered his spade-like hand in greeting. The office was warm and welcoming, white painted walls and a slate grey carpet gave it a professional look. There was a tense atmosphere in the air.

'Ron Mason.'

'I'm Henry.'

'Patrick.'

'Sit down, gentlemen,' Big Ron growled, his accent thick. 'Apologies for the delay in making contact but I needed to know who did what. We were all ripped off, you lost your skipper and I lost my brother and my cousins.'

'Any news of them?' Henry asked cordially.

'Not yet. I am not holding my breath on seeing them alive again.'

'Hope for the best but plan for the worst.'

'Something like that.'

'They made a bloody mess of things, so they did.'

'They did and I want the bastards that did that.'

'We're sorry for your loss,' Henry spoke gently. 'Truly we are.'

'That's appreciated.' Ron nodded, uncomfortable with Henry's politeness. 'Anyway, you're here now. I hope we can put things right between us.'

'Of course, we can. We're reasonable men. We understand your initial reluctance to talk. Of course, we do.'

'Obviously, I wanted to find out what happened and who was responsible first. I had to be sure in my own mind before I started pointing the finger at anyone.'

'Of course, you did. We understand all that.' He paused and smiled. 'Do you know who did what?' Henry asked calmly.

'We think we do, yes,' Big Ron said, glancing at Rickets. He nodded his huge head confidently and a smile touched the corner of his lips. 'Rickets had a little chat with one of our Russian friends last night.' Rickets closed the door and stood with his arms folded. His chest seemed to inflate with pride. The Irishmen glanced at him and then at each other.

'An informer?' Henry asked.

'No.'

'An employee of the firm that hit us?'

'Yes.'

'Was he taken under duress?' Henry asked, shaking his head.

'Yes.' Ron frowned. His eyes narrowed. 'What difference does that make?'

'It makes a big difference.'

'Why does it?' Ron sat back. The chair creaked under his weight.

'In my experience it makes a huge difference to the quality of the information.' Henry held up his hand in a calming gesture. 'It is a proven fact that information gained under duress is unreliable. Volunteered information is always more reliable.'

'Why would he volunteer the information?' Ron snapped. 'That is the whole point. No one was volunteering any fucking information. That is why we took him.'

'And I understand that, of course. Was he tortured?'

'Of course, he was.' Ron shrugged, irritated. 'What do you think we did, have a chat over tea and biscuits?'

'How far up the organisation is he?'

'Was he,' Rickets corrected him and grinned.

'Apologies, my mistake. Was he?' Henry shrugged.

'He worked the doors at their clubs.'

'He was a bouncer?' Henry sighed. 'Not exactly the font of all knowledge, was he?'

'They're tight that lot,' Ron intervened. 'The grapevine never fails. Sooner or later everything filters down to the troops.' The Irishmen exchanged glances but remained quiet. 'He told Rickets that he had heard on the grapevine that the Russians had a hand in the hit.'

'A hand in it? What does that mean, exactly?'

'From my point of view, it means that they did it!'

'That doesn't sound conclusive to me. Did he say that the Karpovs killed your brother or not?' Henry turned to look at Rickets.

'Not exactly in those words.' Rickets flushed. 'He didn't actually admit that it was the Karpovs.'

'But?'

'He works for the Karpovs, he's bound to say that isn't he. After a little persuasion, he admitted Russian involvement, but he wouldn't give up his boss. He was loyal to the end, wasn't he, Rickets?'

'Let's just say that he didn't give it up easily.' Rickets grinned coldly.

'Information gained from torture is rarely reliable,' Henry said, shaking his head. 'I wouldn't act on it alone. I would want more than that.'

'You weren't there were you?' Ron was trying to stay calm. 'You two were playing with yourselves in a nice warm hotel room while Rickets put his neck on the line to get this information.'

'Oh, I wouldn't be questioning your man's ability at all.' Henry raised both palms and shook his head. 'Heaven forbid that I would come here and criticise your employees.'

'Heaven forbid,' Ron repeated, sarcasm heavy in his voice. His eyes flickered to Rickets, who was grinning and shaking his head.

'I am merely questioning the quality of the information that you have, nothing more than that.'

'I am happy with it.'

'I can see that.' Henry nodded slowly. 'And that concerns me.'

'Listen, Henry. I have worked with Rickets for a long time,' Ron said. 'If he is happy with it then I am too.'

'Okay. It is your funeral.' Henry shrugged. 'So, you are convinced that you know who took your drugs?'

'Absolutely,' Ron said. He didn't look as convinced as he said he was. 'No doubt about it. They killed my brother and I'm going to come down on them like a ton of bricks.'

'Good,' Henry said. 'Good for you. Look, the bottom line is that you are clear that you know who took your shipment?'

'Yes. We do.' Ron frowned. He detected something in Henry's tone had changed.

'Then you will have no problem paying us what you owe us. 'He sat back and smiled widely. 'For the drugs, that is.'

'What are you talking about?'

'We did our part. We delivered the goods to the place that was agreed between Patrick and your brother. We need to be paid for the goods.'

'Are you having a giraffe?'

'You ordered a shipment. It was delivered.'

'A shipment, which was stolen, remember?'

'It was delivered safe and sound. What happened once it arrived is your problem,' Henry said straight-faced. His tone was no longer friendly. It was cold and sharp. 'We need payment for the goods.'

'Our money was stolen with the drugs,' Ron growled.

'That is unfortunate but I'm afraid that you still owe the money.'

'Don't come that one with me, Paddy.' Ron slapped the desk. The noise sounded like a whip being cracked.

'Let's keep this professional.' Henry held up a hand. 'The shipment arrived. We need payment.'

'Don't fuck around with me, Henry. You're fucking with the wrong man.'

'Oh, I am not fucking around at all and I'm not easily intimidated.' Henry smiled thinly. 'We delivered the goods. You owe the money and it needs to be paid this week.'

Ron laughed. 'Can you hear this idiot,' he said to Rickets. Rickets scowled and grinned. 'I could crush you in a minute.'

'You're a big man, right enough,' Henry said coolly. 'I am not here to fight you.' Henry pointed at Rickets. 'Do you think we would come here for a fist fight with you and your goons?'

'I am not sure why you came here to be honest, but you are wasting my time and yours.'

'We have to try, you see.' Henry shrugged. 'Nobody wants to part with their money. I understand that but you owe us. I have to ask you to pay what you owe. You can see that, surely you can?'

'I suppose it was worth a try, but I am not paying again and I'm not playing games with you.'

'Playing games?' Henry frowned. 'I am here to conclude our business. Are we playing a game, Patrick?'

'No.' Patrick shook his head. 'We are not playing a game.'

'What game do you think I am playing?' Henry raised his eyebrows in question.

'I don't know what your game is.' Ron stood up and leaned over the desk. He stabbed his index finger towards them. 'Coming in here and demanding money for gear that was stolen. Who the fuck do you think you are?'

'Oh, I am nobody special. I'm not here to do anything but conduct business,' Henry said, shaking his head. 'I am baffled that you can't understand that.'

'You're baffled?' Ron scoffed. 'He's baffled, Rickets.' Rickets laughed, his hand across his mouth. 'You're baffled, are you? My head is totally fucked. I can't believe you can sit there and tell me that I owe you money.'

'Allow me to help you to understand,' Henry spoke slowly and loudly as if Ron was hard of hearing or stupid. 'As I said earlier, we delivered the drugs as arranged. You were hit by whoever and that is regrettable however that is your problem. We wish you good luck with it, but we need payment.'

'Fuck you!' Ron laughed coarsely. 'Have you lost your fucking marbles, old man?'

'He's going senile,' Rickets sneered.

'Do you really think I'm going to hand over more money for stolen drugs?' Ron shook his head. 'My brother made this deal with this fucking idiot here.' He leaned over and pointed a thick digit at Patrick. 'My brother is dead. My cousins are feeding the fishes somewhere. Your captain is dead, strung up like a prize pig, his crew nailed to a fucking table. The drugs and the money are gone. Yet you think that I owe you money. Are you cracking up, Henry?'

'Not at all but I can see that we are going around in circles. I had to give you the opportunity to square your side of the deal.' Henry checked his watch. He took a piece of paper from his inside pocket and placed it on the desk. 'This is the bank account number where you will transfer the money.'

'Stick it up your ring piece!'

'Charming,' Henry said, not offended.

'Get out, you fucking idiot. I am beginning to lose my rag.'

'We're on our way.' Henry stood and turned away from the desk. 'Don't forget now, you have until Friday.'

'Fuck Friday and fuck you!'

'My mobile number is on there too.'

Ron picked up the paper and screwed it into a ball. He tossed it into a wastepaper basket. 'Get out!'

'You shouldn't have done that,' Henry said, shaking his head as if he was talking to a child. 'You'll need it shortly.' He turned to Patrick. 'We are not making any progress. We need to go.'

Patrick stood and followed Henry to the door, a confused expression on his face. Ron scowled, shaking his head in disgust.

'You're mad, old man,' he grumbled.

'I'll keep an eye on that bank account,' Henry shouted cheerily from the corridor.

'Don't hold your breath. You won't see a fucking penny from me,' Ron shouted back, kicking the wastepaper basket across the room. It clattered off the wall just missing Rickets and landed spinning of the floor.

'Hope for the best but plan for the worst, Ron.'

'Fuck off!'

'You'll pay. You will,' Henry called from the car park. 'You'll see, Ron. You will.'

'Will someone please shoot the silly old bastard,' Ron shouted.

Rickets laughed but there was no humour in it. Ron stared at Henry through the window as they climbed back into their car. The old man waved and smiled. The gates opened and they pulled out and drove away. As they drove out of sight, Ron's mobile began to ring. He didn't recognise the number.

'Who is this?'

'Henry. Are you missing me yet?'

'What the fuck do you want?'

'I forgot to mention that you might want to make a call to your nightclub. I think you should.'

'My nightclub?'

'Rotter's, I believe it is called.'

'Why would I need to call them?'

'I just think that you should. I think they will want to talk to you,' Henry said happily. 'Go on, give them a call.'

'What are you talking about, you fucking lunatic?' Ron growled.

'Oh, now you're mad with me again, aren't you? Call them,' Henry said. He hung up and left Ron looking at the screen.

'I don't think he's a full shilling,' Ron said, shaking his head.

'Fucking looney tunes, Ron,' Rickets said, making circles next to his temple with his finger. 'Absolute fucktard.'

Rickets' mobile phone began to ring. Closely followed by Big Ron's. He looked at the call waiting on the screen. Rickets answered his and took the call out of the room. Ron looked at the screen on his phone. The screen showed 'Rotter's' flashing. A shiver ran down his spine. How could the silly old fool have known about a call from Rotter's? He sat down and shifted uncomfortably on his chair as he answered the call.

'What?' Ron answered angrily.

'Is that you, Ron?'

'Of course, it is! You rang my phone.'

'Sorry, Ron.' The nightclub manger sounded shaky. 'There's been an explosion at the back of the club.'

'What?'

'One of your vans blew up, Ron!'

'One of the vans?'

'Yes.' The manager was flapping. 'One of your lads had a few drinks after work last night and left his van around the back. It has just fucking blown up.'

'For fuck's sake!' Ron hissed. 'Could it have caught fire?'

'No one saw any fire, Ron.'

'You're sure it wasn't the petrol tank?' Ron ran through the scenarios in his mind. They kept coming back to Henry.

'I don't know much about cars,' the manager said nervously. 'All I know is that the van exploded, and the toilet block windows blew out. The van is fucking rubble, Ron. I think it was more than a petrol tank fire to do that much damage. It was an explosion.'

'When did it happen?'

'Just now. Literally two minutes ago.'

'Is anyone hurt?'

'No. It was parked in the yard at the back next to the bins. It wasn't a big explosion, but the van is scrap.'

'Fucking bastards!'

'Who is? Did someone do this on purpose?' the manger asked, confused. 'Do you know who might have done this?'

'I have a good idea. Don't worry about that for now,' Ron growled. 'Are the police there yet?'

'Not yet. I called the fire brigade. They will be all over the place in a minute.'

'Everything that needs to be hidden is hidden, yes?'

'Of course.'

'The last thing I need right now is the filth all over the club. Say fuck all to the police. I'll call you back!' He looked out of the window angrily. The muscles in his jaw twitched. His face was purple. Rickets walked back into the room.

'Ron,' he said with a shake of the head. 'You won't believe what has happened, Ron,' Rickets said in disbelief.

'You fucking bastards...' Ron was oblivious to him, ranting to himself and snarling at the window.

'Ron!' he interrupted him.

'What?' Ron snapped at Rickets.

'You won't believe what has happened.'

'I know about it,' he grumbled. 'Nigel has just rung and told me.'

'Nigel?' Rickets was confused. 'From Rotter's?'

'Yes!'

'Not Rotter's. There's been trouble in town, Ron.'

'I know there's been fucking trouble.' He walked across the room and picked up the wastepaper basket. Tipping it up, he fumbled for the piece of paper that Henry had left. There were bank details and a phone number just as Henry has said.

'Ron, listen to me!' Rickets tried to get his attention.

Ron pointed to his phone. 'I need to make this call. That Irish cunt has blown up one of our vans.'

'A van?'

'Yes.'

'Where?'

'Behind Rotter's. It's taken the toilet windows out!'

'Ron!' Rickets called louder. 'Will you fucking listen to me for a minute, please!'

'What is the matter?'

'Before you make that call, you need to know what else has happened.'

'Why, what has happened?'

'There's been more, Ron.'

'More what?'

'Explosions.'

'You're fucking kidding me. Where?' Ron went quiet. His face flushed purple.

'The bins at the back of Wetherspoons have blown up,' Rickets said, panicked. Ron glared open mouthed.

'Bastards!'

'And behind the Grapes and behind the Central Hotel and The Ship and Mitre!'

'I don't fucking believe this!' Ron reached into his desk drawer and pulled out a Glock. His face was like thunder as he pointed it at the window. 'I'm going to shoot him in the face. I am going to kill them both.' Punching the phone number into his phone, he called Henry. The phone rang for a few minutes. 'Answer your phone, you senile old goat!'

'Hello, Henry speaking,' he answered jovially.

'Was that you?' Ron asked Henry angrily.

'Yes, that was me,' Henry tilted his head and smiled thinly. He looked at Patrick and winked. 'You didn't take me seriously, did you, Ron? Do we have your attention now?'

'You do but it isn't the kind of attention that you will like.'

'As long as we have it, eh!' Henry chuckled.

'You won't be laughing when I get my hands on you. I do not believe you two. You two are a pair of fucking jokers aren't you.'

'Jokers? Far from it. I blew up a few skips with some old fireworks this time. They were no more than a big bang. Just imagine what could happen next time when I use the real stuff.' A sinister tone crept into his voice. 'We're not joking, Ron. You need to understand that straight away. This is anything but a joke.'

'You're fucking dead men,' Ron shouted, waving the gun around in the air. Rickets stepped back in case it went off. 'I don't know who you're used to dealing with, but nobody fucks with me. You've crossed the line, old man.'

'Before you go making things worse,' Henry said calmly. 'Incidents like this can be made to happen anywhere we like, anytime we like. Shoot me and a boat load of men like me will be here by the morning.' Ron looked furious but his eyes flickered with understanding. 'They will come after you and your family and bring your business to its fucking knees before the weekend.' Ron remained silent. 'Once word gets out that it's you we're targeting, not the businesses, you have contracts with, they will drop you like a turd. You'll be out of business permanently.'

'You stupid old cunt!' Ron hissed. Spittle flew from his lips. His face was dark with anger, but his eyes showed confusion. Confusion and fear. 'You fucking...'

'Enough!' Henry snapped. Ron looked at the phone surprised. There was a moment of silence. 'That's better. You need to realise exactly what your situation is. After my little demonstration, I expect you to get a grip and give your big fat head a wobble.' Henry paused. Ron looked set to explode. 'You know who took your drugs, pay us what you owe us and go and get your shipment and your money back from them.'

'They will be dealt with, don't you worry about that,' Ron scowled. 'In the meantime...'

'In the meantime,' Henry interrupted loudly. He gestured to Patrick to turn left. 'You'll pay the money into that account. You have until Friday before your world starts to collapse around you.'

'You're dead men.'

'Friday, Ron.'

'Fuck you!'

'You're a stubborn man, Ron.'

'You're a dead one!'

'Stand up and look out of the window.'

'What?' Ron said nervously. He stood up and peered out of the window. Rickets looked confused. They looked at each other and frowned. 'What are you talking about?'

Four small explosions went off simultaneously, blowing the hinges off the compound gates. They were lifted three metres off the ground before crashing onto the concrete with a deafening clatter. Ron stared at the phone; his face darkened. His jaw tightened with frustration.

'Now that was the real stuff, Ron and there's plenty left.'

'I'm going to kill you.'

'Once you've calmed down, you'll see sense and pay us.'

'Fuck you!'

'You have until Friday, Ron,' Henry said calmly and hung up.

Ron put his hands to his head, gun still in hand. He walked around the desk and sat heavily in his chair. His eyes were squeezed tightly closed. He held his breath in his chest, trying to keep his temper under control. His head went down slowly until his forehead was resting on his desk. Rickets had seen him angry before but not to the level where he was debilitated by it. He waited ten minutes until he dared speak.

'What are we going to do, Ron?'

Ron lifted his head up and stared at him. He looked almost surprised to see him. His eyes seemed slightly glazed as if he was looking through Rickets into the wall behind him.

'Are you okay, Ron?'

'Where did you bury that fucking Russian?'

'Delamere Forrest,' Rickets said frowning. 'Why, Ron?'

'Go and dig him up.'

'What?'

'You heard me,' Ron said gruffly. 'Dig the cunt up.'

'Why would we do that, Ron?'

'I've heard that Yuri Karpov is in town tonight.' Ron stood up and looked at his gun. 'It is time we sent the Karpovs a message that they won't forget. Dig the fucker up. Get the men together. We're going to get our drugs back. And when we've done that, I'm going to skin that Irish twat with a cheese grater.'

CHAPTER 26

JO

Jo watched the tech hit the print button again and she heard the printer whirl into life behind her. Steff Cain's laptop was yielding valuable information. She knew that it would. That's why she had posted it to Braddick before she killed herself. It was her last act as a police officer, sticking two fingers up to her tormentors. Jo couldn't fathom how frightened she must have been that her family would be harmed. If the Karpovs had threatened her, then she would have been under no illusions that their threats would be carried out. If they had said that her parents would be tortured to death and that her sister and her children would be killed or worse, then they would have carried that through without blinking. Cain would have been helpless. It wasn't something that she could imagine.

Having a family was something that Jo had forgone a long time ago. She was an only child. Her parents had died in a car crash when she was at university and that was that. She was alone in the world with no relatives to speak of. Her father had a brother, but he had emigrated to Australia thirty years before and they had never heard from him since. She joined the force straight from university and was fast tracked to detective. When the opportunity to join Matrix came, she jumped at it and took to it like a pig in muck. The more she delved into the city's serious crimes, the more she wanted to become an undercover. She wanted to sink into the mire and live and breathe the filth. Her training had been intense. An ex-undercover had drilled her one on one until her head hurt. Even other UC's didn't know the identity of an undercover. No one but her handler and his superior officer knew. He taught her how to survive on the streets, becoming invisible and insignificant to other human beings. He showed her how to blend into the underworld and float through it like a ghost, always watching, always listening, always learning.

She rented out her two-bedroom terrace via a letting agency and told them that she was travelling the world. Closing the front door and disappearing into the bowels of the city was simple for her. She never felt alone, and she never felt afraid. The streets embraced her, and she embraced them back. She became Lilly. Lilly was a part of her life that she loved. Lilly was like the sister that she had never had. Two people in one body. She missed being her. When she had been sucked back into the real world, adjusting wasn't as hard as she thought it might be. She felt like an actress who had finished her stint on Broadway. It was time to take off the makeup and hang up the dress and go home to be herself again. It seemed like the most natural thing in the world.

Trawling through Steff Cain's laptop was like dissecting another life. Everything was there, professional and personal. Her cases, her boyfriends, her girlfriends, her photos, her memories, everything that she was, was there. It made her sad to think that her soul was stored on a hard drive while her broken body rotted in a mortuary. The woman pictured smiling, skiing, scuba diving, laughing with friends, dancing, drinking, living, was gone. Everything on her laptop was nothing more than an echo of the past, a shadow of a life ended in a painful second. Jo looked at her photos and smiled sadly. She had been a beauty. The world would be slightly dulled by her loss although it would continue to turn, nonetheless. Her mobile rang. The screen flashed 'Braddick'.

'Hello.'

'Any joy with Cain's laptop?' he asked.

'I can't see the joy but there is lots of information,' she said, walking to the printer. 'We're printing off everything relevant from the last two weeks.'

'Any details on the informer?'

'Not yet. It will be there somewhere on there but unfortunately there's no file set up under 'informer'.'

'If only things were that simple.'

'There's plenty in her Karpov file but it is old news, mostly from our archives.'

'What about day to day stuff?'

'Most of that was backed up on the server anyway but I've got plenty of reading to do to catch up with her case files.'

'It took me a month to get a grip on things when I moved to MIT.'

'I've talked to all my sergeants and all my UC's are accounted for bar two. I am assuming one of them is the missing link.'

'That's good news.'

'I suppose you could say that,' Jo said. 'One of the missing UC's is listed as, George.'

'And?'

'The last few months of my time undercover, a guy began to frequent the seedier parts of town. He appeared to be a down and out on the surface, but he always had cash, buying the working girls coffee and cigarettes. My instinct told me that he was Matrix, you know, making friends with the addicts. You make friends with the addicts and you soon know who all the dealers are. Some of the girls used to call him, gorgeous George. He had a way about him that people liked, always smiling.'

'Could be a coincidence.' Braddick didn't sound convinced.

'One thing that my time as Lilly taught me, the city might be vast but the underbelly and the people who live there make up a community. Six months on the streets in the city centre and you know everyone that there is to know. I'm trying to work through her files, but I think it might be him.'

'Would you be able to find him?'

'I remember that he was always hanging around the Jamaica Street area.'

'The Baltic Triangle?'

'Yes. He used to hang around the girls who work near the old mills,' Jo explained. 'It's less than five minutes from the station. I'll asked uniform to keep an eye out for him around there.'

'Good idea. Can we assume he knows that Cain is dead?'

'Not really,' she said matter of factly. 'It would take a while for that to get around. He may have been rattled by the lack of communication though.'

'What makes you say that?'

'When communications breakdown, UC's are given a location to hook them back up with their handler. There are several in the city and they rotate them from time to time. Cain changed it last month to a new location. Have a guess where that was?'

'Not a clue.'

'The old Kodak building,' she paused for effect. 'The canteen in the old Kodak building to be precise.'

'You're kidding me?'

'I am not even joking.'

'The same canteen where the fishermen were nailed to a table?'

'The very same.'

'What does that mean to you?'

'It means that they knew Cain and Pilkington were handling a UC. And they knew that with them gone, the UC would eventually have to break cover and go to that address. I think that they were trying to identify the UC.'

'So, you think George could be the tramp that found the fishermen?'

'Exactly. I think he was one of our UC's. Maybe not George but certainly one of them.'

'Who knew about that location?'

'Only the Matrix Team sergeants and above. Four people at the max.'

'So, they could have got to one of them?'

'They must have. They left the fishermen there to scare the shit out of the UC when he turned up and to let us know that they are onto us. I don't think that they know who the informer is but they do know that they have one.'

'If that was your UC, they were trying to identify him and make him break cover,' Braddick said. 'They wanted to force him to do something that he wouldn't normally consider. Something rash.'

'Like warn the informer,' Jo said, following his train of thought.

'Exactly.'

'They want him to lead them right to him.'

'That's what I think. There's nothing I can do about it right now,' she sighed. 'I'll keep going through the laptop and keep you in the loop.'

'Do that.'

'How's things from your side?'

'I'm going to bump into Yuri Karpov tonight at a charity event,' Braddick said seriously. 'I'm going to rattle his cage and see what falls out.'

'You need to be careful,' she warned. 'Their lawyers will crucify you.'

'I'll keep them in mind,' he joked. 'I just want to look in his eyes when I mention Cain's name. I'll know if they had anything to do with it.' Jo stayed quiet. He decided to leave it there. 'Any sign of Ron Mason yet?'

'Not yet. He won't give us anything anyway. I want the witness. We'll get him from social media, eventually. People can't help themselves on there.' She sounded distracted. 'I'd better get on. Try not to stab Karpov in the eye with your fork.'

'I'll do my best.' The line went dead.

CHAPTER 27

YURI KARPOV

St George's Hall is a rectangular, sand coloured building that could have been taken from a movie set in ancient Rome. With a flat roof, wide sweeping steps lead up to sixteen huge Corinthian columns, three massive doorways and a myriad of giant bronze statues. Inside, red polished granite columns hold up a tunnel vaulted ceiling and multicoloured Minton tiles adorn the floor. As Braddick entered the main hall, the acoustics reminded him of a leisure centre swimming pool, voices echoed from the ceiling. Security was tight. He had to queue to be scanned and searched before giving in his ticket and overcoat to a greeter, who had a fixed grin on his face. The entrance was busy, and he stood aside and waited for Ade Burns to be processed.

'Sorted,' Ade said as he cleared security. 'Where is the bar?'

'On the right over there.'

'Do you want a pint, Guv?'

'No,' Braddick said, looking around. He couldn't see any sign of the main sponsor. 'And neither do you. I want you focused tonight. We shouldn't be here. Any fuck ups and we're for the high jump. I don't want you half-cut, shooting your mouth off, okay?'

'When have I ever done that?' Ade looked hurt.

'Every work function you've been to for the last twenty years,' Braddick said matter of factly. 'Do you need me to list them?'

'No thanks. Orange juice?'

'Diet Coke for me, please.'

'I'll get a receipt for my expenses,' Ade grumbled sarcastically. He walked into the crowd near the bar, hands shoved deep into his pockets. Braddick sensed that Ade was uncomfortable when surrounded by the city's movers and shakers. He was out of his comfort zone. Throw him into an interview room with a hardened criminal and he could dissect them with clinical precision but ask him to have an intelligent conversation with a VIP and he would implode. 'I'm sure that one or two vodkas won't hurt,' he muttered as he approached the bar.

Braddick ignored him and scanned the room. He nodded hello to a council official and waved to the town centre manager. The men in the room all looked smart in dinner suits and black ties and the woman looked spectacular in their evening dresses. He could smell perfume and aftershave. The air was thick with the scent of a hundred brands drifting like a cloud in the huge concert room. His mobile rang and he took it out of his dinner jacket and looked at the screen. It was an MIT number.

'DI Braddick,' he answered.

'It's Google, Guv,' one of his sergeants said. 'Sorry to disturb you. I know you're at a function, but I thought that you would want to know straight away.'

'It's no problem. What's up?'

'CSI found a gun at Mike Pilkington's gaff.'

'A gun, what type?'

'It's a nine-millimetre Makarov.'

'A Russian weapon.'

'Yes, Guv. I thought you should know.'

'Where did they find it?'

'In the glove box of his MG.'

'That's where I keep mine,' Braddick scoffed.

'Me too,' Google chuckled.

'Ballistics?'

'Not back yet. I'll let you know as soon as it comes in.'

'Thanks, Google.'

Braddick put his phone back into his jacket and looked for Ade.

'Inspector Braddick.' A female voice interrupted his thoughts. He turned to see the Lady Mayoress approaching. They had met at a police charity ball a few months earlier. Whoever had first coined the word 'cougar' to apply to an aging temptress, was thinking about women like her. He was embarrassed that he couldn't remember her first name. 'What a lovely surprise to see you. I didn't see your name on the guest list.'

'I'm a last-minute substitute,' he joked, kissing her on each cheek. 'It's nice to see you again. You smell good. I like that perfume.'

'Thank you,' she said, grinning. 'So, do you. What are you wearing?'

'Creed.'

'Oh,' she looked disappointed. 'I've never heard of it.'

'Good,' he smiled. 'Then no one else will be wearing it, will they? That's a beautiful dress by the way. You look amazing.'

She smoothed her dress at the hip and blushed. 'Thank you, Inspector.'

'Drink, Guv,' Ade said, approaching. He nodded to the Mayoress and stared at her cleavage. She hoisted her neckline, conscious of his gaze. Her smile faded. Braddick could smell vodka on Ade's breath.

'Can I get you a drink?' Braddick asked her, taking his drink from Ade.

'Oh, that's very kind of you,' she said smiling. 'I'll have a glass of pinot please.'

'Could you get the Mayoress a glass of pinot, please.' Braddick grinned sarcastically. Ade nodded silently and sulked off into the crowd again.

'Oh, call me Jan,' she said, touching his shoulder. 'There's no need for formality.'

'Okay, Jan it is. What table are you sitting on?' he asked.

'I'm on the sponsor's table. They are Russians, you know?' she said with a sigh. 'I think there's two of them coming along with their entourage. They don't step out of their hotels without being surrounded by bodyguards.'

'Yes. I'm familiar with the Karpovs. They have a lot of enemies in their own country and some of them wouldn't think twice about coming here.'

'They have a lot here too from what I hear.'

'The super-rich always have enemies, Jan. It depends on how many people they squashed on their way to the top.'

'That's true. I know businessmen can be ruthless and dull but oh my God, it was so painful last year. They were so bloody miserable,' she whispered. 'I'm going to have a few wines before we sit down. I can't face it stone cold sober.'

'I don't blame you one bit. I wouldn't mind five minutes with them. Could you introduce us at some point after the meal?'

'Of course,' she said, looking intrigued. 'Official business?'

'Good heavens no!' Braddick smiled. 'This is neither the time nor the place for that. We have dark damp interview rooms for things like that.' He joked. 'I wanted to meet him and mention the new wing that they're building at Alderhey,' he lied. 'These functions do great work, but the money raised is a drop in the ocean. The Karpovs could build that wing without blinking about the cost.'

'I'll give you a nod if someone leaves the table after we have eaten. Where are you sitting?'

'We're on table twelve,' Braddick said.

'One large glass of pinot.' Ade returned and handed her the wine. He stared at her cleavage again. She took it and smiled uncomfortably. 'That glass of wine costs more than an entire bottle in Aldi.'

'Really?' the Mayoress said, trying to sound interested. 'I have never bought wine from there.' She smiled thinly, clearly uncomfortable. 'In fact, I've never bought anything from there. I would expect to pay more at an event like this. It is a charity fund raiser after all.' Ade was about to reply but Braddick threw him a look that said 'don't'. 'Would you excuse me, Inspector. I'm being waved at furiously by my husband. I'll give you a nod later.'

'Of course. My regards to your husband. Enjoy your evening.' Braddick kissed the back of her hand. She blushed a little and walked away. Ade followed the movement of her hips.

'I could do that some damage. I'd smash her back doors in,' he said, almost drooling. 'She's not bad for an older bird, eh Guv?'

'It's nice to see romance isn't dead,' Braddick said, shaking his head. 'How long have you been single again?'

'Nearly eight years now.'

'It's hard to understand why,' Braddick muttered to himself. 'I can't understand it at all.'

'What's that?'

'I said I've just had a call from Google about Mike Pilkington. They found a Russian made Makarov in his MG.'

'Fucking hell,' Ade said, looking shocked. 'That's not good. Any ballistics yet?'

'They're running it now.'

'I can't put my finger on it, but something isn't right with him.'

'Keep that to yourself for now. There's no evidence that he was dirty.'

'Not yet,' Ade mumbled.

A murmur ran through the crowd. Braddick looked towards the door. Three gorillas in leather overcoats parted the crowd, flanking two men in dinners suits.

'They're here.' Braddick recognised Yuri Karpov immediately. His bodyguards had an air of menace about them.

'I recognise Yuri Karpov,' Ade said. 'Who is the younger bloke?'

Braddick thought that the second man was vaguely familiar from observation photos that he had seen when he was seconded to the NCA. It came back to him in a flash.

'The name Sergei Karpov springs to mind. He is a generation younger than Yuri.'

'What tier is he on?'

'He's right at the top. He was allegedly in charge of operations in the Balkans.'

Ade glanced at Braddick. 'The Balkans. Bloody hell, the UK will be a like a theme park after running that place.'

'That's if he is here permanently. Let's hope he isn't, or we had better order some more body bags.'

'Nice guy then?'

'He was in the Russian military when the Bosnia/Serbia conflict was settling down. Interpol have a file on him starting after the conflict ended, that reads like a manual on how to establish a drug network. There was no hard evidence of course, just rumour and speculation, but Interpol were desperate to nail him. It never happened.'

'Of course, it didn't.'

'He always seemed to be there whenever anything bad happened. The Balkans were virtually lawless for years. When the borders were redrawn, the infighting in the underworld was brutal. The Karpovs came out on top. From what I read about it; Sergei was the main man.'

'What do you think he is doing here in the UK?'

'Let's hope it's leisure and not business,' Braddick said. He didn't take his eyes of the Karpovs. 'I think we should head to our table' As they turned, Braddick came face to face with the Chief Constable. He was wearing his full-dress uniform. 'Evening, Sir.'

'Inspector Braddick,' he said, shaking his hand. The position of his thumb told Braddick that he was a mason. 'I didn't know that you were coming.'

'Last minute thing, Sir,' Braddick said. He could feel his face redden. 'I didn't realise you would be here either.'

'I've had the Mayor and Jim Barnes on my case all week.' The chief lowered his voice. Jim Barnes was the local MP. 'You know what a pain in my backside Barnes can be. He mentions the word 'funding' in every sentence. To say that I didn't have much choice would be an understatement. Sharing a table with those Russian upstarts is the last thing that I want to do but I'm afraid our job is as much politics as it is policing nowadays.'

'Isn't that the truth,' Braddick said, nodding. He felt gutted. Trying to get to the Karpovs would be virtually impossible now. 'Still we soldier on, Sir.'

'Indeed, we do, Inspector, indeed we do.' He tapped his hat with his forefinger in mock salute. 'Enjoy the evening. I'm damn sure that I won't.'

'Have a good night,' Braddick said as he walked away. He turned to Ade and gestured with his head. 'I won't be able to get near the bastards now.'

'Another time, eh Guv. Does that mean I can have a pint?'

Braddick ignored him again. They walked to table twelve and sat down. Ade sipped his diet coke and hoped that Braddick wouldn't smell the vodka in it. They watched as the Karpov entourage made their way slowly to the top table, shaking hands with the local dignitaries along the way. The Chief Constable looked uncomfortable as they were introduced by the Mayor. The handshake looked less than cordial. Another murmur announced the arrival of eight stunning females dressed as serving wenches. They were wearing short black dresses, fishnet stockings and white pinafores. Each pushed a trolley stocked with bottles of premium vodka and crystal shot glasses. Their minders followed at a discreet distance, standing stony faced when their progress came to a halt. The Master of Ceremonies banged his gavel on the top table and the room fell silent. He made some introductions, the sponsors, the Mayor and Mayoress, councillors, the Chief Constable and VIP's. He announced that the sponsors had kindly provided the vodka and that everyone was encouraged to try the unusual brands. He added that the meal would be served as soon as everyone was seated. Braddick's mobile rang again.

'DI Braddick.'

'It's Google, Guv.'

'What have we got?'

'The gun was used in a double murder two years ago, brothers by the name Rakov.'

'Russians?'

'Ukrainian. They were found shot dead in a Range Rover on a farm near Tarbock Green. The investigators found wheel marks on the field consistent with an aircraft landing. They reckoned it was a drop that was hijacked. The case is still open.'

'Did they have any links with the Karpovs?'

'No. They were with the opposition apparently.'

'Good work. Keep me posted.'

'Will do,' Google said, hanging up.

Braddick put his phone away and looked at Ade.

'What was that about?'

'The Makarov was used to kill two Ukrainians a few years back. They were found in Range Rover near Tarbock Green.'

'I remember that, Guv. Alec Ramsay worked that case. You would have been in London then.'

'I was. See if you can dig out the murder-book on it tomorrow will you.'

'No worries,' Ade said, distracted as the vodka was distributed.

The vodka girls took one row of tables each and began handing out the shots, one table at a time. One of the women approached Braddick's table. She flicked her long blond hair as she showed her wares, Vestal, Belvedere, Grey Goose, Crystal Head, Sipsmith, and

Beluga. Ade looked like a kid in a sweetshop. He rubbed his hands together and smiled at her.

'They've got Golovkine there, Guv,' Ade said, rubbing his hands together again. 'I've never tried that. I know you said no drinking but we're not going to get to the Karpovs tonight and it's free. Surely I can have one?'

'Just don't overdo it.'

The server overheard them and poured Ade a large shot of Golovkine. He downed it and she filled it up again while Braddick was distracted, tipping a flirty wink as she did. 'What is your name?' she asked. She had a foreign accent. Definitely Russian, Ade thought.

'Adrian but people call me Ade,' he said, smiling. 'What is yours?'

'Irina.'

'Nice to meet you, Irina.'

'Nice to meet you too, Ade,' she said smiling. 'I'll be back shortly.'

'See you then.' Ade grinned.

The meal arrived in three courses, each one lukewarm and bland. Ade had his shot glass filled every time Braddick was in conversation with someone or went to use the bathroom. He was building a rapport with the server, who was downing her fair share of shots too. Ade was convinced that he could pull her, and it felt good. It had been too long. He hadn't lost it. Not yet.

Braddick waited patiently for Jan to summon him over to the table. The Karpovs seemed relaxed, joining in conversation with the people on their table and others, who approached them. There were far too many people around them for him to speak to them. Rattling their cage was looking more unlikely as the evening past. The people on his table were keen to chat but he had one eye on the sponsors all night. He noticed Ade leaving the table. It was obvious that he was becoming intoxicated as he weaved his way clumsily through the tables. The gent's toilets were at the far end of the hall, past the sponsor's table.

'How long have you worked in the Major Investigation Team?' Braddick heard the question coming from the lady sat to his left. She was drunk, her eyes glazed, and speech slurred. From the corner of his eye, he noticed Yuri Karpov leave his chair. He walked at a tangent and intercepted Ade at the washroom door. They exchanged words and headed into the toilets. Braddick got the impression that they were familiar with each other. He frowned and answered the lady's question, his attention on the washroom door. His stomach clenched in knots. He questioned if what he had seen was what it appeared or if his mind had turned a simple greeting of strangers into something more.

CHAPTER 28

LIQUID

The manager at Liquid nightclub, Jack Clark, parked his car at the rear of the nightspot. He always made sure that his Porsche was left underneath the security cameras. Running a city centre club had its downsides and his car had been targeted several times. The first time was the previous manager, who had been sacked for arguing with Viktor Karpov. Viktor didn't tolerate being challenged so he sacked him and promoted Jack on the spot. Later that night, Jack noticed that his car had been scratched and he identified the culprit on CCTV. The bouncers paid him a visit at home at four o'clock in the morning. He ended up in the Royal with eight broken fingers and missing his thumbs. Another time was by a disgruntled employee, who he had dismissed for dipping into the tills. He had disappeared completely, never to be seen again. Jack had told Viktor that he had stolen a substantial amount of money, which was an exaggeration. Then he pocketed the balance. He hadn't thought much about it until the employee's parents came looking for him a week or so later. They had filed a missing person's report, which led Jack to believe that the

Karpovs had dealt out their own justice. That particular incident had cost him over nine hundred pounds to grind out the scratches and respray the entire driver's side. The time before that was an angry dealer, who had been beaten badly and relieved of his money and stock by the bouncers. On that occasion, the bonnet had to be replaced completely. That had cost over a grand. The dealer was pulled out of the Mersey estuary a few months later. His arms and legs had been crushed to pulp and were the thickness of cardboard, the cause of death, drowning. The coroner had said that his injuries could only have been caused by an industrial press. There was no need for a human resources department and employment tribunals were unheard of. Those foolish enough to cause a problem were dealt with. Jack knew that he had to manage the day to day running of the club but that he was in charge of nothing. The security team reported directly to the Karpovs and they watched him like hawks. His position was fragile at best. If he was to put a foot out of line, he would lose it. The skill was keeping them onside. With the security team onside, the job was enjoyable enough. Managing them sometimes taxed his people skills to the max but that was what he had to do to survive.

On the flipside, the perks of the job were myriad. He had a different woman every week. He earned more money than he had ever imagined possible and he could nearly double his salary by skimming from the Karpov's profits and taxing the dealers who were sanctioned to sell their products inside. The dealers were monitored by the bouncers, but it was Jack who employed them. He had the final say on who stayed and who went, and he milked it. The pros outweighed the cons despite the risks. He had to be careful, every penny accounted for meticulously. Any hint that he was skimming would cost him his life. He couldn't get away with it forever and he knew that. If he was clever, he could build up a nest egg and walk away while the going was still good. When the time came, parting company with the Karpovs on good terms was essential. He didn't want to be pulled out of the river with arms and legs like Mr Tickle.

Jack turned off the engine and switched off the lights. The St John's tower loomed above him like a giant sentinel. As he opened the driver's door, a security light illuminated the yard. He swore beneath his breath as he looked at the state of the place. The bottle bins were overflowing, and the cardboard skips were full to the brim. He made a note to call the refuse company as soon as he got inside. They were beyond useless. He had lost count of the number of times that they had failed to fulfil their contract. They seemed to turn up when they felt like it. This was the last straw. He was going to put the contract out to tender and refuse to pay what they were owed. No one would chase the debt. It was under the umbrella of the Karpovs after all.

He closed the door and set the alarm. The car beeped and the indicators flashed once. He reached for the keys to the back door of the club and walked towards the entrance. The security light went out and he cursed again. He had told the maintenance man to adjust the timer. It was like talking to a brick wall sometimes. He would be going the same way as the refuse company if he didn't sort his head out. His priorities were always the easy options first. Anything that involved a little hard work was put to the back of the queue. The lazy bastard would be getting a flea in his ear when he came in. His mood was darkening, and he hadn't put the key in the door yet. It was going to be a long night, he could tell.

He waved his arms above his head and the light came back on. A siren sounded nearby, and he turned to look behind him. He watched as an ambulance whizzed by the rear gate, closely followed by a fire engine. It was still relatively early in the evening. As the clocks moved towards midnight, the number of sirens would grow. It always did. He turned back towards the club and walked to the door. As he neared it, he heard a bottle clink and roll across the concrete. He looked around and saw an empty green bottle spinning in a circle. It slowed and then came to a stop near his car. He wondered what had made it fall but then remembered that the bins were overflowing. It wouldn't take much to make the entire pile clatter all over the yard. He selected the key and slid it into the lock. It clicked open and he inserted a mortise lock key beneath it. He pulled the handles and the heavy metal door creaked open. The alarm panel began to flash. He had thirty seconds to punch in the code to disable it before the claxons started to blare. It was deafening when they did. Jack entered the six-digit code and the lights stopped flashing. He turned back towards the door to close it and looked into a pair of deep brown eyes through a slit in a balaclava. The urge to run and scream was overwhelming, but he was frozen to the spot. Fear blocked his brain from telling his body to move. Fifty thousand volts surged through the muscles in his neck. His teeth clenched together, biting a lump from his tongue. The taste of blood filled his senses as another belt from the Taser switched his lights out.

CHAPTER 29

GOLD

While the manager of Liquid nightclub was jerking around on the floor, his skin blackened and charred, Rickets was already hitting Gold with his team. They had arrived fifteen minutes earlier and used two men dressed as policemen to trick the staff into opening the back door. Inside were the manager and two staff, who were bottling up ready for the night ahead. Rickets and his men had tied up the staff, frightened the living daylights out of them and then dragged the manager into her office. She was a stern-faced brunette with Botox, breast implants and luminous white teeth. Her nails were perfect, her clothes expensive and her tan came from a bottle. She didn't look like she had ever pulled a pint in her life.

'Open the safe,' Rickets ordered. He pushed her hard and she stumbled to her knees in front of a green metal Chub safe, that was the size of a family refrigerator.

'Do you know who owns this club?' she hissed angrily. 'They will find you and kill you.'

'Can you see me shaking?' Rickets grinned beneath his mask. 'Open the fucking safe. I won't tell you again.'

'And if I refuse?' she asked defiantly.

'I'll knock those shiny teeth out and then carve your face up so badly that you will look like you've been in a car crash,' Rickets shrugged. 'It's your choice how we do this, but you will open the safe at some point. 'Her expression changed from stubborn to terrified. It was obvious that her vanity was more powerful than her loyalty. 'Now, open the fucking thing before I lose it.'

'You are dead men,' she muttered as she turned the dial forward and backwards. She inserted the key and unlocked it, twisting the handle with practised ease. The door swung open.

'Good. That wasn't too difficult, was it?'

'Fuck you.'

'Sit against the wall there and shut your mouth,' Rickets said, pushing her away from the safe. He opened the door fully and looked inside. Bundles of notes of all denominations sat next to bags of pound coins. 'Bag the lot. Take it all,' he ordered his men. They began to empty the contents into holdalls. Rickets turned to the manager.

'What's your name?'

'Anna.'

'Are you Russian?'

'Yes.'

'Okay, listen to me, Anna. We're going to have a question and answer game,' he growled. 'I'll ask you a question and you will answer me. Tell me a lie and you'll lose a nail. Then we'll start on the teeth.'

Her face changed colour when he produced a pair of pliers. 'Do you understand the rules?' She nodded her head. 'I asked you if you understand the rules?'

'Yes. I understand.'

'Good. Where do you keep the drugs?' Anna looked at her feet and shook her head. Rickets grabbed her left wrist and put the pliers against her hand. 'One last time. Where do you keep the drugs?'

'Don't hurt me, please!' She gestured with her head towards the desk. 'There's a floor safe underneath the desk. The code is 1978.'

One of the men walked across the room and lifted the desk. Another peeled back the carpet and uncovered the safe. He entered the code and the door opened. 'Two kilos of coke, a few hundred E's, a bag of brown and four bottles of Ketamine. There's a lot of money in here, Rickets.' The man held up a thousand-pound bundle of fifties. 'There must be a hundred bundles here.'

'That is a bonus,' Rickets smiled. A gold tooth glinted in the light. 'No zombie?'

'No.'

'Zombie?' Anna frowned.

'Your bosses haven't told you that they have come across a shit load of zombie?'

'No, they haven't. I don't know what you're talking about.'

Rickets stared into her eyes. He didn't think that she was lying. The sound of hammering was coming from the club. 'Take it all.'

'You are so dead,' Anna chuckled sourly.

'Like I said earlier, can you see me shaking?'

'Oh, you will. You will shake like the shitting dog that you are when they track you down.'

'Do you want to keep that pretty smile?'

'Yes.'

'Then I suggest that you speak when you're spoken to and keep a civil tongue in your head or I'll rip it out, understand?' She nodded. 'I asked you if you understand.'

'Yes. I understand.'

'Good. Where do the Karpovs keep their gear?'

'You have it.'

'That is enough for a few nights, a week at the most. We both know that.' Rickets crouched in front of her. 'I mean their main store. Where do they keep it?'

'It is never in one place. You know how it works. They split up the supply and spread the risk.'

'There is always a main supply.'

'If there is, then I don't know it. They keep gear all over the place. It moves around. I just run this shithole. I only know what I overhear.'

'You're talking about the club supply. I am talking about their large shipments, not what they sell in here. Where would they stash a large shipment?'

'I wouldn't know that.' Rickets moved towards her; pliers raised. 'Wait!'

'I don't have time to fuck around. Answer me or we'll take you somewhere quiet. If we do, you will talk and then I'll get my men to take you out, remove your hands, head and feet to slow down identification and then they'll bury your remains randomly across the city.' Tears filled her eyes and she bit her bottom lip. 'Of course, they will probably take turns on you before they kill you. Perks of the job. I might have a go myself,' Rickets said, touching her breast with the tip of the pliers. A tear broke free and ran down her cheek. 'I know you're loyal to your employers. We all are in this business but they're not worth what will happen to you, trust me. They don't give a fuck about you. Think about it carefully. Where would they keep a large amount of gear?'

'I don't know where they would keep a shipment, honestly I don't.'

'Okay.' Rickets stood up. The hammering noise started again. 'Put her in the van. She's coming with us.'

'No, no, no, no!' she panicked. 'Wait a minute.'

'Quickly, Anna. I'm in a rush.'

'It would have to be somewhere big but near the city, yes?'

'Yes. It would be nearby.'

'I know that they have a laundry that supplies their hotels. It is huge. I went there last year. I can't think of anywhere else locally, please don't take me with you.'

'Where is it?'

'Warrington, just off the M62 near Ikea. It is a huge place. The lorries are blue. It is called Pristine.'

'I now the place,' Rickets said, nodding. Her face relaxed. She breathed a sigh of relief. 'Tie her up and put her with the others.'

One of the men pulled her up and fastened zip ties to her wrists. The tough plastic bit into her flesh. He bundled her towards the door. Her two staff members were bound and gagged; tears streamed down their faces. They were staring at something above the bar. She followed their gaze and then wished that she hadn't. The bloated body of Leonid was crucified to the wall.

* * * *

Ron Mason and Rickets watched as they unloaded their hoard. Ron was grinning as the cash was counted and loaded into his stash. They had welded a panel into the back of a transit van so that they could conceal their gear and keep it mobile. To the naked eye, it couldn't be detected. There was over four hundred thousand in cash and nearly the same again in drugs. Once the drugs were sold on, the street value would double their take. It was a major haul. He had almost replaced what had been taken from Holyhead.

'That is karma, Rickets.' Ron grinned. 'That is one in the eye for those Russian bastards. Payback time, my friend. A couple more of them and they will be reeling.'

'What do you mean, a couple more?'

'It was so easy,' Ron laughed. 'We should have thought of it years ago. They have been doing it for decades. It is about time someone hit them back.'

'I think that we should lie low for a while, Ron,' Rickets said. 'They will be going ballistic trying to find out who hit them. We should sell the drugs on cheap to get rid of them. Having that much coke around is bad news.'

'Fuck that,' Ron said, shaking his head. 'That is quality gear not the shit we get. We'll get top dollar for that. They won't have a clue who hit them. You worry too much.'

'One of us needs to worry.'

'Everything will be fine, my friend. I feel like we have squared things up a little bit, but I'm not finished yet.'

* * * *

Henry and Patrick were sitting outside the Mason Security building. Patrick watched vans arriving through night vision glasses. The gates had been repaired and they slid open as another van arrived. Roller shutters clanked open on the main building.

'What are they up to?' Henry asked.

'They are unloading vans and putting it into another one.'

'Are they now?' Henry chuckled. He reclined his seat and closed his eyes. 'Wake me up when they have finished. This could be a long night.'

CHAPTER 30

ADE BURNS

Ade sensed the change in Braddick as soon as he returned to the table. His expression was dark and moody. Ade felt drunk and vulnerable. He had definitely overdone the vodka. If his inspector started pecking his head, he wasn't in any position to respond. He couldn't risk dropping the ball now. Luckily, Braddick was being harangued by the woman sitting next to him. She was more pissed than Ade. It was obvious to everyone on the table that she had the hots for Braddick. She was making a fool of herself but was too pissed to realise it. Braddick was clearly not interested. He was politely answering her questions, the epitome of professional but he had one eye on the Karpovs all the time. Ade watched as Sergei Karpov took a phone call. It was obviously bad news. Something had happened. His face looked like thunder. He turned to Yuri and whispered in his ear. Yuri screwed up his napkin and threw it on the table angrily. They both stood up at the same time and gestured to their minders. The other guests at the table looked concerned as they quickly shook hands, said their goodbyes and headed for the door. Braddick stood up and thought about following them but the Chief Constable was walking towards him. He summoned Braddick over to him and Ade watched as they made for an empty table and sat down. Ade was glad to see the back of him.

'Do you want another shot?' Irina had returned. Her eyes were smiling. 'I noticed that your boss is busy,' she winked as she filled up his glass again.

'Thanks,' Ade said, trying to speak without slurring.

'You're very welcome.'

'I'm ready to get out of here.'

'Me too.'

'What time are you finishing work?'

'Ten minutes,' she smiled. 'I'll be on the front steps if you want to walk me back to my hotel. We're staying across the road in the Holiday Inn. I have my own room.'

'I'll meet you outside in ten minutes,' Ade said, beaming from ear to ear. 'Bring a bottle with you. It will keep us warm on the way back to the hotel.'

'I was kind of hoping that you would do that,' she teased. 'See you outside. 'She winked again, more exaggerated this time and then turned and walked away. Irina swung her hips to let him see what he was getting later, looking over her shoulder, she flicked her hair seductively. Ade smiled and congratulated himself inside. His smile was fixed to his face. He caught Braddick's eye and made a thumbs up sign. Braddick nodded, unaware of his sergeant's success. The Chief Constable was still bending his ear about something or another. Quite frankly, Ade didn't give a shit. He stood up and felt sick. Ade waited for the dizziness to pass. Braddick stared at him, suspicion in his eyes. Ade made a cutting gesture across his throat and pointed to the door to let Braddick know that he was leaving. Braddick nodded and waved briefly. He didn't look happy but so what? At that moment in time, Ade only had one thing on his mind. He wobbled a little as he made his way towards the door, handed in his coat ticket and walked to the steps. The wind was blowing off the river, so Ade pulled his coat on and fastened his buttons.

Irina was leaning against one of the columns. She had a fur lined parka on, but Ade was delighted that she still had her maid's uniform on beneath it. He walked towards her, hoping in his mind that he didn't get too turned on too quickly. She was half his age, pretty, sexy and dressed in stockings and a maid's outfit. He was scared that he would cum in his pants as soon as she touched him. A few more vodkas might slow things down a little, numb the parts that other drinks can't reach. It was either that or running the Istanbul European Cup winning squad through his mind. He wasn't sure that he could do that sober, never mind drunk. As far as problems to solve went, it was up there with the best ones.

'Hi,' Irina said, smiling. She waved a bottle of Sipsmith vodka in her hand. 'Sorry, I know it isn't your favourite, but it was the only one that I could get.'

'Don't be sorry,' Ade said. He leaned in and kissed her cheek. Her lips were full and shiny, and he wanted to kiss her full on the mouth but thought that it might be more gallant to wait until they got to her room. Once they got to the room, all gallantry would be forgotten. It had been a long time. Too long. 'It's cold out here. Shall we head to your hotel?'

'Let's go,' she said, linking his arm. Ade felt happier than he had in years.

* * * *

Young Ronny Mason stared at his phone. He had a million notifications on *Facebook*. His family had been messaging him constantly, trying to get information about what had happened in Holyhead but all he could say was that he was with his dad and that he would be back when everything had calmed down. Ignoring his family was simple enough. They all took the piss out him anyway. The only time that they spoke to him was when they wanted something or to take the piss again. They could all go and take a flying fuck. He wasn't bothered what they did or what they said but the text message from Alex had sent his head into a spin. Alex wanted to see him.

Alex had messaged and asked him to go over to his house. He loved seeing Alex. Alex was the closest thing to a relationship that he had experienced. The opportunity to see him was too good to miss. Big Ron and Rickets had gone out in the car and told him not to call anyone or to go out. They treated him like a child. Alex lived about twenty miles away on the edge of the city and Ronny knew the bus route like the back of his hand. He had been there many times before. The first time that he went there was as an errand boy for Eddie Farrell while he was still at school. He had gone there to drop off a parcel, which he later found out was full of drugs. It was one of the first times that he realised that it wasn't just a phase that he was going through, he was sexually attracted to men. Especially older men. It had been an epiphany. Alex was pushing forty then, but Ronny was blown away every time he saw him. He would blush and stutter whenever he saw him. Over the next few years, Alex was kind to him and didn't take the piss and Ronny had a massive crush on him. He never expressed his feelings. The thought horrified him. He was happy to worship him from afar.

Then one day it had happened. They had been searching online for the answer to something to do with the origin of a phrase. It was a naval reference. Something that he couldn't even remember anymore. Alex had left the room to make a drink and Ronny looked on his browsing history. He was shocked and thrilled that most of it was gay pornography. Alex had come back into the room before Ronny could exit the history and they both knew then that they had the same interests. Although they were friends, for Alex, it was just casual sex with a younger man with no strings attached. It meant much more to Ronny. Ronny would have moved in with Alex in a heartbeat but that was never an option. They both flew beneath the radar, neither wanted to come out to their families and friends. Alex kept the relationship going because Ronny was discreet. He had to be; he was Big Ron Mason's son. For Ronny, it was different. He was ensconced despite the fact that Alex would only message when he wanted sex. The sex was quick and one sided. Alex would get what he wanted, which was usually oral and then make excuses as to why Ronny had to leave. Ronny was always left hanging, unsatisfied but every time Alex messaged, he went running. Sometimes they talked about things before but not often. Ronny took what he could get, enjoying the time when it was on offer. He hadn't heard from Alex for over a week and after all that had happened, his message had made his heart skip a beat. He needed a break and he needed to be away from the farm. It had also made him horny. Very horny. Ronny stared at the message and thought about it. He could be there and back within a few hours, maybe less. Forty minutes on the bus, less than ten for the sex and then forty minutes back to the farm. He added it up in his head. Maths wasn't his strong point. Ninety minutes. That was over an hour but less than two. Actually, it was an hour and a half. He was sure. There was no way that Big Ron and Rickets would be back by then. They were never back before the early hours of the morning. He replied to Alex, put his phone into his pocket and ran upstairs. Alex replied straight away. Ronny ran into his bedroom. His towel was still damp from the day before, but he needed a shower before he went to see Alex.

* * * *

Ade sat on the bed and smiled at the ceiling. Irina had been everything that he could imagine and more. She had been eager and excited. He felt rejuvenated, attractive and virile. She certainly knew her way around a man's body. There was no doubt about that. She was catapulted to the top of his all-time best fuck list and the night wasn't over yet. He downed the vodka that she had given to him before she went to use the bathroom. It burned as it slipped down. He heard her running the taps and brushing her teeth. She sounded like she was talking to someone too. He thought about asking her who it was but decided to leave her to it. She was cleaning her teeth. That was a nice touch. Some of his exes didn't brush their teeth from one day to the next. Irina was different. She was different in every way. Her tits were magnificent, false but magnificent. They defied gravity. As for the rest, he had nothing to compare her to.

The other women that he had been with were not even in the same league. She was perfect. The way she moved, the way she felt beneath his touch, the way she breathed and moaned as he moved inside her. He loved her accent, her voice, her perfume, the scent of her body. Everything about her was perfect. He closed his eyes, suddenly very tired. In fact, he was exhausted. His muscles felt drained. He opened his eyes and felt his vision blur and his head spin. The nausea hit him like a bus. The toilet flushed and the bathroom door opened. There she was, silhouetted against the light. A vision of ecstasy. A vision that darkened at the edges and then warped, like the image in a funhouse mirror. He saw her phone in her hand and then heard a knock at the door. His lips quivered when he tried to speak. He wanted to ask her what was going on, but nothing came out. She opened the door and two huge figures entered the room. They spoke in a foreign language; Russian he was sure. He knew that he was in grave danger but there was absolutely nothing that he could do about it. His heart raced as the men approached and their shadows loomed over him.

CHAPTER 31

Sergei looked up at the swollen face of Leonid Ivankof. The stench of decomposition hung heavily in the air. Yuri stood next to him. The muscles in his jaw twitched.

'Get him down from there and get rid of the body,' Sergei ordered his men. 'Make sure that he cannot be found.' He turned to Anna. 'Was anyone hurt?'

'My staff are badly shaken, but they will be okay.'

'Will they talk?'

'I have spoken to them. They won't say anything.'

'Make sure that they don't.'

'I don't want the police involved, understand?' Yuri added.

'Of course.'

'Did you recognise any of them?'

'No but the man who was giving the orders was black and he had funny shaped legs.'

'Funny how?'

'Bowed.'

'There can't be many men fitting that description. He shouldn't be too hard to track down,' he said, turning to one of his men. 'Did you hear that?'

'Yes, Sergei.'

'Find out who he is.'

'Yes, Sergei,' the man said, turning and taking out his mobile.

'Did he say anything that would help us to find him?'

'He asked a lot of questions, Sergei.'

'Questions about what?'

'He was asking about drugs.'

'Go on.'

'He kept asking about where my employers would stash a big shipment of drugs.'

'Did he indeed?'

'And he mentioned something about zombie.'

'Zombie.' Sergei raised his eyebrows in surprise. He looked at Yuri. Yuri watched Anna intently. 'And what did you tell him, Anna?'

'He threatened to kill me, Sergei.'

'Of course, he did. He wanted you to talk.'

'I told him about the Pristine site.'

Yuri and Sergei exchanged glances. 'Make sure your staff get a decent bonus. I want this kept quiet.'

'Sergei.' A man approached. 'The black man with misshaped legs. He works for a guy called Ron Mason.'

Yuri nodded and smiled. 'Eddie Farrell's cousin. So, he has obviously worked it out.'

'Obviously,' Sergei agreed. 'I'm not concerned about Mason. He is nothing but a Neanderthal. We will keep him in his place.'

'Poor old Leonid,' Sergei said as the body was taken down. 'He was interrogated before he died. I wonder what he told them.'

'He didn't know anything worth knowing. He was door security, nothing more.'

'They returned him to us. Let's repay the favour,' Sergei said, thoughtfully. 'We need to silence all of our little rats for a start and then thanks to Anna here, we know where they will be going to next. We will give them the welcome that they deserve.'

CHAPTER 32

Young Ronny Mason knocked on the door, nervously looking around as he waited. The journey had taken five minutes more than he had anticipated but he was excited and eager to please Alex. He waited a few minutes and then knocked again. There was still no reply. The property was rented by one of his companies and he used it when he had business in the UK. Ronny remembered that Alex sometimes sat in his conservatory at the side of the bungalow, reading and listening to music. He couldn't hear a thing when he had his music on. He walked to the side gate and peered over. The conservatory was empty, and the lights were out. Ronny walked back to the front door, his hands were in his pockets and he kicked at the doorstep with his trainers while he mulled over what to do. He took out his phone and messaged Alex that he was at the front door. There didn't seem to be any lights on anywhere inside the house. He was beginning to think that Alex had gone out when he heard the door being unlocked. He smiled and his heart began to beat faster as the door opened but it faded when he saw the muzzle of a gun pointing at his head.

'You must be Ronny?' the man said. 'Step inside. I'm sorry but Alexei is a little tied up at the moment.'

* * * *

Braddick stepped out of the lift and came face to face with two uniformed officers. They nodded hello and looked sheepish. There were no words when something like this happened.

'Have you cleared this floor?' Braddick asked.

'The last room has just left.'

'Where is he?'

'That way, Sir,' one of them said, pointing down the corridor to his right. It was typical hotel decor, neutral colours and random prints on the walls, repeated every fifty yards or so. Braddick could see a detective from the Vice Squad and two members of his MIT standing outside of a bedroom door. They all looked tired and dishevelled; their sleep interrupted by an urgent incident. He walked towards them, warning voices echoing around his mind. Half of him wanted to run to see what had happened, the other half wanted to run the other way so that he couldn't. This could not be happening. Not now, not never. The detectives saw him coming and stopped talking. Their faces said all that he needed to know. He had seen that haunted look too many times before not to know what it meant.

'Morning, guys. I won't say good because it isn't.' Braddick turned to a young DC, whose name he couldn't remember. 'Why is vice here?'

'The woman's ID flagged up a previous, Guv. She was a brass, part of a ring that was busted last year. They were run from saunas on Smithdown Road. It was a Russian operation.'

'That is no surprise. Okay, what have we got, Pete?' Braddick asked flatly. He directed the question to one of his sergeants from MIT.

'It's not a pretty picture,' the sergeant sighed, with a shake of his head. He pushed open the door and stepped back for Braddick to enter. Braddick felt his nerves tingle. He looked around. The familiar smell of death clogged his senses. The hotel room was a mess, clothes were strewn everywhere. A stiletto lay on its side in the bathroom doorway next to a black sock and a discarded towel. Ade's trousers had been tossed over the arm of a chair, a pair of dark boxer shorts still inside as if they had been removed in one motion. The matching dinner jacket was crumpled beneath them, his wallet protruding from the inside pocket. A handbag lay open on the bedside table. He recognised the female from the charity function at St George's Hall. She had given out vodka at their table; a lot of vodka, especially to Ade. Braddick hadn't given her a second thought at the time. She had been flirting with Ade, but he figured that she was fishing for a tip or a sugar daddy. He didn't think that Ade would be the right man for either job. The room had been booked in her name, which surprised Braddick. He took a step forward and looked closely.

Her arms were tied to the bed above her head with her own fishnet stockings. Red welts circled the wrists where she had struggled to escape. Three of her false nails were missing from her right hand. She had put up a fight. There was blood congealed around her nose and her mouth hung open at an awkward angle, indicating that her jaw was broken. Her eyes were open, dull and staring. She seemed to be looking at Braddick, pleading for help, asking why did he does this to me? He shifted position so that she wasn't staring at him anymore. There was a bruise on her forehead and her eyes had blood spots at the corners. The bruising around her neck was dark and deep and uniform. Something had been wrapped tightly around her throat and then removed post-mortem. Her thighs were apart, the knees bent slightly. He moved closer to see the soft flesh inside her legs and could see more bruising there. Sticky fluid glistened on her skin. Finger marks lined the outside of her thighs. Whatever had happened had been rough.

'I'd smash her back doors in,' he heard Ade's voice in his head. *'I could do that some damage,'* bounced around his mind. The crudity of his words was more poignant now. Was it poolroom 'banter' or something more?

The maid's outfit and her bra had been ripped open at the chest, exposing her breasts. The skirt was pushed up to her hips. Braddick stepped forward to look at scratch marks on her thighs.

'Fucking hell, Ade,' he said, his voice almost a whisper. 'What did you do?'

Ade didn't answer. Ade was next to the girl, sitting up against the headboard. He was naked, his arms by his side. His head was tilted slightly at the neck. A black leather belt dug deep into his throat, fastened to the bed rail above him. His eyes were open, bulging, the whites flecked with red. His tongue lolled from the corner of his mouth, already blackening.

'Autoerotic gone mental or suicide?' his sergeant asked. 'What do you think, Guv?'

'I don't know what to think. I think I need another DS,' Braddick said quietly. He shrugged. 'Who knows, sex game gone wrong? Murder suicide? Or maybe someone wants us to think that is what happened.' Braddick shrugged again. It didn't feel right. Ade Burns was stupid enough to be suckered into taking a brass to a hotel but killing her? That might have been a game gone too far but Ade wasn't the type to top himself. Something didn't sit right. 'Let's get the experts in, eh? Are CSI on the way?'

'They are downstairs. We wanted you to see him before we let anyone else in. I'm having all the CCTV checked.'

'Good man. There's nothing we can do to help him now except to find out what happened. Get them in and we'll see what they find. It will be what it will be.' Braddick patted his sergeant on the arm. He walked out of the room and nodded to the other officers. 'I don't want any fucking gossip flying around the station. If anyone asks, tell it as it is. No dressing it up. Once the forensics are back, the truth will come out anyway. Are we all clear?'

'Guv.'

Braddick nodded and walked away. There was no anger, no sense of loss, no feeling of shock, just complete numbness.

CHAPTER 33

Braddick looked up from his screen when the door opened, and Google walked in with a laptop under each arm. He had called two minutes earlier to say that he had something. Braddick cleared some space on the desk and pulled a chair up next to his.

'I hope you have something good for me, Google,' Braddick sighed. 'I feel like we're swimming through mud at the moment.'

'I heard about Ade this morning,' Google said, shaking his head. 'Fucking unbelievable. Everyone's stunned. So soon after Cain and Mike Pilkington too.'

'I know. No funerals for years and then three turn up at the same time,' Braddick said sourly. 'We need a break on this.'

'This might give us some leads,' Google said, sitting down. He turned the laptops at a better angle. 'At first we couldn't find anything on the CCTV from the bridges that stood out. Nothing obvious jumped out crossing the straits and then returning to the mainland in our time window. Until we found this,' he said, pointing to the left-hand screen. Braddick looked and frowned. He shrugged for Google to expand. 'See this big articulated lorry?'

'Yes.'

'Here it is crossing the bridge onto the island and here it is again driving through Holyhead twenty-five minutes later. At first glance there is nothing unusual in that. Hundreds go through every day.'

'Okay. Go on.'

'What is unusual is that this truck never reaches the ferry terminal itself and it never parks up on the truck stop, which is located here next to the Road King. They have to register when they arrive. Four hours later, here it is crossing back over the bridge to the mainland.'

'I'm not getting this, Google. What am I missing?'

'It stopped somewhere, and I think I know why.'

'Go on.'

'Watch this bit. We know that the lorry reached here at least.' Google pointed to a stretch of road on a map. 'We have it on CCTV from the petrol station here, you can see it driving past now but it doesn't go any further.' Google took off his glasses and pointed to the screen. 'Now in this bit of CCTV, three black SUV's drive past the railway station here but they didn't pass the petrol station. This road that they are on heads to the old harbour.'

'And that is where the fish factory is?'

'Yes. It is at the end of this road here.' Google used the map again. 'Then on this footage, two and a half hours later, the three SUV's go back past the railway station, but they never go past the petrol station but,' Google paused and raised his forefinger. 'The lorry does, here.'

'You think the SUV's are in that lorry?'

'I am sure they were. Either that or they sprung rotor blades and flew off the island.'

'That would explain what the fisherman said to me.'

'Pardon?'

'One of the fishermen from the trawler said the engine noise was muffled.'

'That's why. They were in the back of that artic.'

'Good work, Google. Who owns it?'

'It is registered to a haulage company in Amsterdam. We have tracked it when it left the island. It uses the A55 along the coast and then the motorway network to Liverpool. We lose it in the city for a few hours and then we picked it up heading north to Hull where it was put on a ferry to Rotterdam. I think that shipment was taken to Holland to be broken up and sold. Less chance of us finding it and a lot less chance of the original owners finding it.'

'I'm not so sure,' Braddick said, shaking his head. 'Why risk exporting it again. The hard work was getting into the country in the first place. I wouldn't risk another border crossing. They could sell what they had in the city.'

'Maybe. We're tracing the owners of the haulage company now.'

'It will be a dead end,' Braddick said. 'They are way ahead of us here. We're going nowhere with that are we?'

'Not really, Guv but at least we know what happened and how.'

'It was like a military operation,' Braddick said. 'I mean look at that,' he said, pointing to the SUV's on the screen. 'They hid a snatch squad in the back of a lorry, hit the drug deal and then they load up again and disappear into nowhere. It is very impressive. It was planned to perfection.'

'It does back up what we know already. This outfit is well-run, well-funded and well-organised.'

'With ex-military personnel in its numbers. These tactics prove that. It all points to one crew.'

'The Karpovs.'

'Without a doubt.'

* * * *

Jo picked up the brown envelope from her post tray. She opened it and tipped the contents onto her desk. A mobile phone and a wireless camera tumbled out. She checked inside to see if there was any paperwork. It was empty. The sender had turned the phone off. Jo turned it on and waited for it to reboot, hoping that it wouldn't be locked, or password protected. It was neither. The log showed that the phone had received three messages and two photographs from a withheld number. She looked at the photographs and recognised the homeless man, who she had known as George.

'Gorgeous George,' she said to herself. 'I knew you were a UC. Now I know who you are, I can look for you,' she said, picking up the telephone. She sent the image to her own phone by text message and then dialled the DS from Matrix.

'Yes, Guv,' he answered.

'I'm sending you an image of a homeless man known as George. The working girls call him Gorgeous George. He's our UC, I'm sure he is.'

'I recognise him. I've seen him around. He is always in the Baltic Triangle down near Jamaica Street.'

'That's him. Can you circulate that image to Matrix and uniform? We need to find him quickly.'

'Has he been compromised?'

'I think so.'

'I'm on it. I'll let you know if we have any joy.'

'Thanks.' She hung up and looked at the image. Gorgeous George wasn't gorgeous at all. He was plain. He was normal, even unnoticeable but then that was why he was accepted as a UC. The girls called him gorgeous because he looked out for them. A hot cup of coffee and a cigarette on a cold night went a long way. He was a well-liked character and as such, people might remember where they last saw him. She touched the screen with the tip of her nail. 'Where are you, George?'

On the picture, George was staring into the camera, looking confused. He looked confused and frightened. The background was blurred, even when she zoomed in but she thought that she could see several pairs of wellington boots. The second picture showed a face that she didn't recognise, badly beaten, cut and bruised. That picture had been sent to the phone via text message. Someone sent the image to the phone. She thought about it as she picked up the phone and dialled the technical evidence lab.

'Hello, tech lab.'

'It's DI Jones here,' she said, looking at the camera. She ran her fingers through the ends of her hair as she spoke.

'Hi Jo, what can I do for you?'

'Who is that?' She recognised her voice but couldn't put a name to it.

'It's Wilks,' the tech said.

'Wilks!' Jo said, excited. They had started cadet training together, but Wilks had dropped out to pursue a career in science. 'I haven't seen you for I don't know how long.'

'Too long. I heard that you were back at HQ. When you went UC, we thought that you had left the force.'

'No, that is just the way it works. No time for goodbyes,' she chuckled. 'But you can't get rid of me that easily. I'm still around. How are you?'

'I'm happy thanks. We'll have to grab lunch sometime.'

'Definitely. That would be great. Look, I know that you're snowed under, but I've got a mobile phone and a wireless camera that I need stripping. It could be linked to the Steff Cain case.'

'Really? I knew Steff. That was devastating news.'

'It was. I need everything that you can get from them and I need it yesterday, please. Any chance?'

'No problem. I'll put it at the front of the queue. On my way.'

'Thanks, Wilks.' Jo hung up and walked to the window to think. Liverpool One was booming below her, the shops and restaurants packed with locals and tourists alike. She missed being down there, missed gliding through the crowds unnoticed and unseen. Life on the streets was a different world. Most of the shoppers down there never gave a second thought to people who lived in the gutters, ate from the bins behind sandwich shops or sold their bodies to survive. George was down there somewhere. It was a harsh life and a short one for most. She didn't want to go back but she missed it. A knock on the door disturbed her. 'Come in.'

'Have you got five minutes?' Braddick said, poking his head around the door. She thought that he looked tired. His stubble was longer, speckled with grey. 'I need to run over some updates with you if you're free. I need your thoughts on where we are at. I feel like my head is going to explode.'

'I know the feeling,' Jo said, gesturing to the chair opposite hers. 'I'm so sorry to hear about Ade Burns.' She didn't want to ask what he thought about the situation. News of how he had been found had trickled through the building. It seemed to be pretty obvious what had happened.

'He was a strange one,' Braddick said with a shrug. 'But he was a good detective. At least I think he was.' His eyes were tinged with sadness for a moment. The silence was awkward.

'Don't worry. I don't expect you to tell me what a perfect DS he was,' she said. 'You think that he may have been bent, right?'

'You don't beat about the bush, do you?'

'What's the point?' Jo shrugged. 'I tend to say what I'm thinking. Everyone knows where they stand that way.' She paused and thought about her next words. 'You do think that he was bent though, don't you?'

'Before yesterday, I didn't know for sure but today, yes I do think that.'

'Trust your instincts. They're probably right. There's no point in pretending Burns was an angel. It will all come out in the wash. Paying him lip service in the meantime won't help. I can't think of anything worse if I am honest.' She smiled. Braddick nodded but didn't add anything. 'I am glad that you are here. I was just going to ring you.' Jo sensed that he was uncomfortable. She picked up the mobile, careful not to smudge any trace and showed Braddick the pictures. Braddick didn't recognise them. 'That is George, the guy I told you about. I think he's our UC and I think that he posted this to me because he knew that he had been compromised. I think he's in trouble.'

'Are they wellington boots in the background?' Braddick asked, squinting at the screen.

'I thought so when I first saw it.'

'So that would mean the picture was taken in the Kodak building with the trawler men behind him?'

'That's exactly where I am at,' Jo agreed. 'They knew that the UC would turn up there eventually and they wanted to identify him. They planted the camera and the phone, take the picture and then send the image to the phone to let him know that they know who he is. He would have crapped himself when that image came through.'

'At least he had the foresight to take them with him.'

'I've got technical on the way. They may be able to pull something off them. I'm worried about him, Braddick.'

'I am too. If he knows that he has been compromised, why hasn't he come in yet?'

'To protect Cain's informer, maybe.'

'In which case we may have another dead copper on our hands. 'He sat back and sighed. Jo nodded that she agreed.

'I've sent the image to Matrix and uniform. If he is still out there, someone will find him. Fingers crossed.'

'What about Mike Pilkington?' he asked. 'Where are we on that?'

'We have some footage from the scene. He was pushed.' She turned her laptop to face him. 'You can see Mike here at the cash point and then here at the crossing. See here,' she said, pointing to his hand.

'He has his car keys in his hand.'

'Yep, then we see this guy stood behind him.' Braddick leaned closer to see a well-built male in sunglasses and a beanie hat. 'He steps forward and looks at the traffic and boom!' She slapped her palm on the desk. 'The timing was perfect. A short hard push in the small of the back was enough to topple him over. Mike drops his keys as he falls so no one notices the killer picking them up.'

'Any chance of facial recognition?'

'They are running it, but they said, 'don't hold your breath'. They are ninety percent sure it's the arse that ARU shot dead at Mike's house.'

'Good. Let's hope it hurt,' Braddick sighed. 'What about the search of his house?'

'You heard about the gun being found?'

'Yes. They called me last night.'

'They told you it was dirty?'

'Yes. Did you know the brothers who were shot with it?'

'The Rakovs,' Jo said, nodding. She played with her hair as she spoke. 'They were Ukrainians trying to break into the big time. I remember them well from when I was UC. They were nice guys, pretty harmless actually but they were always swimming upstream.'

'What do you mean?'

'They didn't have the steel that it takes to make it on the streets. The local dealers didn't trust them, and the foreign muscle only worked with their own. They bounced around town from club to club for months. I heard they had taken a few good hidings for selling in the wrong places, but they kept coming back. Rumour has it that the Turks gave them some courier work. They would sometimes use foreigners to transport gear. If they got caught in transit, it wasn't a Turk that did time. Apparently, they set up a delivery of heroin to be brought in on a light aircraft but it was the first time that they had used the importers, so they were nervous. There were whispers of a police sting. They coerced the Rakovs to meet the flight and bring the gear into town, but they were hijacked, and they got wacked. The killers emptied fourteen, nine-millimetre cartridges into their vehicle.'

'Messy.'

'There wasn't much left from the shoulders upwards. Most of them was scraped off the windows.' She nodded. 'I remember whispers on the streets after the killings. Some said that the Turks had done it themselves to cut them out and to stop them eventually establishing themselves as competition.'

'It wouldn't be the first time the Turks squashed the opposition.'

'I'm not sure. I didn't buy into it. The Rakovs were a couple of cocky wannabies. They could never have cut it. They were never big league and never would be, not in a million years. I fed back what I was hearing to my handler, but no one ever mentioned who the hit man could be, which is unusual. People always speculate and gossip but there wasn't even a whisper about who had done it.' She leaned back and stretched. 'A couple of months later a wave of heroin hit the streets. It was Turkish brown. I knew that whoever hit the Rakovs had kept the smack.'

'That's no coincidence is it,' Braddick scoffed. 'They just sat on the gear for a while until the dust had settled.'

'Exactly.'

'Who was selling it?'

'The dealers linked to Liquid and Gold.'

'The Karpov's clubs. For fuck's sake!' Braddick snorted. 'Where do they get off the fucking bus?'

'They have got it stitched up from Moscow to Manchester. Their intel is amazing. I have to take my hat off to them,' Jo said. 'They must have eyes and ears in every outfit in the city. There were no end of people working for them when I was on the streets. Even people who didn't work for them claimed that they did. It gave them kudos and a little protection too. They connect to the underworld and hear where the deals are going down and take the lot, drugs and money. Nice work if you can get it and less risky than importing. Why smuggle it in when you can steal it from someone else?'

'They have it down to perfection, I'll give them that. I'm just fucking sick of hearing their name.'

'It's a proven business model.'

'It's a joke from where I am sitting.'

'That is what they see us as.'

'What?' Braddick laughed.

'They see us as a joke,' Jo shrugged. 'They can operate here without any hassle because we need hard evidence to be able to do anything. We can't touch the Karpovs and as long as they don't get their hands dirty, we never will. It is a fucking joke!' she chuckled dryly. 'Can you see them getting away with this in their own country? Under Putin?'

'Not a chance. They would have been taken off the streets and sent to a Siberian gulag where no one would even know that they were there. Their files would be lost, and they would be buried in the dirt before the ink was dry on their warrants.'

'Exactly. Our hands are tied. It's a joke. As long as they can keep officers on the payroll, they are way ahead of what we are investigating. They can react and cover their tracks,' Jo said, turning her palms skyward. She shrugged. 'I don't know if Ade Burns was bent but someone is.'

'I didn't want to believe that, but it is hard not to.'

'Hard not to?' Jo shrugged. 'Are you kidding me? The gun that killed the Rakovs turns up at a dead officer's house?' Jo rolled her eyes to the ceiling. 'Are you telling me that he put it in the fucking glove box?' she asked no one in particular. She was ranting. 'Of all places to hide a murder weapon, in the glove box of your car. He was an experienced detective. I mean, are you joking?'

'You're right. It was planted. Whoever planted it must have been in a rush?' Braddick thought for a moment.

'What are you thinking?'

'Who was the lead CSI at his home?'

'Holly Evans, why?'

'How well do you know her?'

'Not very well.'

A knock on the door interrupted them.

'Come in,' Jo called.

The door opened and her friend Wilks walked in. Her black hair was silver at the roots and her chins had multiplied. Jo stood up and embraced her. Her smile could light up the night.

'This is Helen Wilkins,' Jo said, introducing them. 'We were cadets together. Do you two know each other?'

'We do.' Braddick shook her hand and smiled. His eyes looked distracted. 'Actually, I am glad you here.' He walked to the door and closed it. Helen looked confused. 'You were at Mike Pilkington's house, weren't you?'

'Yes, why?'

'We have been discussing it,' Braddick said. 'Did you see DS Burns at the scene?'

'Yes,' Helen blushed. 'Why, what has he said?'

'Don't worry. He hasn't said anything, Helen,' Jo reassured her. 'He's dead.'

'Oh, my word. What happened?'

'We don't know yet, but it looks like he killed a brass and then hung himself.' Jo lowered her voice as if others could hear. Braddick looked horrified. A thin smile touched his lips. 'What?' she asked him. He just shook his head. 'That is what happened isn't it?'

'That is terrible,' Helen said, looking suitably shocked. The truth was that she wasn't bothered by the news in the slightest.

'So, you did you see him at Mike Pilkington's house?' Braddick asked. He made it sound like an innocent question.

'Yes.' Helen appeared concerned again. She looked like she wanted to say more.

'And?' Jo asked.

'And what?'

'I have known you long enough to know when you're holding something back.' Jo smiled and nodded. 'Come on. Spit it out.'

'It seems unfair to cast aspersions now he's dead. Even if he was a prick.'

'You didn't like him then?' Jo smiled. She exchanged glances with Braddick. It was the general consensus of most of the women in the division who knew him. He was a misogynist pig and a sex pest. Helen looked at Braddick. 'Don't worry about DI Braddick. He thinks that he was bent, don't you?' She looked at him for confirmation. Braddick had his mouth open, a little bit stunned by her bluntness. 'Let's just say that there was more to DS Burns than meets the eyes.' She shrugged. 'You did see him there?'

'Yes,' Helen relaxed. 'He was sneaking about. I had to have a word with him.'

'What do you mean, sneaking about?'

'I caught him going through Mike's bedside table. He was searching through the drawers. I told him not to touch anything until we had finished.'

'Then what?'

'Then he did that squeezing past way too close thing that he always did, and he went.'

'Did you see which way he left?' Braddick asked. His face had darkened, he looked angry.

'It was getting on and we didn't want the press walking in. The front and back doors were locked up. We were using the garage to come and go. He must have left that way.' Helen looked from one to the other. She read their faces. 'Is this about the gun that we found?'

'We shouldn't say anymore,' Braddick said.

'Yes, it is,' Jo cut across him.

'Jo?' he sputtered. 'We can't…'

'What?' she said turning to face him. 'I don't do the 'don't talk in front of the children' bollocks, okay?' she said, smiling. 'We're discussing the options with a fellow professional, nothing more. Stop being so worried about what people will think. They will make their own minds up anyway.'

'Fine. I get that. We shouldn't be pressurising a CSI to make assumptions on our behalf.'

'I am not under pressure and I'm not making assumptions on your behalf. I am making them on mine,' Helen said. 'We all knew that gun had been planted, especially when the ballistics came back. It was obviously a plant to muddy the waters. I must admit, I didn't think that it was Burns who put it there though.' She smiled at Jo. 'Anyway, where are the things you want me to strip?'

'Here.' Jo pointed to them and Helen put them into evidence bags and labelled them. 'Thanks, Wilks.'

'No problem. I'll run them this afternoon and get back to you before I leave. Don't forget that catch up.'

'I won't and thank you,' Jo said, walking to the door. She opened it and hugged Wilks. 'I'll talk to you later.' She closed the door and walked back to the desk. 'Have we just had our first disagreement?' she joked.

'Not really,' Braddick said, shaking his head.

'Good. DS Burns planted that weapon. There is no other explanation. Either we have it completely wrong and Mike Pilkington was on Karpov's books or the copper that planted it in his car was?' she said, looking at Braddick. He nodded. 'One way or the other, the Karpovs have police officers from our division on the payroll. There's absolutely no doubt about it. We might be wrong about Burns, but I don't think so and neither do you.'

Braddick blew air from his lungs and closed his eyes tightly. He shook his head as he thought about it. She was right and he knew it.

'Who else could be on their books though?' Braddick asked. 'Cain, Pilkington, the UC's or all of the above?'

'We may never know. Pilkington's bank accounts are all kosher. His father was a successful insurance salesman who made his fortune in the nineties. He died before he was fifty and left his money in trust. Apart from the gun, Mike was clean and so far, Cain is too. I don't think that they were bent for one second. They were taken out because they were bringing in an informer. The Karpovs know that they have one, but they didn't know who it was. They may know now.'

'That's the problem,' Braddick stood up and looked out of the window. The river was slate grey, moving sluggishly towards the sea. 'They know more than we know.'

'People talk when they are terrified.'

'Take this Holyhead hit for instance,' he said, turning towards Jo. 'Look at the number of people involved in that deal. The chances of one of them being pressured into talking were huge.'

'Information is valuable. There are addicts out there queuing up to sell it.'

'As long as the Karpovs keep that information coming in then they will keep wiping out opposition supply lines and will always be ten steps ahead of us. We've hit a brick wall.'

'Did I tell you that they pulled the surveillance on Ron Mason's properties?'

'I heard that this afternoon.'

'He hasn't done anything wrong and he wouldn't talk about what happened to his brother anyway. It was a waste of time and money.' Jo looked thoughtful. 'My money is on the informer turning the case. If we can find him that is. We still have no idea who he is.' Jo shrugged. 'He will surface eventually, dead or alive. If he is still alive, he will take us a lot closer to nailing these bastards.'

'I have been thinking a lot about Cain's informant.'

'I'm listening.' Jo raised her eyebrows.

'I was thinking about what the ACC said about it when we first spoke about it. He said that Cain said the informer's evidence could bring the Karpovs down, right?'

'Something like that.'

'That would mean that the informer would have to have vital information, right?'

'Right.'

'We are talking about bank accounts, dealer's names, supply lines, witnesses to murder or the like and they would have to have evidence. Hearsay would not be enough. It would have to be solid evidence.'

'For Cain to take it as seriously as she did, I agree. He would have to be tier three or above and that would be the minimum in my book. No one below that level would have that kind of information. And she would have to have seen it. There's no way that she would have acted without seeing sample evidence.'

'That's what I've been thinking. I couldn't see why anyone would want to turn evidence against the Karpovs. It would be a death sentence. Even if we managed to put some of the top tier away with the evidence, they would find the leak eventually.'

'Agreed. What is the point?' Jo twiddled her fingers through her hair repeatedly. He had noticed that she did it when she was thinking.

'The informer would know that too, right?'

'We would have to assume so.'

'I'm trying to rationalise the decision to come in.' He shrugged. 'I mean, why turn against them? What would make someone want to do that, knowing that they would wipe out their family first and then go for them.'

'Maybe they have a grudge. They might have been screwed over by them,' Jo suggested. 'We all know what absolute bastards they are.'

'I think it is more than that.'

'What do you mean?'

'I hadn't given it much thought until last night. It was when I saw Sergei Karpov.'

'I'm not getting this yet?'

'I don't think it's a coincidence that Sergei Karpov comes to the UK and suddenly an informer comes forward. I think that they think they will be killed anyway and that is why they're not afraid to give evidence. Sergei is here for a reason. The informer thinks that he is dead anyway.'

'That would put them high up the chain?'

'I think so. Right near the top.'

'Another thing,' Jo said. She raised her forefinger in the air. 'Who would not worry about their family being wiped out.'

'Someone with the surname Karpov,' Braddick nodded. 'That's what I was thinking. They are right near the top.'

'Right near the top?' Jo ran her fingers through her hair again, just next to her right ear. 'Right near the top of a list?' She reached for her phone.

'What happened?' Braddick asked, confused.

'You gave me an idea?'

'I did?'

'Yes,' she nodded and held up her hand to quieten him. 'I told you that Cain had a Karpov file on her laptop.'

'Yes.' Braddick nodded, confused.

'I didn't pay much attention to it because most of it was archive information. She had her folders laid in alphabetical order. There were the usual names, nothing new,' she explained. Braddick shrugged that he didn't understand. 'Except for one, which wasn't at the top of the list. It was way down the list, and it shouldn't have been.'

'And?'

'It was a file on Alexei,' she said, shrugging. 'It should have been at the top of the list.' The call was answered. 'Hi, it's Jo.'

'Hiya, Jo. What's up?'

'How are you getting on with that list on Cain's laptop?'

'The Karpov folder?'

'Yes.'

'We're working on it. You were right, it is mostly archive information. If we find anything, I'll call you.'

'Try the Alexei folder for me.'

'I'm well past the A's.'

'It's near the bottom.'

'Let me scroll down.' The line went quiet for a minute. 'I've got it. It won't open, Guv. It's password protected.'

'Try her name in lowercase.'

'No.'

'Uppercase?'

'Nope.'

'Date of birth?'

'Nope.'

'Shit!'

'Do you want me to try that?'

'Don't be ridiculous,' Jo groaned. She looked at Braddick and then looked at the space where the mobile phone had been. The UC's face flashed in her mind. 'Try George uppercase.'

'Nope.'

'Lowercase.'

'Nope.'

'Try gorgeous George,' she said. The line went quiet.

'I'm in, Guv. It's *gorgeousgeorge*, all one word, lowercase.'

'What is it?'

'It's a Criminal Informer file. There are sixty odd pages here. I'll print it all off and bring it over to you.'

'What does it say about Alexei Karpov?'

'He is forty-seven years old and is an accountant by trade. He is listed as working out of Amsterdam. That's all I can see about him.

There may be more in the meat of the file. I'll send it all over to Google, shall I?'

'Thanks,' Jo said with a smile. She looked at Braddick 'Bingo! We're in. They're printing it off. We need to find Alexei Karpov if he's still alive.'

'We need to stop and think about this,' Braddick said. 'Let's run a search and wait and see what is in that file before we do anything. Everyone who has been near this is dead or missing.' Jo nodded and sat down. She sighed and bit her thumbnail. She knew that he was right. Rushing in now would be dangerous. 'I think that the first thing we should do is call in the NCA and get that file to them. They might be able to act against the Karpovs on what's in it. If anyone gets burned on this, let's make sure that it isn't anyone from here. We've lost too many people already. I don't want to lose anymore.'

CHAPTER 34

Big Ron Mason pulled into the farm; the rough track slowed his progress. There were potholes and rocks every few yards and the Shogun rocked from side to side. The sun was beginning to rise, chasing the darkness away. Everything was a dull misty grey. A rotting combine-harvester loomed out of the night. Its lime green paint had been turned to rusty brown by the elements. It hadn't moved from where it had broken down twenty years ago. The woods to his left were deciduous, their branches bare. To his right, the trees were evergreen, conifers and Leylandii. He could smell the needles rotting beneath them. The farmhouse was silhouetted against the dark grey sky. A light burned in the bathroom upstairs. He was approaching the house when his mobile rang.

'Is that you, Ron?' a female voice asked nervously.

'Yes, who is this?' He didn't recognise her voice.

'This is your neighbour, Lesley from next door to you,' she explained. She had a mild scouse accent that she tried hard to disguise but there was no hiding her roots. 'I was wondering if everything was all right. I mean, were you in?'

'What are you talking about, Lesley?' Ron was tired and grumpy. He had only met the woman a few times and she looked down his nose at him. The last thing that he wanted to do was chitchat with Mrs Bucket from next door.

'Well, I couldn't see your car, so I was worried if you were in or not. Do you even know about it?'

'Know about what?' He pulled the van to a stop and turned the engine off. The nosey old bat was winding him up.

'The fire. I wondered if you knew about it.'

'What fire?'

'At your house. There are fire engines all over the place. Your house is burning down.'

'What?'

'And there are three dead bodies on your front lawn.'

'Three dead bodies on the lawn?' Ron knew that they were his cousins, the Farrells. The Karpovs had done a tit for tat for Leonid. 'Fucking hell!'

'They have been buried upside down. I can see their legs sticking up in the air. I wasn't sure at first, but they are there. The glow from the fire is illuminating them now. I gather that you weren't in then?'

Ron felt the anger rising. He hung up and punched the steering wheel. For the first time since he was a child, he suddenly felt scared. Scared and alone. Gary had always been there, but he wasn't there now. Rickets was his lieutenant, but he wasn't his brother. He needed help. The Karpovs had found out who had hit them much quicker than he had expected. He hadn't planned for that. The Irishmen had made him so angry, that he hadn't thought things through properly. He had rushed in because he was so pissed off and now, he saw it was a mistake. His outfit was tight knit and made formidable enemies, but he knew that the Karpovs were too much for them to take on. He had always known that. That was why he had always played second fiddle to that wanker Eddie Farrell. It was too late for regrets. He had to face up to whatever they would throw at them. One thing was for sure, the Karpovs would know that they had been in a fight.

CHAPTER 35

Rickets sat in the van and watched the huge linen warehouse through binoculars. He had driven east along the M62 and then exited the motorway at the Burtonwood services. From there, he followed a tree lined road. It winded its way through farmland towards Burtonwood Village. He carried on slowly until he reached an elevated section of road that overlooked the industrial laundry. A copse of trees offered him some cover. The building was enormous. It was the size of four football pitches with parking and loading bays that were half the size again. There were at least sixty articulated tractor trailers on the parking bays. The entrance was monitored by two gatehouses and a small army of uniformed security guards, who checked the paperwork for everything going in and out. Vehicles queued in both directions to be processed. Lorries were arriving and leaving every few minutes, the incoming vehicles carried soiled linen, the outgoing carried freshly laundered sheets and towels all over the UK. It was the ideal setup for distributing contraband across the country. The drivers would have no idea what was stashed beneath their vehicles. Everything would appear to be above board. If the Karpovs had hidden a shipment in there, it would take a dozen police handlers with sniffer dogs to find it.

Storming in with shotguns was not an option. It was a legitimate operation turning over millions of pounds a month. The employees would have no idea whose money backed it or what was behind the Pristine logo. Any attempt to use force would bring armed police, helicopters and police interceptors. There would be no escape. They may as well have hidden it in Fort Knox.

On top of all that, he had watched men arriving at regular intervals. Eighteen vehicles so far, people carriers, vans, SUV's and a minibus had pulled onto the site and parked up. The passengers had walked into the building and then fifteen minutes or so later, they climbed back into their vehicles and drove away. It was obvious to Rickets that the Karpovs were responding to their clubs being attacked and they had called in their cavalry. The prefixes on their registration plates showed that they were from all over the country. He had watched nearly a hundred men arrive and leave. They had all headed west towards the city. Against this outfit, Rickets knew that Big Ron Mason's crew didn't stand a chance. They were outgunned and outnumbered. The Karpovs had steamrollered every outfit that took them on, and they had no qualms in chasing them and their families to extinction. He was getting ready to leave, when his mobile rang. The screen showed 'fun police', which was his nickname for his partner, Becky.

'Hiya,' he answered. 'Sorry I haven't rung. It's been a busy night.'

'It has been a busy night all around,' a man's voice said. It was thick with an accent. 'Your lady friend, Becky has been busy too. She has been entertaining us. There were four of us. I'll text you the pictures. We're putting some of them onto her Facebook too. I don't think she enjoyed it very much. She cried a lot. I think she wants you to come home now.' The voice paused. Rickets felt his stomach knot. He wanted to speak but he was fear-struck. His muscles were frozen stiff. Tears of anger filled his eyes. 'Hurry up home now before it is too late for her.'

CHAPTER 36

Henry and Patrick parked at the rear of the Mason compound. They carried their tools in a holdall and a rucksack. Henry took out a Glock-17 and checked the magazine. It was full. Patrick watched as he slotted the automatic into the back of his trousers.

'Where did you get that?' Patrick asked in a whisper.

'A friend of a friend,' Henry replied with a wink. 'Don't go soft on me now, Patrick. This is our chance to go home with our heads up and you get to keep all your limbs.'

'In the meantime, I don't want to be banged up for murder.'

'Don't worry your little head. Let's hope we won't need to use it. Now shut up and let's get this done.'

'After you.' Patrick said, resigned to what they had to do. 'If we are confronted, let's tie them up. Don't shoot anyone, please.'

Henry smiled as they approached the perimeter fence. He crouched down and studied the links. There were motion sensors attached to the pillars. He followed the cables until he found a section out of their field of vision. He took a wire with a crocodile clip on each end and bypassed the power supply. Cutting the data link, he rendered them blind, although they had the appearance of functioning. The lights flickered and then came back on.

He nodded and smiled. Patrick stood beside him and watched as Henry took a laser pen from his pocket. He pointed it at a motion sensor and let it rest there for a few minutes. It heated the sensor and rendered it useless.

'Okay, cut the links,' Henry whispered. Patrick cut from the ground up until the gap was wide enough for them to pass through. 'That will do. Get in there.'

They crouched low and reached the back of the building. Henry reached into the bag and took out a thermal lance and a gas bottle. He attached the gas and ignited the flame, narrowing it until it was at its most effective. The flame cut through the metal sheet cladding like a knife through butter. It crackled as it burnt through. Henry had cut an arch within minutes and he kicked it down. He took out the Glock and gestured for Patrick to follow him into the building. Patrick checked around behind them and then ducked into Mason Security.

****

Young Ronny was bundled into Alexei's dining room. Three men stared at him, two standing and one seated. Alexei was sitting on a hardback chair, his feet tied together, and his hands bound behind his back. A small blowtorch was on the floor next to his feet. The blue flame hissed as it burned. His toes were blackened and blistered, the nails burnt to cinders. Tendrils of smoke floated from his big toes and the stench of burning nails filled the air. His chin was on his chest as if he was sleeping; blood was running from his nose. Ronny was shocked and sickened by the scene.

'Alex, are you all right?' he stammered. 'Why are you doing that to Alex?' Ronny shouted at the men. 'You horrible bastards!' A blow to the back of the head sent him sprawling across the floor. He landed facedown at Alexei's feet. The stench of burning flesh was overpowering and he gagged. He felt blood trickle down his neck from a wound in his scalp. 'Who are they, Alex? What the fuck do they want?' he moaned as the men pounced on him and tied him up. They dragged him onto a chair opposite Alexei, pulling his hair painfully tightly. 'That hurts!'

'Really?' the man behind him said. He pulled harder, ripping the hair from the roots. Tears filled Ronny's eyes, but he couldn't move away from the grip. 'We've been talking to your boyfriend, haven't we?' he chuckled evilly. The other men grinned and nodded. 'We guessed that you two were queers. Of course, he denied it at first, but we found the photographs on his phone. You know the ones where you're on your knees?'

'I don't know what you're talking about,' Ronny muttered. His face turned red with embarrassment.

'Don't you?' the man sneered. He grabbed a mobile and flicked through the images. 'Here look. That is you there, isn't it?' Ronny looked away. 'What is that in your mouth, eh?' He kicked Alexei in the shin and put the phone in front of his face. 'What is that in his mouth, Alexei?' The men laughed coarsely.

'Fuck you,' Ronny said, beneath his breath.

'Don't be like that. He even has some videos of fucking you from behind. Did you know that he had filmed it or was that for his own pleasure?' Ronny cried out when he ripped his head backwards again. 'I said, did you know?'

'Get off me!' Ronny shouted but he couldn't move. 'You don't want to admit that you're a faggot, eh?'

'Either way, your dad is going to be so proud of you when he sees these pictures,' another man said. 'I can imagine what he will say, can't you?'

'Leave me alone!' Ronny shouted in frustration. 'My dad will fucking kill you. Just you wait and see.'

'Your father won't kill anyone.'

'Oh, he will. He'll kill you.'

'No, he won't. Your father is an idiot.'

'You'll see who the idiot is.' Ronny couldn't believe that he had called his father an idiot. That word was usually aimed in his direction. 'Cheeky cunt, you'll see.'

'We will?' The man shrugged. 'He doesn't have a very good record so far. We took his money, we took his drugs and now we have his son,' the man sneered. 'He is a fucking idiot.'

'He'll break you in half.'

'We will wait, and we will see.' The man shrugged. 'In the meantime, we need to know if what Alexei has told us is the truth.' The man moved towards Alexei. 'He's having a little nap, aren't you, Alexei?' The man slapped Alexei hard around the face. He moaned in pain but didn't look up. 'Wake up. Your faggot boyfriend is here to see you.' The man put his fingers beneath his chin and pushed his head backwards. Alexei opened his eyes and a tear ran from the corner. He focused on Ronny and began to shake his head. Saliva dribbled from his chin.

'Don't hurt him. He doesn't know anything,' Alexei slurred. Blood ran from his nose into his mouth. 'He's only a boy.'

'Oh, that is so sweet, isn't it?' the Russian said sarcastically. He punched Ronny in the face, splitting his top lip open. Ronny moaned in pain and spat blood onto the carpet.

'Don't!' Alexei shouted.

The man grabbed Ronny's hair and wrenched his head backwards.

'Alexei told us that you told him about a drug deal that happened last week.' The man looked into Ronny's eyes.

'I don't know anything about any drug deal.'

'You told him when and where it would happen?'

'No, I did not.'

'You told him that you would be there?'

'No.'

'You told him that you would be a lookout?'

'I don't know anything about it.'

'You know what I am talking about. The drug deal,' he said, leaning closer to his face. 'The one where we killed your uncle and your cousins.'

'Fuck you!' Ronny spat into his face. The man wiped the blood and phlegm from his cheek with his sleeve. He smiled at Ronny and shook his head slowly. The smile disappeared a millisecond before he smashed his forehead into Ronny's nose. There was an audible crack as the bridge splintered. 'Aah!' Ronny cried out. He felt blood running down his face and he could taste it at the back of his throat. White light flashed through his mind and bolts of pain streaked through his brain. 'No more, please,' he whispered.

'Good girl,' the man said, grinning. 'Let's start again. Alexei said that you gave him the information about the drug deal. Is that true?'

'Yes.' Ronny flushed red, embarrassed and ashamed that he had ratted on his family. He had been trying to impress Alexei. 'You said that you wouldn't tell anyone no matter what!' he snapped at Alexei. 'I can't believe that you told them that. If my dad finds out that I told you, he'll kill me. They killed my Uncle Gary.'

'I didn't know that would happen, Ronny,' Alexei slurred. 'They said that they might monitor it but that nothing would happen.'

'They lied.'

'They did and I am so sorry.'

'You lied too,' Ronny snapped.

'Don't be surprised that he is a liar, Ronny. Your boyfriend has been talking out of turn to people a lot lately.' He slapped Alexei hard. His head rocked back sharply, and blood sprayed up the wall. 'He has been talking to the police, eh Alexei?'

Ronny frowned and shook his head. 'He's one of you lot. He's not a grass. No way. Alexei wouldn't talk to the police. You've got that wrong.'

'No, we are right. He's a grass all right. So, you did tell him about the drugs coming from Ireland?'

Ronny nodded. 'Yes, I did. He said that he had to mention it to his bosses but that nothing bad would happen if he did. He said that they wouldn't be interested but that they had to know who was doing what. He said it was the rules. They had to know what was happening. They said nothing bad would happen, but they lied.'

'Everyone lies, Ronny. Especially our cousin Alexei. He is the worst type of liar. He lies to his family, to his own flesh and blood.' The man punched Alexei hard in the stomach. It knocked the wind from his lungs. He gasped for air and vomited. Yellow bile splattered onto the laminate floor.

'Leave him alone. I don't believe it. He wouldn't turn on his family.'

'Why not? You did.'

'It wasn't like that,' Ronny said, shaking his head. He hadn't felt like a rat when he told Alexei. He was just showing off. 'We were just talking. I didn't know that he would tell the others but when he did, he said that he had to and that nothing would happen.'

'He lied.'

'But why would he do that?' Ronny was genuinely confused. He was in pain, physically and emotionally.

'Because he is a rat. He was talking to police.'

'I don't believe that.'

'It doesn't matter what you believe. Alexei was passing on your information to hide the fact that he was about to turn himself into the police, didn't you, Alexei?' the man sneered again. 'It was all a smoke screen, wasn't it, you old queer.' He stepped back and punched Ronny this time. 'So, we have two rats in a trap. Now then, let's have your phone. We need to speak to your dad.' The man checked Ronny's pockets and took his mobile. 'Where is your dad?'

'I don't know where he is,' Ronny said. His lip was swollen and bleeding. His voice was shaking with fear. 'He went out before I left.'

'Left where?'

'What?'

'Where were you?'

'Where we live,' Ronny stuttered.

'Liar.' The man punched him again. Ronny felt a tooth crack. The pain in his nose intensified by a hundred times.

'Were you at his house?'

'Yes.'

'Liar,' the man said, smiling. He punched Ronny in the ear. His full sovereign ring ripped through the cartilage leaving the top hanging loose from his head.

Ronny rocked sideways, almost toppling from the chair. His eyes widened in shock and he had to blink to clear his vision. The man waited a few seconds for him to recover.

'Let's try again. His house is burning to the ground as we speak. We know he wasn't in it. They searched it before they torched it. You are obviously too stupid to feel the pain. Alexei feels it though, don't you, Alexei?' He bent down and picked up the blowtorch. The blue flame hissed noisily. He put it beneath Alexei's left foot and turned up the heat. Alexei screamed, the sound piercing. He twitched in his chair; his body jerked violently with the pain. His eyes rolled backwards in his head. 'Try again. Where were you staying?'

'Okay, okay!' Ronny sniffled. The man took the flame away. The sweet smell of singed flesh filled the room.

'Where were you?'

'He has a farm on the outskirts of the city. I don't know the address, but I can take you there.'

'You don't know the address?' The man put the blowtorch close to Alexei's other foot.

'Don't burn me,' Alexei pleaded. 'He isn't good at remembering addresses and the like. He has learning difficulties.'

'So, the son of the idiot is actually an idiot?'

'I am not an idiot. I know where it is,' Ronny mumbled.

'We don't need the address. We'll make your father come to us. He's stupid enough to do it.'

CHAPTER 37

RICKETS

When Rickets arrived home, it was like a scene from Law and Order. A fire engine was parked in front of his house, the hoses trained on his roof. Blue lights flashed off the surrounding houses. Orange flames climbed through a gaping hole where the trusses had burned through and collapsed. The first-floor windows were nothing but black holes, flames roared skywards, the glass and frames gone. Scorch marks ran upwards from the ground floor, the entire structure an inferno. An ambulance screamed past him in the opposite direction. He saw three police cars to his left; uniformed police officers were holding back the neighbours. Anger, rage, hatred and worst of all, guilt burned inside him, hotter than the flames. His heart was broken.

The Russians had sent him pictures of Becky being raped and they had lived up to their promise to post them on her Facebook too. Facebook had gone into meltdown and his phone hadn't stopped ringing, friends and family horrified by what had happened. Becky's father had been particularly clear about who was to blame. He had always hated her being with Rickets and said that nothing good would come from living with a criminal. He said that it would end in tears. In hindsight, he was right. Rickets had to hang up and ignore any further calls. It was difficult enough to cope with what they had done to Becky without being blamed for it too. The truth was, it was difficult to cope with the fact that it was his fault. It wasn't a random attack. She had been targeted because of what he had done. He should have talked Big Ron out of it. Attacking the clubs was a huge mistake, one that Becky had paid for dearly. He knew that it wouldn't end there. They would not stop hunting Rickets until he was dead. What happened to Becky would happen to every female member of his family until he was caught, shot and buried in the woods. His guts were twisted with anger and regret. Tears ran freely down his cheeks and saliva dribbled from his mouth, down his chin and onto his chest. He was almost hysterical when he first saw the photographs. It was impossible to comprehend her suffering captured on camera. The expression on her face would break the strongest mind.

He had called the police immediately; they could be there in minutes whereas he was an hour away. The switchboard operator could hardly understand him because his sobbing rendered him incoherent. His vision was blurred all the way home, the tears hadn't slowed down or stopped once. He parked up and wiped his eyes. Becky's father was across the road arguing with a police officer. He saw him and began a tirade of abuse. Rickets ignored him and opened the car door, not knowing whether Becky was alive or dead. Her phone had been switched off and the neighbours that they knew were away or at work. He walked towards the police cordon, a sense of dread in his heart.

Darkness began to spread from the pit of his stomach, through his veins and into his very soul.

CHAPTER 38

HENRY

Henry crept around the edge of the warehouse keeping close to the walls. Dozens of security vans were parked inside the cavernous building. Apart from the light from his torch, the place was in darkness.

'The guards will be in the office.'

'Good,' Patrick said. 'Let's get the gear out of the van and get out of here.'

'Are you sure that you can hotwire it if we need to?'

'I had a misspent youth,' Patrick said, grinning nervously.

'Which van was it?'

'That one there.' Patrick pointed to a black Transit. It was the only vehicle with no logo on it. They crept towards it and crouched down next to the driver's door. He tried the handle, but it was locked. Henry shook his head in disbelief.

'Did you think it would be open, really?'

'It was worth a try,' Patrick sighed. He took a wire from the bag and began to work on the lock. Henry moved away and checked the roller shutters. They were locked from the inside. He could see the glint of light coming from the corridor which led to the office. The drone of a television reached him. 'I'm in,' Patrick whispered.

'Good man,' Henry said, walking back to the van. He looked inside the cab and frowned. There was a bulkhead separating the front from the back. 'Now what?'

'We need to get the back open.' Patrick shone his torch around the steering wheel.

'What are you doing?'

'There should be a catch under here that opens the lock on the back doors. It's been removed. They have adapted the van so that no one can open the rear doors from the inside.'

'Clever bastards, eh?' Henry muttered. 'I'll burn our way into it.'

Patrick shook his head. He knocked on the bulkhead with his knuckles. 'This has been plated. It's been reinforced. Your lance won't cut through that.'

'What about the back doors?'

'Try it but I think there's a better option.'

'What's that?' Henry raised his eyebrows.

'We take the van. If we get it out of here, we can take our time getting into it. We need industrial cutting gear to get through this plate.'

'Can you hotwire this?'

Patrick looked at the steering column and shook his head. 'They've plated that too. See here,' he said, pointing to it. 'If I bust the ignition block, I could fuck it up completely. We need the key.' Henry nodded and stood up. He walked towards the corridor. 'Where the fuck are you going?' Patrick hissed.

'To get the key, Einstein. Where do you think I am going?'

'Shit!' Patrick whispered to himself. 'We don't know how many men are down that corridor.'

'I have fifteen bullets in this magazine and another four magazines in my jacket.' Henry paused and counted on his fingers. 'Do you think there will be more than sixty?'

'Funny, very funny,' Patrick said. 'Don't kill anyone!'

'I'll try,' Henry winked. 'Are you coming or are you going to stand there with your thumb up your arse?'

Patrick shook his head and followed. He stayed close to his shoulder. They reached the door, which led to the corridor and peered through the glass. The corridor was empty. A light burned from the office. The reflection of a television screen flickered off the glass. Henry turned the handle and pushed the door open slowly. The hinges creaked and he stopped, holding his breath. Patrick froze to the spot. They waited for the office door to open and a horde of angry security guards to run out, guns blazing but nothing happened. Henry grimaced at Patrick, a thin smile on his lips. Patrick breathed a sigh of relief and they moved on down the corridor. They were five yards from the office door, when a shadow appeared on the glass and it opened.

'What the fuck?' the guard hissed. He reached into his jacket with his right hand. Henry raised the Glock and fired once. A dark hole appeared in the centre of his forehead and the back of his head exploded. Pink goo sprayed up the wall. His eyes widened as his knees buckled and he fell forward onto his face.

Henry moved quickly. He stood in the doorway and aimed the Glock, both hands on the weapon. Patrick watched in horror as he fired two shots to the left, two to the right and another two straight ahead. His ears were ringing as Henry disappeared into the office. He was stunned and stared at the spreading pool of blood on the floor.

'Get in here,' Henry called. 'I need your help!'

Patrick moved towards the door, stepped over the dead guard and looked into the office. Three bodies were sprawled on the carpet. Blood splatter covered the walls and ceiling in crimson arcs.

'Jesus Christ, Henry!' he snapped. 'I thought we weren't going to kill anyone.'

'I changed my mind when he reached for his weapon.' Henry glared at him. 'What the fuck is wrong with you, don't you want to live?'

'Of course, I do.'

'Good. There's a board full of keys over there. Have a look for what we need. We might need to move some of the vans from in front of the doors.' Patrick was staring at the dead men. 'Patrick!' Henry shouted at him.

'What?'

'Get a fucking grip, will you!'

'Okay,' Patrick mumbled.

'Get the keys!'

'Okay. What are you going to do?'

'We're on candid camera,' Henry pointed to a bank of monitors, 'I'm going to wipe it while you get the van out of here.'

'I can't believe you killed everyone.'

'Shut up and get the keys.'

'You didn't need to kill them all.' Patrick searched for the right keys. They all looked the same until he spotted the labels. Then the system made sense. He found the keys for the transit and put them in his jacket. 'You didn't need to do that.'

'I did, Patrick.'

'Why did you?' Patrick said taking the other keys from the board. The vans between the transit and the roller shutters were Fords. He took all the Ford keys and put them into another pocket. 'I don't get it.'

'Because that is what the Karpovs would do,' Henry said with a wink. He tapped the side of his head with his forefinger. 'Up here for thinking, Patrick and down there for dancing. I want Big Ron Mason to think that the Russians fucked him again.'

* * * *

Jo walked into her office and nearly bumped into Google. Her black trouser suit touched her curves in the right places. Google looked red faced and excited. He held up a sheet of paper and smiled.

'You need to see this, Guv,' he said, waving the paper.

'Take a seat, Google,' she said, pointing to a chair. 'You look like you're going to wee yourself.'

'I nearly did when I saw this,' he said, sitting down. He straightened his tie. 'Steff Cain was a genius.'

'Calm down and talk me through what you have.'

'It was in the file that technical brought over,' he began. 'I had a scan through it all quickly, but this stood out straight away.'

'What is it?'

'It is mobile phone acquisition,' he said, holding up the sheet. 'Cain took it out three weeks before she died. There are calls made to Cain's number up to the day before she died. Some of the calls are over an hour long. She didn't answer the last three.'

'Tell me that you think that the phone was for her informer.'

'Why else would she need it?'

'Tell me that you have the number.'

'I have the number.'

'Tell me it is still active.'

'It is still active.'

'Tell me it is switched on.'

'It is switched on.'

'Now tell me that you have triangulated it and you know where it is.'

'I have triangulated it and I know where it is.'

'I love you, Google.' She slapped the desk with her hand. 'And I'm not even joking. Well done, Google.'

'Thank you, Guv.'

'Does Braddick know yet,' she said, reaching for the phone.

'Not yet. Do you want me to gather the troops?'

'Yes. Everyone and his dog. Get an ARU Inspector up here too.' She dialled Braddick. Google stood up and walked towards the door. 'Google!'

'Yes?'

'You had better call the ACC too. We will need his authorisation for this.'

'No problem.'

'Google.'

'Yes.'

'Well done.' Google blushed and nodded and hurried off. Braddick answered the telephone. 'You are not going to believe this!'

CHAPTER 39

BIG RON

Big Ron pulled up to the entrance of the compound. The rollers were down, and everything looked okay until he realised that the gates were unlocked. What were the men inside thinking? Maybe one of them had gone to the chippy or sneaked out to the pub. It wouldn't be the first time that type of thing had happened. He was beyond rage to the point where he couldn't think straight. The Karpovs had gone for them all out, no holds barred. They had dug a hole in his front lawn and buried his cousins headfirst in it, leaving their legs sticking up. Then they had torched his home. The bastards had no class. He was fuming that he hadn't torched their clubs. Hindsight was a bitch. They had let everyone at the clubs go unharmed. All he wanted was the drugs and money and to piss them off. They had responded with the wrath of the devil.

One of his men had called him and told him about the pictures on the internet. Becky had been raped and Rickets wasn't answering his phone. He had no more information than that. She had been taken away in an ambulance, but he didn't know if she had made it. He should have known better. He should have let sleeping dogs lie but it was too late for regrets, too late for hindsight and too late for sorry. Sorry wouldn't cut it for Rickets and Becky. Rickets adored her. He would be devastated. Ron knew that he needed to consolidate their position or the Karpovs would bury them all. Whoever all was. He wasn't sure who was behind him and who wasn't anymore. His men seemed to have deserted him like rats leaving a sinking ship. Despite leaving a dozen messages, none of his men had returned his calls and looking at the empty car park, no one had turned up at the compound. He was bitterly disappointed but hardly surprised. All those years that he had looked out for them and where were they now?

He thought about the images of Becky. They were horrific. She had been through an ordeal that was beyond description. They had terrorised a gang member's partner and published the pictures for the world to see what happens to people who fuck with the Karpovs. Those images would be out there forever. That was the nuclear weapon of retaliation and it had the desired effect. If he was honest with himself, it was no wonder that his men hadn't turned up. They had probably packed up their families and left town and who could blame them? Ron was alone and that was that.

He opened the driver's door and climbed out, walking to the gates he inspected the CCTV cameras. The gates squealed as he pushed them open. He wondered why the guards hadn't seen him. If they were asleep, he would give them a good kick up the arse. Ron climbed back into the vehicle and drove up to the rollers. He turned off the engine and climbed out. The roller shutters were open at the bottom. It was only a few inches, but it was enough to set the alarm bells ringing in his head. The shutters could not be closed and locked from the outside. It was a feature of their design. It was only then that he realised that the compound had been compromised.

He stormed towards the rollers, angry beyond description and reached down to lift the shutters up. They rattled loudly and the noise echoed from the walls. He reached inside to switch on the lights, fumbling blindly in the dark until he felt the panel. One by one the long fluorescent light tubes flickered to life and illuminated the interior. He looked at the spot where the black transit had been parked and roared like a silverback gorilla. His cries were carried on the wind into the night. The safe van had gone with two months takings and what they had taxed from the Karpov's nightclubs and he had a good idea who had taken it.

Ron turned towards the corridor door and kicked it as hard as he could. It crumpled like cardboard; the hinges were ripped from the frame. The door rattled down the corridor and came to a stop near the dead body of the security guard. Ron stopped and looked at him. A single shot through the forehead had killed him, the entry wound dead centre. Whoever had shot him was ex-military. He reached the office door and looked inside. The three bodies were still warm, the blood still running from their skulls. They had been shot from the doorway, one shooter, six shots, all on target. He couldn't see any bullet holes in the walls. The shooter hadn't missed with a single shot. That kind of marksmanship was very rare indeed.

Ron froze when he heard the sound of an engine approaching outside. He ran to the desk and took out his gun before running down the corridor towards the vehicle bay. He raised the gun and aimed just above the approaching headlights. The van stopped in front of the open shutters and the engine was switched off. Ron blinked as the driver turned off the lights and opened the driver's door.

'Fucking hell, Rickets,' Ron said. He felt emotional and relieved to see him. 'I didn't expect to see you.' Ron walked towards him and they embraced. Rickets was weeping like a child. Ron closed the shutters and waited for him to settle down. 'How is she?'

'She's at the Royal. She's alive but she won't see me,' Rickets sniffled. Ron felt awkward. Rickets was the hardest man that he knew but he was broken. 'Her father is blaming me. He said that he is going to get an injunction against me so that I can't contact her.'

'What a cunt,' Ron said, shaking his head. 'He can't do that.'

'I can't say that I blame him to be honest.'

'You can't put this on yourself.'

'Can't I?' Rickets shook his head. 'Who else is to blame, Ron?'

'This is not your fault,' Ron said. 'This is down to those Russian bastards. They did this. They started this and we need to finish it before they do anything else. We have to stop them.'

'Who exactly are you going to stop, Ron?' Rickets snapped. 'There are hundreds of them, and you can't get near the Karpovs. If you kill a few of the top dogs, another one steps up into their place before they're cold. You can't win.'

'I have to do something. These bastards are well out of order and I'm not having it.'

'What are you going to do, Ron?' Rickets stepped back and wiped his eyes. 'Are you going to take them all on single handed?'

'If I have to.'

'Then what? They won't stop coming back at you. You hit them hard and they come back even harder.'

'They burned my gaff down and dumped the Farrells on my lawn.'

'That's just the start. They're not finished yet, Ron. If they can't find you, they will go after young Ron. They'll come here next.'

'They already have.' Ron pointed to the empty space where the safe van had been. 'Our stash has gone.'

'The safe van?'

'Gone.'

'What about the guards?'

'They shot them all.'

'Fucking hell. We're finished, Ron. It's all over.'

'We can't do nothing, Rickets.'

'Look around you, Ron. This is it. The men have all left town. You're the only one left with any fight in you. Everyone else saw what they did to Becky and they have run for the hills and I can't blame them. We're finished.'

'I'm not finished. What about you, Rickets?' Ron tilted his head. 'You've never rolled over for anyone before.'

'This is different, Ron. We can't fight them. The dirty bastards don't play by our rules.'

'When did we play by anybody's rules?' Ron scoffed. 'We always made up our own rules.'

'When, Ron?' Rickets shrugged.

'What do you mean, when?'

'When did you make up your own rules?' Rickets took a deep breath and sighed.

'I've always made up the rules.'

'You're kidding yourself.'

'What are you talking about?'

'Eddie Farrell made up the rules and he worked for the Karpovs.'

'Bollocks!'

'It's the truth and you know it.'

'Bollocks.'

'We were dancing to their tune all the time and do you know why?'

'Go on. It sounds like you're going to tell me anyway,' Ron growled. His face reddened with anger.

'Because you always knew that we were out of our depth. We could never have fronted out the Karpovs, not then and not now and you know it. Look at what they've done, for fuck's sake!'

'Careful, Rickets.'

'Careful?' Rickets shrugged. 'It's a bit late to be careful, isn't it?'

'Look, you're upset,' Ron said quietly. 'We can't do nothing. We have to end this.'

'There is only one way to end this, for me, for Becky, for my family, for everyone.'

'And that is what?' Ron said, shaking his head. 'Are you walking away?'

'I'm not walking away. No one can walk away completely, can they?'

'Okay, I'm listening. How do we end this?'

'We can't win, Ron. We have to end it.'

'How?'

'I'll have to do what they told me to do,' Rickets said, pulling out his gun. 'I'm sorry Ron.' He fired three bullets into Ron's chest before he could react. Big Ron Mason staggered backwards, clutching his chest.

'Why?' Ron gasped as his legs gave in and he fell backwards onto the floor.

'Because they said that they would do it again if I didn't,' Rickets said, raising the gun again. He emptied the clip into Ron's head. 'Bye, Ron. Forgive me but I had no choice.'

CHAPTER 40

MIT

The briefing room was packed. Braddick and Jo walked to the front and stood beneath a bank of screens. The ACC was pacing up and down, looking stressed and tired. He was talking to an inspector from the ARU and a DI from the Tactical Entry Unit. A buzz of conversation echoed across the floor. Braddick picked up the remote and turned to face the room.

'Can we have your attention please,' Braddick said. Silence fell across the gathering. 'We have a lot to catch up on and not much time so let's get started.' The image of a burning house appeared on one screen and Big Ron's body appeared on another. 'I'm sure you have all heard that we finally found Ron Mason. He was found shot dead with four of his men at his security compound in Liverpool 8. His home was fired, and the bodies of Brian, Jimmy and Frank Farrell were found dumped on the lawn. We know that this is the aftermath of what happened in Holyhead.' He changed the images again and Jo took over.

'This is Rebecca Thomas, partner of Lawrence Mann, better known to us as Rickets. Rickets is an enforcer for the Masons. Last night Rebecca Thomas was brutally raped, the assault was filmed, and the images were posted online. She is certain that her attackers were Russian. They left her for dead and set fire to her home. She's recovering in the Royal.'

'We know that this is all tit for tat retaliation, but we are struggling to prove that the Karpovs are responsible,' Braddick carried on. 'What we know from all this is that the witness, who made the emergency call from Holyhead, is Ron Mason's son. When we notified his family of his death, they told us that Ron junior, known as Ronny, is still missing.'

'The good news is that a call was made to his father's mobile from Ronny's phone last night. We have traced the number to this property on the edge of Woolton Village.'

He nodded to Jo to take over. The image of a huge bungalow appeared on the screen. It was set in a few acres of land and surrounded by trees.

'This is the target property,' Jo began. 'You all know that Steff Cain was working on bringing in an informer from the Karpov family.' Nodding heads and serious faces told her that they did. 'Three weeks ago, Cain gave the informer a mobile. It is active and it is switched on and it is in that bungalow.' A picture of Alexei Karpov appeared on the screen. 'When we enter that building, we need to do everything possible to make sure that Alexei Karpov comes out of there alive. We don't know what the connection between Karpov and Ronny Mason is yet, but they are both at this address. The ACC has given us a green light to enter and search the place with the support of the ARU and we'll have air support. We don't have much time. You all know what we are dealing with.'

She looked at the ACC and he nodded for her to continue. Images of Yuri and Sergei Karpov appeared.

'I am at liberty to tell you that Yuri and Sergei Karpov were arrested at Gatwick airport this morning on the strength of the sample evidence recovered from Steff Cain's laptop.' A cheer went up around the room. Applause echoed through the department and expletives filled the air. When the noise subsided, Jo carried on. 'The NCA are on their way to take charge of Alexei Karpov. Remember that Steff Cain died believing that bringing Alexei Karpov in could bring the Karpov cartel down for good.' Determined faces looked back at her. 'You all know what to do. Let's get on with it.'

CHAPTER 41

RONNY

Ronny couldn't hear the helicopter that hovered above the bungalow, its engines running on stealth. Its thermal imaging cameras had identified six bodies, four mobile and two static. The static bodies alerted the tactical unit that they would have to encounter hostiles on entry. They had used snake cameras to pinpoint where all the occupants were and to identify their targets. It had been hoped that Alexei could be brought in without a shot being fired but now it appeared that would not be the case.

Ronny looked at Alexei, but he couldn't see his eyes. His head was lolling onto his chest again. Blood and saliva dripped from his mouth onto his trousers. His toes had stopped smouldering but the stench of burning flesh still hung heavy in the air. He didn't like seeing Alexei being hurt. It had ripped him apart inside. He knew that he had strong feelings for him, but he hadn't realised just how strong they were until now. He loved him. It was that simple.

The windows exploded inwards, covering Ronny with shards of glass. He felt a piece embed itself into his cheek. Gas canisters hissed and his eyes began to sting and water. His nostrils burned inside, and his lungs constricted, making breathing almost impossible. He held his breath and listened to the chaos around him. Men's voices boomed all around him. British voices and Russian voices. Orders were screamed and shouted. Shots were fired, more glass shattered, more voices and more shouting. He closed his eyes tightly and tried to make himself invisible.

Ronny felt his hair being pulled and then his head was jerked back violently. He felt a strong arm around his neck, and it pulled him upwards. The chair came up off the floor and he felt himself being spun around one hundred and eighty degrees.

'I'll kill him! 'He heard a Russian voice in his ear. The man squeezed tighter, cutting off his air supply.

'Put the weapon down!'

'I'll fucking kill him!'

'Put the weapon down!'

'Drop the weapon!'

'Fuck you!' Ronny heard the exchange and then felt a very brief moment of red-hot pain as a nine-millimetre bullet entered his skull through his cheek and exited through the back of his head. Then all was shadows.

CHAPTER 42

NCA/KARPOVS

Braddick and Jo watched the helicopter take off from the roof, Alexei Karpov safely on board. The ACC clapped his hands together and patted them on the back. Braddick looked at Jo and she half smiled. Her blue eyes seemed a little sad, but they hadn't lost their sparkle. The energy behind them was still there. She had an aura around her, an inner strength that only a few possess. The NCA had taken possession of Alexei Karpov.

'He should have been taken to hospital,' Jo said as the helicopter disappeared over the city.

'He will be,' Braddick said. 'Just not here. It's too risky. The Karpovs will be desperate to shut him up.'

'Where will they take him?' she asked.

'Foxley Hall first,' Braddick said, turning away from the window. 'He'll go to the medical unit and then they will process him before they whisk him away to some secret location where he will be interviewed until he is of no more use to them.'

'Europol are gagging to talk to him,' the ACC said. 'I think he'll be farmed out to agency after agency and bled dry until the information that he has becomes of no consequence. That will be a very long time from now.' There was an awkward silence as they all reflected on the day's events.

'When is Steff Cain's funeral?' Braddick changed the subject.

'Next Tuesday,' Jo said. 'Mike Pilkington's is Thursday. I haven't heard anything about Ade Burns.'

'They won't release the body,' Braddick said. He shrugged. 'I spoke to his sister this morning. The coroner hasn't ruled yet. She said the family are devastated. They want him buried as soon as but because of the suspicious circumstances, he's still in the fridge.'

'Suspicious?' Jo chuckled dryly. 'Suspicious like a dead woman in the bed?'

'The NCA are all over it,' the ACC added. 'They have found a PayPal account with a lot of money in it. Regular payments have been paid in for the last two years.'

'So, he was on the take.' Jo sighed. 'That worked out well for him didn't it?'

'If you make a deal with the devil then you can't complain about the heat,' the ACC said. 'The NCA are making a point of finding out what happened to our missing Matrix officers. Apparently the Karpovs aren't talking.'

'No surprise there,' Jo said flatly. 'As much as it pains me to say it, they are gone.

'We can only hope. Whatever happens, you have done a marvellous job,' the ACC said quietly. 'I will remember this day for the rest of my days. I feel like we squared things for Steff Cain.'

'I don't think we did. Not really,' Jo said, thoughtfully. 'Not even nearly.'

EPILOGUE

After securing some cutting equipment from Clint, Patrick and Henry burned their way into the safe van. It took them less than an hour. Henry was overjoyed with the amount of drugs and cash that they had recovered. Clint secured a buyer for the gear and they converted them into cash before they left the city. Patrick wasn't sure exactly how much cash had been recovered but he could see that Henry was happy. He looked like a huge weight had been lifted from his shoulders.

When they left Liverpool, they split the haul into two vehicles for safety and headed for Anglesey once more. The roads were quiet, and they stopped at a roadside Starbucks for coffee. Patrick had followed Henry along the North Wales coast, keeping to the speed limit all the way. They stayed in convoy in the slow lane allowing the faster moving traffic to overtake. When they reached Holyhead, Henry weaved through the back roads, through narrow lanes and warren like housing estates to avoid CCTV. They weren't being chased by the police or Ron Mason, but it was better to avoid the cameras just in case. He followed Henry along Land's End and then they navigated the speed bumps for half a mile along the Newry Beach before taking the road towards the quarry. A mile on, the road split into two. The left-hand road took tourists to the coastal park, right took locals to a couple of disused boatsheds and some little know fishing spots. They took the right turn. The road was no more than a track, grass and weeds formed a green strip down the middle. Overhanging trees formed a canopy above the road. Henry slowed as they reached a sign, which pointed towards the Rocky Coast. They trundled on for another mile before Henry indicated left and turned into a yard. The gates were hanging off the hinges and thistles the size of grown men surrounded a tin hut. He saw a torch being switched on; the beam swept from side to side. Patrick wasn't aware that they were being met by anyone. Henry had kept him in the dark but then he did that a lot.

Henry switched off the headlights and turned off the engine. He climbed out of the vehicle and reached inside for two large sport's bags. Patrick watched two men emerge from the darkness. Both wore black waterproof jumpsuits, the type worn by lifeboat crews. They greeted Henry with a handshake and took the bags from him. He couldn't hear what they were saying but they turned and looked in his direction. Patrick turned off the engine and the lights. He felt a wave of relief wash over him. The journey from Dublin had been a long and dangerous one. He opened the door and climbed out, popping the trunk to retrieve his bags. The men walked towards him as he reached the boot of the car. Patrick grabbed the bags and placed them on the ground. He felt scared as the men approached. He didn't know why, he just did.

'Patrick Finnen?' one of them asked.

'Yes.' Patrick looked at Henry, but Henry wasn't watching. He felt a prickle of fear touch his soul.

'I watched you boxing a few times,' the man said. He reached out his hand in greeting. 'You were good!'

'Thanks,' Patrick said. He relaxed and shook his hand.

'We'll take the bags for you.' Patrick hesitated. 'Don't worry, we'll look after them for you.'

Henry looked up and nodded that it was okay to hand them over.

'We're going to take you home,' the other man said. 'We've got a rib waiting off the breakwater. It shouldn't take more than a few hours to cross. I bet you're looking forward to getting back, eh?'

'I am that,' Patrick said.

'Over here, Patrick,' Henry called. He was walking towards a path in the heather. The path was narrow and led steeply down to a shingle beach. Patrick could see white stones glowing in the moonlight. The breakwater loomed in the darkness. It snaked out to sea for a mile and a half. The lighthouse at the end shone a rotating beam that warned ships miles away. They walked across the beach to the breakwater and climbed up a stone staircase. The steps were covered in cockles and seaweed. 'We need to divvy up, Patrick.'

Patrick reached the roadway on top of the breakwater and turned to face Henry. Henry put out his hand and Patrick pulled him up the last few steps. The older man bent over to catch his breath.

'I'm out of breath,' Henry panted and smiled. 'I'm too old for this shit, Patrick.'

'You and me both, Henry.'

Henry stood up and looked at the stars. A crescent moon hung in the inky sky to the west and Venus twinkled like a diamond above the Skerries to the North.

'We did okay, Patrick.' He turned and smiled. 'You're a good man.'

'We got there eventually, eh?'

'We did,' Henry said, nodding. 'How much cash did you put into the original deal?'

'I put two hundred and fifty thousand euros in and raised the rest.'

'Another seven hundred thousand euros?'

'Yes.' Patrick kicked a stone into the sea. It splashed, the concentric circles in the water shimmered in the moonlight. 'Why, how much did we recover?'

'One point two million.' Henry smiled and shook his head. 'Pounds, Patrick. Not euros.'

'That's what?' Patrick worked it out in his head. 'One point four million euros?'

'There or there abouts.' Henry smiled and patted Patrick on the arm. 'One point four million!'

'It was worth the trip,' Patrick sighed.

'Now listen to me.' Henry stopped laughing and lowered his voice. 'The General is only expecting what the investors put in.'

'What do you mean?' Patrick asked. He frowned but the cogs started turning. His heart started to beat a little faster.

'The investors want their money back, right?'

'Right.'

'That is seven hundred and fifty thousand euros. That is what we tell the General that we recovered. That leaves you with your initial investment and us with four hundred thousand to split down the middle.'

'Two hundred thousand each?'

'Yes.'

'Plus, my money back?'

'It was your money in the first place, Patrick.' Henry offered his hand to seal the deal. Patrick shook it with both hands.

'Deal,' Patrick said, smiling. 'Thank you, Henry.'

'You don't have to thank me, Patrick,' Henry said, looking serious again. 'I did this job for you.'

'What do you mean?'

'I came out of retirement because of you.'

A bullet went through Henry's back and exited his chest, splaying his ribs open and leaving a hole the size of an apple. Blood splattered Patrick's face. He blinked and looked at Henry. He was still holding his hand and looking into his eyes. Henry looked confused as the light began to fade. A second shot hit Patrick in the jaw, shattering his teeth before spiralling upwards into his brain. He was already dead when the two men in waterproofs emptied their magazines into them until the guns clicked. Silence fell again.

'The General said that they would try to cut a deal between them.'

'He did?'

'He did indeed. He guessed they would.'

'Clever man.'

'Not really. Blood is thicker than water.'

'What are you talking about?'

'Blood is thicker than water and you're thicker than both, so you are,' the man said, shaking his head. 'They were father and son.' He shrugged. 'It's a crying shame really but some people are just plain greedy. Let's get the chains on them and dump them in the water.'

Printed in Great Britain
by Amazon